ONLY HUMAN

TOUCHED BY HELL

EMMA SHADE

Touched by Hell
By Emma Shade
Copyright © 2019 Emma Shade
All Rights Reserved

Cover designed by Book Cover by Design
Cover model: Alaina Justice
Photographer: Evond Photography

"Hope is being able to see that there is light despite all of the darkness."
Desmond Tutu

CHAPTER 1

The stink of death.

My sword slid through the demon's neck in one quick slice.

Vomit rushed up my throat as I breathed in the sulfuric stench from the aftermath. I wiped the orange gelatinous blood from my face with a gag.

"God, I need a new job," I groaned, flinging the goop from my hand. "What should I wash my skin with this time?

Raven laughed. "Mara, I'm not sure bleach will remove that disgusting odor."

I glared at my best friend, who happened to be the daughter of Death. Yep, that's right. She was the child of the Grim Reaper. For as ancient as old Grim was, he had some sex appeal. It appeared my friend's looks ran in the family, too. Raven was beyond beautiful if you could see past her dark, dramatic makeup and her scary as hell Reaper performance.

Shoving past the fact that I had thought the Grim Reaper was hot, I grunted. "A shower is a must."

"Look, girlie, I like you and all, but you're not getting in my car. No way. Nuh-uh." Raven's blonde hair bobbed in her ponytail as she shook her head. "I'd never get that smell out."

I sighed. "Where am I supposed to go?"

"There is a small pond about a half mile from here."

"Raven, don't make me walk to a pond when you have your car. We rode together, we leave together. I promise I'll clean your car tomorrow."

Her eyebrows lifted. "I think I remember you saying that with the demon from last week. I had to have it professionally cleaned, and hedge questions when the detailing shop asked why my car smelled like vomit and death."

As a last-ditch effort to get a ride home, I rushed from behind the building in an attempt to beat her to the vehicle. However, because I was human and she wasn't, she beat me to it, locked her car so I couldn't get in, and then gave me a smirk. "Sorry, babe. Love ya!"

With a poof, she disappeared, leaving only a whiff of black smoke and her locked car in her wake.

"Dammit, Raven!" I shrieked and flipped my middle finger at her last location.

With a scream of frustration, I made my way to the pond I hoped was there. Otherwise, I was walking all the way home reeking like a sour fart. Damn Raven, and damn the stupid demon I had killed.

This wasn't what I had planned with my life, and I sure didn't expect to be doing this at twenty-six. No, my mother made that decision for me. When I was a kid, she tricked me and sold my soul for money. Useless paper apparently worth more than her child. However, as with most deals with the big man downstairs, it's never what it seemed. There were always catches and loopholes. Ten long years after I signed my life over, she finally got her riches as promised, but she also died the next day. Life was a bitch, wasn't it?

That's how I had met Raven. The young reaper in training was with her father the day they came to collect my mother's soul. I don't think I was supposed to see them, but the damn loophole in my mother's contract allowed me to see all matters of supernatural creatures. I gave myself away when I screamed, not really grasping what my mother had done to me. I was just a child, an innocent and a deal with the Devil. I hoped she was rotting in hell for all eternity.

Shortly after seeing my mother's black soul screeching as they ripped her away from this world, an enormous, familiar man came to see me. I knew I had met him before, but couldn't remember when. He had felt creepy, powerful, and old. That's when I found out what had happened. I didn't own my soul anymore. I was the property of the devil himself. My own mother had sold my soul to Satan, all for something she got for less than twenty-four hours. Remember that life is a bitch thing? Yeah, it applied to me too.

Instead of being dragged to hell – literally – I had somehow talked my way out of it with Raven's help. Then again, there was that loophole bullshit. In exchange for my soul to stay on Earth, Raven had to train me on weapons and demonology. Then I had to hunt the unruly demons that slipped to the surface after my eighteenth birthday. The pay was shit, demon blood coated my hair and skin more than I wanted to admit, and the only true friend I had was Death's daughter. After all, I couldn't hunt down demons with human friends. That was a disaster waiting to happen. Possessions were the real deal, even if they were rare.

By the time I reached the pond, my feet screamed at me for wearing heeled boots on a hunting trip. And, of course, the pond was in the middle of a residential neighborhood. Go figure.

"I'm going to kill you, Raven," I grumbled and dropped my sword and scabbard on the ground as I wobbled my way down the muddy embankment.

I jumped in and let the cool water wash off my stink. Okay, most of the stink. At least I wouldn't be heading home smelling like I'd spent the night in a sewer, right?

Floating along the water, I stared up at the glittering sky and wondered if my biological father was still alive. I'd never known him and I assumed my mother never told him about me. I also speculated how my life would've turned out if my worthless mother hadn't sold my soul and my father was there for us. With an exhausted breath, I sighed. I didn't need a father, not after all this time. I could take care of myself.

Closing my eyes, I tried to ignore the moon and my wandering thoughts. The upcoming full moon was a calling card for the lower demons and I had a job to do. Still, it would've been nice to know my father before all this bullshit started. On the other hand, my mother probably would've done it anyway or sold his soul instead, so his presence didn't mean anything.

"You know, I can tell when you're in a melancholy mood," Raven said, scaring the living daylights out of me.

Water splashed as I attempted to right myself and calm my beating heart. "Good God, don't do that to me."

She sat on the grass near the pond, her face obscured by her hooded sweatshirt. I guarantee she smirked as she said, "I know God. He's nice. Way too nice. Too bad you won't get to meet him."

"Don't remind me," I barked, splashing water in her direction. "Now, help me out of this water so I can go home and shower."

"So cantankerous." Raven tsked. She helped me as I stumbled out of the muddy embankment and onto the grass to take my ridiculous boots off. She held her nose. "You still reek."

"That's because of the putrid orgallas demon." I peeled off my soaked socks. "I don't see how you can even smell it, seeing as how you grew up in the underworld."

"Febreze, girl. Febreze."

"Febreze can't even mask that," I said, wringing out my wet, multicolored hair. I removed myself from the ground and attempted to wipe some of the water off my arms. "Now, how am I going to get home if your car is still next to that bar in town?"

She grinned and then let out an evil laugh.

"Oh, no. No, no, no!" I cried, taking a step back as she reached for me. "I'm not taking a ride on the reaper express."

Raven laughed again and snatched my arm with supernatural speed. My body screamed in pain as my skin splintered, and right before she transported me out of there, I called her every name in the cussword dictionary.

A few seconds later, I landed unceremoniously on the hardwood floor of my bedroom, my elbow banging the nightstand in the process.

"You still haven't figured out how to land after transportation?" Raven said with a giggle. "Even lesser demons know how to do that."

I cut a glare in her direction. "Yeah, well, I'm not a demon. That shit hurts."

She opened her mouth to say something but sighed instead. "Daddy's calling. Gotta go." And with her little magic trick, she vanished the hell out of my room.

With a sigh, I stood up and headed to the shower. As I stripped, I cussed Raven again. I had a distinct feeling she had lied because she didn't want to hear me yell at her again for the awful joyride to my apartment. For such a badass, she hated confrontation. I often wondered how she brought souls to the veil when they tried to stay. Then again, when they're dead, I doubt they put up much of a fight.

Cleaning the dirt and demon stench from my tattooed skin in the shower, I let the hot water wash away the night. Once I entered my room, I noticed my sword and shoes had miraculously arrived. Instead of cleaning the blood from the blade, I crashed on the bed in only a towel. I needed as much rest as possible to prepare for what laid ahead of me tomorrow evening. I'd make the sword shiny in the morning, or leave it covered in demon blood out of spite. Maybe leaving the blood would be a warning for the assholes to leave me alone.

However, I knew that would never happen. I apparently had a sign on my forehead that read, "Demon hunter, kill me."

CHAPTER 2

Let the bridges burn.

Insomnia made me clean.

That's why I cleaned out a closet at four in the morning. The number of boots I had was shocking. Some I still wore, while others appeared too worn to be salvaged. A few ruined because of demon blood. At least I had gotten my money out of them.

I threw some old boots in a black garbage bag and tackled the top shelf. Sandals, high heels, and a few boxes sat covered in dust. I threw some shoes I could donate to a local charity in a separate bag and then looked inside the first box.

I sat cross-legged on the floor and smiled as I read my first love letter from a boy in high school. He was a cute football player with freckles and killer abs. My smile fell as I read the letter for a second time. How normal my life could've been. I may have married this boy and had children, or maybe owned a furry, loving pet.

With a morose sigh, I flipped through the pictures of my past life. My old friends together at parties, at school, at the Friday night football games. Unbelievably, I had been a cheerleader. I snorted at the audacity of it all. Now I killed demons and could handle a sword better than I was able to do a backhanded flip.

Slamming the lid down on the box, I shoved it to the side and moved to the next. At first, I saw myself as a child in a few of them, my pale gaunt face staring back at me from the image. The last one was my mother and me. Anger surged at the sight of the vile woman. I hadn't realized I had any mementos of her.

Without warning, the memory came flooding back.

A deep voice echoed down the hall. Curious, I peeked around the corner. A large man with dark eyes sat across from my mother, his leg bouncing in impatience.

"There she is," he said. "Come on out, Mara."

I stepped out from behind the dingy wall as the microwave dinged. Mommy's smile made me smile too.

"Hi, baby, why don't you come here for a minute, okay?" she asked.

I bounced over to her and giggled at the man sitting on the opposite side of the coffee table. He looked too nicely dressed to be on the ugly couch.

"Do you love me, Mara?"

I hugged my arms around her neck. "Of course I love you, Mommy."

The man smirked and slid a yellowish paper across the scratched wooden surface of the table.

She wrapped her arms around me and kissed me on the cheek for the first time in a long time. "If you love me, would you do anything for me? Even give up something very important?"

"Yes!" Leaning into her embrace, I looked at the creepy guy on the couch.

She gave me another kiss on the cheek. "Can you show this man how you can sign your name like a big girl?"

My nostrils flaring, I shredded the picture. I tossed the scraps in the bag with the ruined boots. Then I dug out all the fragments of the picture and decided to burn them. I stepped out on my balcony with a candle lighter and began to incinerate every shred of evidence that she existed.

The ashes floated on the breeze and I took a deep cleansing breath.

Raven's voice was soft so she didn't startle me. "What are you doing?"

"Burning a picture."

She stood next to me and watched the charred remnants float on the breeze. "An ex-boyfriend?"

"My mother." I wiped the ashes from the balcony ledge.

She was silent for a few minutes, and said, "Good riddance."

"I hate her for what she did to me," I whispered, my gaze traveling over the twinkling lights of the city below. "Along with the abuse."

Raven slung an arm over my shoulder. "If it makes you feel any better, I hate her for what she did to you, too. But, without that horrible woman, I wouldn't have met you. So there is some silver lining to the whole ordeal."

I didn't reply. The night was becoming more emotional than I had wanted to deal with. Life sucked. That's how it was, and there was nothing Raven, her father, or I could do about it. Still, I thanked my lucky stars I had saw Raven and her father that fateful night. That damn contract with Lucifer had ruined and blessed my life at the same time. The inevitable double-edged sword known as my existence.

As the sky lightened with the impending sunrise, I watched the headlights of the early morning commuters. Something blocked the light from the passing cars and I squinted to see better in the low light. A shadowed being stood unmoving on the sidewalk below my building. The humanoid shape appeared oblivious to its surroundings, but I had an unnerving feeling the thing watched me with red, glowing eyes.

I glanced at Raven to see if she had spotted the same entity I had, but she seemed oblivious as she observed the sun slowly rise. I glanced back down, but the shadow was gone.

"Well," Raven said, causing me to start, "I better get some rest before I have to reap souls again. I suggest you do the same."

Nodding, I kept inspecting the sidewalk to see if the dark mass came back. I had spotted them occasionally, but thankfully, they hadn't done more than disappear. Maybe they were ghosts of some sort.

My friend surprised me when she wrapped me in a hug. I remained stiff and uncomfortable at the show of emotion.

"Don't do anything stupid," she said.

Letting out a laugh, I replied, "I never do. I only fight demons and send them back to hell. It's an awesome stress reliever, and very few humans get to let out aggression with violence."

"Just don't let the years of violence change your heart, Mara."

I whispered, "Never."

She faded away, her arms dissipating from around me.

I strolled back into my small apartment and slid the glass balcony door closed. Yawning, I went to slide the blinds shut and fear rocketed through me. Standing on my balcony was a tall shadow. The being was so dark I couldn't see through its form. While the one on the sidewalk hadn't moved, this one tilted its head as it watched me crimson eyes on the other side of the glass.

"Get the hell off my balcony," I growled with more courage than I felt.

With what appeared to be a nod, the thing vanished. I slid the lock closed and placed the bar at the bottom of my balcony entrance. That thing was not getting inside.

There was no way I was getting any amount of sleep now.

CHAPTER 3

Magic is the devil.

The supernatural being hanging from my ceiling barely registered as I went to start the coffee.

The machine gurgled and spewed the black concoction into my mug that said "I like my coffee as black as my soul." I added the necessary sugar. The spook clinked against the glass as I stirred slowly. Then I finally glanced up to see a light-haired figure plastered against the ceiling.

I took a long, slow sip before I said, "Nice try, Raven. Will you stop screwing around and get down from there?"

"You're no fun." She let herself fall and land on nimble feet.

"Well, you're lucky I didn't stab you with a butcher knife for trying that stunt before I've had a full cup of coffee at," I glanced at the clock on the microwave, "ten in the morning."

I gave her my best death stare. She beamed at me.

"A butcher knife would hurt, but you know it wouldn't kill me." She shrugged. "You want to get breakfast?"

Raven rarely was up this early after a late night, let alone hungry enough to eat. I raised a brow. "Why are you up this early?"

"I never went to bed."

Both my eyebrows lifted this time. "Why the hell not?"

"Well," she sighed before she continued, "political crap mostly, but my father decided he wanted a night off."

"Can he do that?"

"Everybody deserves a day off."

Of course they did, and my first day off in over a year was coming up. November first couldn't get here fast enough. I nodded and began lifting my shirt to put on the bra currently hanging from my kitchen chair.

"You're going to put that on here?" Raven asked, her cheeks tinged with red.

"Yes," I lifted my shirt off, "you've seen me half-naked and bleeding more than once."

"At least turn around so I don't see the nips."

With a sigh, I did as she asked and only turned around once I was fully dressed. For someone who brought souls screeching to wherever they go, Raven cared about modesty more than she should.

I grabbed my boots. "What happens if you have to take a naked person to their... destination?"

Her face wrinkled and her cheeks went rosy. "I don't stare, of course. That's rude. Why can't people die with their clothes on?"

Chuckling, I adjusted the laces on my boots. "I have a feeling you've seen your share of senior citizens who pass in the throes of passion."

"I mean, good for them, but I don't want to talk about it." She shuddered. "It's hard enough trying to calm them down and bring then to heaven or hell with a boner."

The visual made me double over with laughter. I know, morbid and awful, but imaging Raven trying to maneuver an old man with a hard on to heaven was hilarious.

"It's not funny!"

"You're right." Still fighting the giggles, I grabbed my purse and sword from the counter. "Where are we going?"

"The Crumble Cafe."

I fought a smile and a fit of laughter. "Thank goodness it's not a nursing home. I've heard those are hotbeds for sexually transmitted diseases."

"Shut up," she grumbled.

"Have I told you how much I love you?"

Raven snorted as we headed out the door.

****

"Are you going to tell me about the political crap you dealt with last night?" I asked with my mouth full of pancake.

"No." Raven took a sip of orange juice. "I don't think it's anything to worry about."

"It has to do with me, doesn't it?"

"I didn't say that."

I pinned her with a glare. "That means a yes if I ever heard one. Tell them all to go fuck themselves."

"Mara!" she warned, her eyes casting worried glances around the room. "You don't know who could be listening. Watch your tongue."

"You know what I think?" I poured enough maple syrup on my pancakes to cause a flood. "I think you're too scared to stand up for yourself."

She looked at me from behind the syrup I was still holding. Her black eyes flashed in warning. "I'm not scared."

My mouth edged into a smirk. I was prodding her with a stick because I knew it would work to my advantage, and if she grew balls while doing so, then it'd be worth it. "Prove it."

"Okay," she threw her fork on to her plate with a clang, "let's go."

Looking down at my half eaten flapjacks, I wished I had finished them before I decided to push Raven. Maybe this was her revenge for my naked senior citizen jabs earlier. They were the best damn pancakes I'd ever had in my life. She was already paying for our meals and motioning me to get my ass moving. Goodbye my sweet syrup, goodbye that buttery goodness...

A few blocks away, Raven sauntered inside an abandoned warehouse across the street as I struggled to stay with her. Okay, so the pancakes were a bad idea when you're trying to keep up with an unnatural being.

"What are we doing in here?" I asked.

She held up a finger to shush me.

Water dripped from somewhere within the building. Broken glass littered the fragmented concrete floors and the roof creaked above us. Colorful graffiti covered the available wall space, and a massive painted mark in red spray paint decorated on the floor ten feet in front of us.

That's when I smelled it. Death. I wondered if a homeless person had died in here at some point, or within the last few days. The floor with the spray paint waved like the hot summer sun beat down on it for hours, or the heat was coming from the painted area itself. Neither was a good sign in the cool October air.

Glancing at Raven, I saw by her facial expression she had expected it.

"Get ready," she muttered.

My sword slid free with a sting of metal and I bent my knees in preparation for whatever was coming. "Mind to tell me what to expect?"

Raven shook her head with a smirk. "You wanted me to be a badass, so I'll prove it to you."

A moment later, a god-awful screech echoed inside the warehouse. The littered glass bounced on the concrete. "What the fuck."

A black mass erupted from the painted markings and hovered eight feet from the floor. Transforming into a ghostly form, it turned in our direction. The woman's black, stringy hair hung around her head in rivulets. Her skin was pale and translucent, her face and body lined with black, ugly veins. Milky white eyes watched at us and I shivered. When it screamed again, I noticed jagged teeth where normal flat ones should be.

I barely had time to scan through my memory bank from Raven's training when it dove in our direction. Raven and I hit the floor, a cold blast of air running along my backside.

"Don't let it touch you," she warned, and then jumped to her feet as it circled back around.

My best friend suddenly transformed into her Reaper form, all black and all deadly. The ghostly figure screamed, its razor-sharp teeth shifting inside its mouth. The ugly bitch focused on me with an evil grin.

When it dove at me, I swung my sword through the form and then followed through with the swing as I twisted away, barely avoiding bony fingers. I suspected I wounded it, but the apparition hadn't died from my blade. That told me two things. One, this thing wasn't a demon and, two; I wouldn't be able to defeat it.

As it came after me again, Raven reached out with her skeletal hand and snatched the thing without an ounce of effort. It fought and shrieked, trying to get out of her grip. Then to my utter horror, Raven lifted the ghoul into the air and opened her skeletal mouth. I watched as she ate the thing. Ate. It.

She morphed back to her beautiful self once again, and then let out a loud burp as if she'd finished a feast. Which I suppose she had.

I gaped at her. Of all the times I hunted with her, she had never swallowed a being. "What was *that*?"

"That was a ghoul." Raven let out a small burp. "Somebody had summoned it here and I hadn't been able to dispatch it for months."

"But you ATE it." My eyes glanced at the floor and then realized it wasn't paint. It was blood. I looked back at her with a frown.

She shrugged. "That's how you get rid of them."

"Wait," I put my hands on my hips, "if you hadn't been able to get rid of that foul thing for months, why did you bring me with you."

Her black eyes met mine and she winced.

Oh. My. God. She had used me as bait. *Bait*! "Tell me you didn't use me for what I think you did."

Raven looked away, her face going paler than it already was.

My eyes widened and I took a step away from her. "What would've happened if the ghoul had touched me?"

"I knew it wouldn't. You're too good."

"What would've happened, Raven," I demanded, my voice dark and deadly.

Although I would never give up our friendship, she had crossed a line today. I know, I asked her to stand up for herself, and she had. Actually, she had shown me she was more than capable of taking care of herself. I knew that, of course, but sometimes she acted weaker than I thought she should.

"Well, let's just say Ol' Luke would've never collected your soul."

"And why is that?"

She finally looked at me. "Because you wouldn't have one to give. You'd be," she pointed to the blood on the concrete, "well, a ghoul."

I stumbled back a few steps in shock, my sword scraping the concrete beside me. "And then you'd have to eat me," I whispered.

"No," she closed the distance between us and placed a gentle hand on my shoulder, "I would make sure you'd get your soul back. Dad most likely knows a way. He's dealt with ghouls for eons."

Snorting, I said, "But that's a big maybe. Let's get out of here."

Raven stopped me. "We have to take care of the summoning spot. I can't do it because I'm not human."

"Nope. I'm not getting anywhere near that thing after what you told me."

"I need your voice and your blood. A deep finger stick will do."

"My blood?" I asked, my hands tucked into my jeans pockets. "And what will you do for me in return?"

"Do you really want to play that game, Mara?" She smirked and gave me a knowing glance.

I sighed, knowing this was part of her payback for me picking on her for being weak and the nursing home joke. More than that, though, Raven had saved my life on more occasions than not, and I'm guessing she fought for my rights with my boss all the time. "Fine. What do I need to do?"

She pulled out a shar- looking dagger with a curved hilt and handed it to me. "Prick your finger with this and run a straight line of blood across the entire mark."

"I don't know what's on that floor, or what is in the blood there now." I wrinkled my nose.

Then I thought about the unsuspecting person who happened to stumble upon the area. *What if it were a child?* My mind made up, I took the blade from Raven and strolled to the center of the mark. The bloody lines were in an exact pattern. A double circle filled about ten feet across with weird symbols in the middle of the two. A weird squiggly mark was in the exact center. What human would've known this? None that I could think of, and when I glanced at Raven, her face twisted with fury as she stared at it, too.

"Stand on the outer edge and begin there."

With a deep breath, I walked to the edge of the bigger circle. The floor swayed with each step. "Now what?"

"Prick your finger, and while you're running your blood across the symbols, repeat exactly what I say."

The sharp point of the dagger pierced my skin and I hissed. Blood welled up and started to drip, so I leaned over and placed the bloody finger over the edge of the circle. I looked at her with raised eyebrows.

Raven began and paused between each sentence. I repeated them and began walking backward with my bloody smeared trail.

"Negate dark with light. Reap the bad blood from this mark."

My finger reached the edge of the middle circle and I felt the entire area pulsate. I ignored it and kept repeating Raven's words.

"We drive you from here. Unclean spirits, all satanic powers," she stretched her arms out and her head fell back, "all infernal invaders, all wicked legions."

When I had only a foot left to go, my blood hummed with wild power. It was a glorious feeling, like being on a fabulous drug and on the verge of orgasm at the same time.

Raven said, "I banish you."

My hands shook with pleasure so unlike anything I had felt before. My breath quickened. My heart beat a rhythmic cadence in my ears.

When tingles covered my entire body, I almost stopped. I wanted to hold onto this feeling forever, but I knew it was only temptation from the original magic. Nonetheless, the power felt better than sex.

I was stronger than whatever dark magic this was. I had to keep going.

Gritting my teeth, I said the last part as I rubbed my blood over the end of the circle. "I banish you."

The intoxicating influence still flowed through me and I bit back a moan. Raven's black eyes watched me, her eyebrows raised.

When the next wave crashed over me, the pleasure turned in to unimaginable pain. An invisible fire covered my skin and I ground my teeth to keep from screaming. I fell onto the concrete as I passed out.

*****

I woke inside Raven's car. My head pounded to the tune of my heart and my skin itched as though I'd rolled in poison ivy. I wasn't sure whether to scratch all over or to grip my head in my hands.

"Stay calm."

I attempted to roll my eyes, but the movement hurt too much. "Stay calm my ass, Raven. You don't have your body going into sensory overload right now."

"Take this," she instructed and pressed something into my palm. "It'll help."

Begging for relief, I lifted my hand and shoved whatever she had given me in my mouth. And instantly regretted it. The foul wafer-like substance melted like butter on my tongue. The taste was akin to rotten eggs and vinegar, and I gagged and held it in my mouth like a child not wanting to take their medicine.

Raven's hand shot up to my chin and tilted my head back. "Swallow it."

I shook my head in absolute refusal. I was not swallowing this nasty stuff.

She took her hand and squeezed my cheeks together so my face resembled a kissing fish. I couldn't spit out the repulsive crap or fight her with my body weak from pain. Left without a choice, I choked down the most awful tasting thing known to man.

"All of it," Raven said.

I coughed and rubbed my tongue with my palm. Again, like a child. "What was that? It's disgusting."

"An herbal mix Dad and I make as a backup plan. It has a little brimstone, a smidge of malted vinegar paste, and some other stuff we'd rather not mention." She shrugged.

She had shrugged, like it wasn't a big deal I had eaten brimstone, which came from the fiery pits of hell. I rubbed my eyes in frustration and let out a slow breath. "Take me home. I need to get some rest."

Raven chuckled. "We're already there."

I looked out the windshield and spotted Mr. Henley walking his poodle. He never cleaned up that dog's poop. If I saw him take a squat (the poodle, not Mr. Henley) and that old man walks away from it, I was going to say something this time. I don't know how many times I had stepped in a steaming pile as I tried to sneak in without a neighbor catching me covered in blood.

Luckily for Mr. Henley, FuFu only piddled this time.

Raven and I said our goodbyes. I was still mad at her for making me swallow the disgusting hell biscuit, but I was too tired to speak. I crashed on the bed without taking off my clothes or boots.

CHAPTER 4

All good deeds go unnoticed.

I woke the next morning and threw on some loose jeans and a baggy red T-shirt. Sure, the demons would be prowling later, but I had something else planned for the day.

As I walked into the back entrance of the small utilitarian building, I smiled. This was my guilty pleasure, my moment to feel completely human. No demons, no death. Okay, no death by my hands or at the hands of the evil these humans rarely see.

"Good morning, Mara," Laura said and handed me a cappuccino while barely looking in my direction. Gray hair in a short ponytail, her crow's feet wrinkled as she squinted over the paperwork sitting on the counter in front of her.

After snatching the cup from her hands, I took the first sip of the sweet concoction and let out a sigh of relief. "Morning."

She finally looked at me and shook her head, her motherly face giving me a once over. "You need to start getting some sleep. Those bags under your eyes look hideous today."

Instead of retorting a smartass comment, I shrugged and replied, "Late night."

"Well, we have enough volunteers for most of the day, but you know what that means for you."

"Gag. Dish duty."

"It's not too bad. At least we have a dishwasher."

A middle-aged woman looking helpless and confused came into the room. Laura scooped her away instructing her where we kept the utensils.

Since the morning had recently started, I only had a few dirty cups to wash. Instead of using the dishwasher, I loaded the sinks with the appropriate cleaning solution according to the health codes and got to work. I stared out over the parking lot, my hands automatically cleaning the cups. The sunshine illuminated the oranges and reds of the falling leaves, the cool October air decaying the once green landscape.

A little over a year ago, I started volunteering at Safety Net, which was a domestic abuse shelter. Once a week I came in to help in some way or another. Nobody knew I came here. Not even Raven. I loved volunteering, and I actually liked doing the dishes, but I'd never tell Laura that. My hands in warm, soapy water felt ordinary, and if I did a good deed while feeling that way, I couldn't complain. When I was here I forgot what I actually did for a living and why. Maybe, just maybe, God would notice my efforts and save my soul from being ripped to shreds in hell.

Little hands tugged at my shirt and broke me from my thoughts. I smiled down at an adorable girl with messy blonde hair and beautiful blue eyes. Her indigo gingham dress was worn and wrinkled, and she twisted her hands in it as she looked at me filled with hope and innocence.

"Can I had anther gwass of miwk?" she asked, not able to pronounce her words very well.

"Of course, princess."

Grabbing one of the clean glasses I had washed, I opened the large fridge and poured her a glass of milk.

After handing it to her and making sure she had a good grip on it, she yelled "Tank you!" and ran back into the commons area, spilling a few splashes of milk in her wake.

The shelter had numerous small apartments and a commons area for meals and entertainment, but I felt awful when I looked into the haunted eyes of a mother or child. They'd seen and experienced far too much in their lives. On my first day, I realized even though true demons came from hell, there were humans who were worse.

With my thoughts on the little girl who had probably seen more than her share of horror, I cleaned up the spilled milk and then continued the barrage of dishes that started coming in from breakfast. The sunshine outside the window above the sink wouldn't clear my head today, no matter how hard I tried. Maybe if I took out some of the filthy demons tonight, I'd feel a bit better about keeping most of the humans safe. I sure as hell couldn't keep them away from the evil humans in the world, even if I wanted to.

*****

I worked until around two in the afternoon and the sleepless night started wearing on me. A yawn escaped as Laura walked into the room while drying her hands with a towel.

She frowned at me. "Why don't you head out for the day? I think we have the rest of the shift covered until dinner. You look absolutely exhausted."

"I can't leave. I have to help with—"

"No, you don't," she chided. "Go home. We'll be fine. I'm worried about you. Sleep is important for your health."

I wanted to laugh at what she had said. My health wouldn't mean shit tonight as I fought the demons who didn't want to leave Earth. They'd end my life to protect their mayhem and destruction. My only saving grace was that Raven wouldn't let them kill me anytime soon. That didn't mean they wouldn't try. I still had a nasty scar on my thigh from last year's Halloween festivities.

"Are you sure?" I asked, hesitant to leave her hanging with chores but my body begging for a nap.

"Go." She shooed me with her hand. "Get some rest. I'll see you next time."

Not wasting time as another yawn spilled out, I gave Laura a hug and headed out the door to get some rest before I had to start my real job.

As soon as I hit a red light, I stared longingly at the coffee shop across the street. The smell of cinnamon, mocha, and vanilla floated out of the shop and straight to my nose like one of those cartoons I watched as a child.

My nap would have to wait.

The bell above the door chimed as I entered. Voices from the wall of people waiting for their caffeine fix assaulted my ears. Ignoring it to the best of my ability, I waited patiently in line. My eyes scanning the area. I noticed a man and woman having coffee with their phones instead of each other. A young woman sat at one of the tables with a laptop, her fingers furiously clacking at the keyboard.

I let out a sigh of relief. No demons or any evil being. I really didn't want to decapitate one with so many witnesses.

After placing my order with the barista, I went to the bank of windows to watch the sidewalk as I waited on my cappuccino.

"Too bad it's so dreary out." An older lady said next to me.

I glanced at her, taking in the slight wrinkles on her face and her blonde hair. I placed her in her mid-thirties. "I kind of like cloudy days. They are good for naps when I can get them."

"Well, let's hope for sunshine and good weather for trick-or-treat tomorrow. I really don't feel like dragging my kids out in the rain."

My eyes widened. How had I forgotten tomorrow was Halloween? The one day a year I really, really hated my job. Well, more than the normal amount.

"Mara," the coffee goddess said, announcing my order was ready.

I gave a polite wave to the woman and told her to have fun with her children tomorrow evening. I'm sure my smile was more of a grimace when I had said it.

Halloween was when the veil was the weakest of all year. All Hallows Eve, Samhain, Halloween, or whatever you called it, was when things *really* went bump in the night. The veil between worlds was so thin; all matters of demons and bad things could slip through. As humans dressed up in costumes and knocked on doors, evil waited within inches of their candy-filled bags.

I strolled out to my car and drove to my apartment, dread pooling in my stomach. If I wanted a nap, now was the time to get one because tomorrow's workday was going to be hell. Literally.

CHAPTER 5

Thin veil at night, demon's delight.

Strolling down the neighborhood streets dressed in the costume Raven had chosen for me, I couldn't help but throw her some choice words as we walked.

"You have to fit in," she said with a giggle.

I swiveled on my boots in the Grim Reaper costume and pointed the cheap, plastic scythe at her. "This is not what I had in mind."

With her hair in pigtails and her makeup bright and cheery, Raven grinned. She had dressed as a damn fairy but picked out the fabled reaper costume for me. I knew it was a joke, but I didn't find the humor in it.

"Come on, live a little. Before you start taking souls to the underworld, that is." She cackled. "You look hot. I bet dear old Dad would get a kick out of it if he saw you." When I stared at her and tried to avoid the burning in my cheeks, she said, "It's a joke. You know? Ha. Ha."

I rolled my eyes and started walking with the trick or treaters as she rushed to catch up with me. Instead of honoring her with a reply, I began visually inspecting the children that passed us. Among the superheroes and princesses, there be monsters. Monsters that liked to prey on humans and their children.

"Don't you think it's awfully quiet for Halloween?" Raven asked after about an hour of scrutinizing the children too. "I figured we'd see something by now."

She was right. Tonight was a night of ruckus and death. However, we hadn't spotted a demon. Not one. I continued to scan the passing children and their parents, hoping tonight might be an easy night.

I was wrong.

My sword quivered against my skin. Heading straight for us was a child dressed in a yellow princess dress, her little pumpkin candy basket swinging next to her as she walked. But she wasn't a child. She was a demon watching the trick or treaters with unbridled anticipation. Tonight was easy pickings, or so she had believed. I nodded in her direction and Raven smiled.

I whispered, "We have to get the beasty away from the kids. And the parents."

Biting her lip in thought, Raven said, "Give me two seconds. I'm going to try something."

She disappeared behind a large shrub. The demon was getting closer. I didn't want to scare the kids around us but I would if I had to. I grabbed the hilt of my sword and...

"Okay, whatcha think," a childlike voice said from beside me.

I glanced down and tried to hide my surprise as my hand fell away from my sword. Raven was no longer an adult, but a cute child dressed in a fairy costume. In addition to looking like an adorable five-year-old, she had masked what she was. "Where did you learn to do that?"

She shrugged. "Dad's been showing me a few tricks."

I watched in stunned surprise as she skipped down an alley between the large row houses. A few minutes later, she cried out, "Mommy! Where are you? I'm scared!"

The demon version of Cinderella perked up, her head whipping in the direction of the alleyway. The evil entity sniffed the air like a hound dog on a hunt. Glancing around to make sure she went unnoticed, the thing made her way into the dark, deserted alley.

"Are you lost, little girl?" she asked, her voice way too deep to be a child's.

Raven's tiny voice wobbled. "Yeah, I lost my mommy and can't find her."

The thing chuckled. "I can help you find her, you know. All you have to do is come closer to me, hold my hand."

Slowly and quietly, I sat down the cheap scythe, pulled the sword out from under my costume, and strolled into the alley to see Raven reach her hand out. The little princess monster chose that moment to morph into something hideous. The dress shredded into scraps as the demon grew. The cute girl had transformed into black, shiny skin and glowing red eyes with gnarly teeth. To my astonishment, the thing still had breasts and a curvy figure. A female demon was odd on Earth, which meant I was in for a terrible night.

Raven's wide eyes swerved to me, her surprise evident from the female demon too. Remembering the task, she shook her head to clear it and then shivered in pretend fear. The ugly thing had no clue I snuck up behind her, not while she had prey within her grasp. Raven mocked a child's cry. The demon rubbed her hands together in glee.

"You smell delicious, child," the demon rasped with a low, croaky tone.

When I was about two feet behind the foul bitch, I said, "She does look good, doesn't she? Too bad you won't get a meal tonight."

The demon swirled to face me and her glowing eyes narrowed. "You think you can stop me, human? I'll just take you instead."

"Come and get me," I taunted.

With an awful, throaty growl, the bitch snaked her long ass tongue out and licked her sharp pointed teeth. "I'll eat you both, you stupid humans."

She charged at me faster than any demon I'd seen yet. In a move that bordered on desperation, I swung my sword with all my might. Her eyes widened in surprise. The blade sunk into her neck and through it, slicing her head from her body. Her red eyes rolled in the air a few times and then the only thing left in the alley was a shredded dress.

"This is going to be a long night. That wasn't a lower demon, Mara." With a worried glance in my direction, Raven shook her head and then poofed out as she collected the demon's black soul to take it back to wherever they go.

My heart thudded from adrenaline, and I thanked whoever would listen for luck being on my side for that one. I shoved the sword back into the scabbard at my waist, took a deep breath for courage, and then headed back into the foray of unsuspecting family members. One down, a lot more to go.

After killing at least a dozen of the vile creatures, I leaned against the brick wall behind a questionable bar in an even more questionable neighborhood. I wiped the sweat off my brow and closed my eyes in exhaustion. My arms ached from the heavy sword, my legs hurt from walking, and I had a nasty blister on my hand from a demon that burned fire when threatened. I just wanted to snuggle in my bed instead of hunting these asswipes. Plus, I was sure I was splattered with some smelly blood, but I was too tired to care.

Raven had disappeared again, dragging whatever was left of the demon trying to steal a drunk woman. I had a few minutes to rest before we were at it again.

A slow clapping sounded from behind me. I snapped my eyes open and turned to face the intruder.

"Bravo, bravo," a gorgeous man said, his hands clapping slowly.

He was tall and handsome. Dark hair, honey-colored eyes, and a chiseled jaw covered in stubble. Dressed in an elaborate prince charming costume, he made his way toward me, the muscles in his arms straining against the white fabric of his tunic.

"Leave me alone and go back to your partying," I said, but he continued to walk in my direction. A hint of warning bells went off in my head.

"Get away from me, asshole," I grunted, reaching for the handle of my sword and waiting for a tingle of awareness, but nothing happened. I wasn't sure what he was, not really. After a night like tonight, you could never be too sure. Looks could be deceiving. After all, even salt looks like sugar. And this guy looked like a whole lot of sugar.

"Nah, I'd rather stay and watch the show," he said with a smile.

"What show? Are you out of your damn mind?"

Hot guy waved his hand to gesture to the alley behind the bar. "Are you not a demon hunter? Because last I checked, that creepy dude wasn't human."

I blinked in surprise. This guy knew about demons? My blood went cold. If he knew about them, that only meant one thing. I hauled my sword out and pointed it at his throat. "Get away from me, Demon," I spit out.

His head tilted back from laughter. I didn't know what he found so funny, but I wasn't laughing with him. I held my sword steady, still aiming the point at his Adam's apple.

"You can't kill me," he said still chuckling. "You can sure try."

Pushing the sword into his neck, I growled, "I will kill you, and you'll beg for mercy."

The demon smiled and kept his eyes on me the entire time. Not once had he looked at the sword currently aimed at his Adam's apple. He winked and said, "I'd like to see that."

Pivoting on my toes, I swirled around and took the sword with me. My momentum was strong, my aim dead on. As I swung the blade around, he was gone. A hand gripped my hilt as my hand came back from the upswing and a strong arm bound around my waist.

"Nice try," a deep voice whispered in my ear. "Want to try again?"

I lifted my free elbow to hit him in the stomach, but he disappeared. "What the fuck?"

"Nice costume, sexy. Easy to remove," he said, his voice floating on thin air. Then he materialized right in front of me with a smile. "But you fight like a girl."

"Last I checked, I am a girl," I growled and lifted my knee before he vanished again. I caught him in the family jewels and he collapsed with a groan. "Suck on that, jerk."

I hefted my sword again to decapitate the dickhead, but I heard Raven's scream. "Mara! Don't!"

However, it was too late; my sword was swinging with full force. Only, instead of the hot, demon looking terrified for his life, he smirked and then evaporated without a hint of smoke or air movement. My shoulder ached, the joint popping at the force of my swing and hitting nothing.

I rolled my shoulder and scowled at Raven. "What was that? He was a demon and you know we're supposed to kill them."

She shook her head. "Not all of them, you know that. And definitely not him."

"Why?" When she remained tight-lipped about it, I closed in on her. "Why not him? What makes him so damn special?"

"You can't, okay?" she said, placing her hand on my shoulder. "Just don't even hurt that guy."

"Why not?!" Raven shook her head and my voice rose an octave. "Tell me!" I demanded, my nostrils flaring in anger.

"No," she barked. "I don't have to tell you anything. And I won't tell you a thing about that guy. I can't."

"Why the hell not?"

Raven sighed and ran a hand over her face, smearing her glittery makeup. "It's complicated."

We remained in awkward silence after the little incident with the hot, demon dude. I slaughtered two demons after him, and when the sun peeked over the horizon, I yawned. The night from hell was finally over, and I could sleep the whole day away. I was utterly exhausted.

"I'm sorry," Raven finally muttered. "I know I tell you everything, but there are some things that I can't out of obligation to my work."

I sighed as we headed back to her car. "You mean the fine-looking jerk that disappeared without an ounce of effort? Lesser demons can't do that. Hell, even the higher ones we saw tonight can't do that. The only person I've ever seen disappear like that before was you and my boss."

She giggled. "You think he was fine?"

"For a vile demon, yes. You'd have to be blind not to."

"Girl, you're hilarious. I love you." She tossed her keys and I caught them in my hand. "I'm going to let you borrow my car. I'm exhausted and don't feel like driving your ass back home. Enjoy." She gave a little finger wave and then vanished with black smoke blowing in the breeze.

I made my way to her car, unlocked it, and sunk into the buttery, soft leather of her blood-red Lexus. She never let me drive her fancy car, and I knew something was up. Rather than question my best friend's motive, I drove home and crashed as soon as I hit the bed.

Chapter 6

No rest for the wicked.

I started my morning reading about demons.

With the insistence of Raven, I checked out a book at the local library to see if I could find some truth hidden between the lines of text. Taking a sip of coffee, I scanned the pages without finding anything particularly useful.

As I flipped halfheartedly through the pages, I ran across a passage about Lucifer's fall from heaven. Apparently, he was a powerful angel in Heaven, and because of pride, he tried to overthrow God. He failed big time. For that reason, he went straight to hell. He was the first fallen angel, or so it says.

Still, there was conflicting information. Some say the fallen angels were in heaven and lusted after women on Earth and God cast them out. If that was the case, where did Satan come from and how is now ruling hell? And when did he begin tricking people for their souls?

I slammed the book shut and slid it across the table in frustration. No amount of written text by humans would have all the information I needed. I took my coffee and went out on the balcony for some fresh air.

The downtown area spread out before me. Platteville, Indiana had its perks. The city had a small-town feel but still had a lot of the amenities I needed. I was within walking distance to restaurants and bars, and I had a parking garage to store my car. Not that I ever had to drive with Raven towing me around, but I had one if I needed it. The only downside to the town was there were demons everywhere. I don't know if the arts brought them out in droves, or if it was because we were close to the river, but you'd think an average-sized city wouldn't have so many demons escaping hell per capita.

"Job security," I said to myself.

As I finished my coffee, my phone chimed in my pocket. Taking it out, I read over the news of a massive pile-up on the highway. No deaths, thank the lucky stars, but there were some injuries. There was a link on the article about an unknown creature on the highway. A grainy video showed something blue loping away from the scene in broad daylight. *Demon.*

Shit.

*****

Breakfast at noon was the best thing in the world.

I listened to the bacon crackle in the pan as I cracked eggs in another. My belly growled and I glanced at the box of donuts longingly. Maybe one or two won't hurt. Actually, four or five during the day made sense. Which reminded me I needed to pick up some more after breakfast. Scraping the partially scrambled eggs inside the pan, I loaded it with crispy bacon and cheese.

Today was my day off and I was going to enjoy my breakfast, then a donut or two, and maybe some cookies. Hell, maybe an entire carton of ice cream for dinner. I deserved it, dammit. Hunting demons for a living sucked colossal, hairy balls.

I began to question life's choices as I heaped a dollop of eggs on top of a cream donut, but I shrugged my shoulders and took a bite.

"God, you gross me out," Raven said, abruptly seated in the chair next to mine.

After jumping from surprise, as a good demon hunter should, I rolled my eyes at her. "Your little parlor trick is annoying. You could knock like a normal person, you know. Shouldn't you be working? Or sleeping? Or whatever you do on your downtime. I know you're not here to take me out shopping or whatever."

She took a deep breath, and then said, "Welllll, about that. Your day off is going to suck."

"No, no. I'm not going to work tonight. It's my break this year. I'm going to sit here, watch sappy movies on TV, and then I'm going to cry into my ice cream."

"You don't cry," Raven stated with a raised eyebrow. She had me there. "You won't be gone long. The big ole boss man wants to have a word with you."

The blood drained from my face as I dropped my half-eaten donut and scrambled egg concoction on the plate. "What? Why?"

Raven shrugged. "Nothing serious. At least I think so. Well, I don't know what he wants. I was just sent here to collect you."

I stood up and huffed. "Hell to the no. Tell that bastard if he wants to see me, he can come to Earth like a normal person. I'm not going to hell to have a chat with him. I'll never get that sulfuric stench out of my clothes."

"I thought you'd say that." Raven sighed. "You know Ol' Luke won't like being denied."

"Luke," I snorted at her nickname for Lucifer. "Can I call him Luke?"

"Not if you like your appendages attached to your body."

"Fine." I stood and threw the plate in the sink, woefully staring at my breakfast. "Tell him I'll meet with him here, on Earth."

Raven sighed, and then shook her head. "He won't like it, Mara. You know he's going to be pissed, and when the guy is pissed, there's fire and brimstone. Pun intended."

"I don't care what he thinks or if he's upset. This is my day off, and I'm not going to come running because the King of the underworld wants to see me." Wiping a hand over my face in frustration, I barked, "He can kiss my ass!"

Raven pecked me on the cheek. "That's why I love you. I'll let him know. Just be prepared for the consequences."

The air quivered as she departed to tell my boss that I had told him to kiss my ass. *Shit on a pancake*. I tended to be grouchy and unruly in the morning, more so than I am on a normal basis. And she'd ruined my breakfast with seeing my boss again. To make matters worse, I may have pissed off the man who had the option of canceling my contract and dragging me straight to hell.

Chapter 7

The mind is its own place, and in itself,
can make a heaven of hell,
and a hell of heaven.

While I waited for Raven, I stared up the steeple of the church near my favorite donut stop as misty rain fell. I wondered if I could pray for donuts, but I think that was frowned upon.

Instead, I went inside and placed my order like a normal human being. While I waited, I wondered if there was such a thing as a donut god, or maybe a coffee god. There could be. I doubted any of them would listen to me anyway. I didn't have a soul to barter with, or one to ask for forgiveness. Besides, I needed something delicious if my day was to suck later on.

The baker loaded the white box with all kinds of goodies after I pointed at them through the glass case. Custard filled ones with chocolate icing, cinnamon rolls as big as my face, and regular yeast donuts.

"Anything else?" he asked with a polite smile.

I shook my head. After I paid for the donuts, I took the box and stepped outside into the rain. Not able to hold back, I opened the box and grabbed one of the custard ones. I took a big bite with a moan. Once that one was finished, I grabbed the next one and glanced up to make sure nobody judged me gorging on donuts.

A man in a dark outfit crossed the road, his head buried in a book. He didn't see the bus coming his way. The road was slick and there was no way the bus would stop in time.

Without thinking, I dropped my box of donuts and ran. The bus honked and the guy finally looked up with wide eyes. Tires scraped on the wet pavement. I dove to move the man out of the way. With just inches to spare, I shoved both of us off the street. I was sure the tire of the bus touched my leg. We landed in a heap of legs and limbs, but we were unscathed besides a scrape or two.

Unwrapping myself from the man, I checked him for any wounds. "Are you alright?"

The gentleman appeared to be in his late forties, maybe mid-fifties with hair the same color gray as the dreary clouds above us. His eyes crinkled as he smiled, and kind brown eyes peered at me behind an average face. He nodded. "Thank you. You and the Lord saved me today."

I frowned and looked down at the book he still held in his right hand. A Bible. Then I took in his dark suit and the white clerical collar. This man was a priest. I had saved a priest.

Standing, I cleared my throat and shifted my feet. "Uh, I'm glad you're okay."

He got to his feet and tilted his head as he watched me. "Would you like a blessing, my child?"

I startled. "A blessing? No, I don't think that's a good idea."

With a grin, he put a warm hand on my shoulder. "Do you think you're not worthy of one? I do. You saved my life."

My mouth opened, but nothing came out. How could I explain to a priest that his competitor owned my soul? That I worked for the enemy? My face paled the more I thought about it. I took a step back, but he steeled his grip.

"I must do this. Please."

With uncertainty, I nodded. A blessing or prayer wouldn't help my predicament, but it was worth a shot. I hoped I didn't burst into flames.

I held still as the priest pulled out a glass container from his pocket. A cross decorated the frosted glass and he whispered something over it so low I couldn't hear what was being said. He popped the cap off and dipped the container with his finger over the open neck.

With a wet finger, he drew a cross on my forehead as he said, "St. Michael the Archangel, defend us in battle; be our defense against the wickedness and snares of the devil. May God rebuke him, we humbly pray, and do thou, O prince of the heavenly host, by the power of God, thrust into hell Satan and all the other evil spirits who prowl about the world seeking the ruin of souls. Amen." He motioned with a hand on his forehead, his stomach, and then each shoulder.

Stock still, I watched as the priest put away his holy water and tucked the bible away in his suit jacket. "What blessing was that?"

"Thank you for risking your life to save another." He grinned, patting his bible behind the fabric of his suit. "You're welcome to join us for mass. We would love to have you."

"Thank you?" Okay, so my thanks came out more like a question. Maybe the priest knew all about me, and maybe he felt the evil along the surface of my being. He dipped his head in way of a farewell and walked into the church across the street from the donut shop.

I remained frozen in amazement as I stared up the church he had entered. The sign read Our Lady of Angels Cathedral. The Gothic-style brick building filled up an entire block, its stained glass glimmering in the sun. I inspected a few windows in confusion, not because I didn't believe in churches and Christianity, but because I didn't understand what any of the symbolism meant.

Maybe, just maybe, this blessing could help me in the end. After a minute of false hope, I snorted. No, I was on a straight track to hell.

After I collected what donuts I could from the dropped box, I waited as I ate a rescued yeast donut. However, Raven never showed on our scheduled time, so I assumed she had a death to deal with. It was, after all, her job. With a deep breath of courage, I slowly ambled to my destination to wait for my boss's arrival.

CHAPTER 8

Working for my boss is hell.

I chewed my thumbnail as I waited outside the coffee house I sometimes met my boss, otherwise known as the Devil himself. This was the first time in over a year I had to deal with him in person.

I was nervous, and if I was honest, I was scared shitless. I knew Raven would tell him word for word what I had said. I liked Earth. I liked my tiny one-bedroom apartment. I liked smelling like perfume and body wash instead of sulfur. If I thought God would help my tarnished soul, I'd pray. He's supposed to forgive all sins, right? I don't think he'd be able to save me, though. According to most Christians, he was merciful and…

Crap on a cracker. A gorgeous, tall man headed straight for me. Dressed in dark, ripped jeans and a "highway to hell" black T-shirt, he drew the eye of every woman near him, and a few men, too. They ogled him as he passed, some more obvious than others.

I wasn't impressed. I knew what he was, where he came from. The man was the same demon from last night, the one behind the bar I had kneed in the crotch. He smirked when he saw me, his eyes sparkling in the sunlight. I resisted the urge to kick him in the nuts again.

"How are your balls?" I asked when he was within a few feet from me.

"Well, they could be better," he said. "They could be on your chin."

"You'll never have those filthy, demon balls near my body. Now or ever." I poked my sharp fingernail against his chest. "What are you doing here, douchebag? If I wasn't concerned about innocent bystanders, my sword would be slicing through your neck right now."

The dude laughed. Again. I yanked my finger back in disgust. "What's so funny?"

"Oh, just that you think you can kill me," he said, still chuckling. "But that's not why I'm here."

I rolled my eyes so hard it hurt. "Then why are you here? I don't have time for games, asshole, I have a meeting."

"Ah, yes. Your meeting. Let's get to it." He snatched my arm with his strong hand.

My skin prickled painfully and the world faded around me. "Son of a bitch!"

*****

I gagged when I crashed on a hard, red brick floor. Oz may have a yellow brick road, but hell had a red one coated with black speckles of blood. The stench of sulfur and the enormous heat of my surroundings filled my lungs. Think of it as walking outside in high humidity when it was a hundred and ten degrees. That, plus a horrible smell of rotten eggs. Not my idea of a good time.

The walls to my right writhed and squirmed, ghoulish hands reaching for me with moaning eagerness. I assumed they were tortured souls, but with the stench and unbearable heat, they could be a figment of my imagination. Hell was like a horrible, ghastly haunted house, only with *real* demons and rotting corpses.

Righting myself, I shoved my hands into my captor's chest angrily. "Where the hell am I?"

He grinned. "I think you know, and besides, you pretty much answered your own question."

"You lowlife, demon scum. I would kick your ass if I could breathe in this nasty ass air." I lifted my hand to punch him. "Stay the fu—"

"Mara,' said a deep, commanding voice, the same voice from when I negotiated my contract to stay on Earth as a child.

My fist fell to my side but stayed clenched. I turned on my heels to face the man, or beast, which had ruined my life. I didn't care if he was a ruler of death and demons. I didn't care if he was the opposite of good and Godliness. He had pulled me away from my carton of ice cream and lounging in pajamas all day, and that time was sacred.

He sat on a throne made of skeletons yellowed from age and probably more blood than I could imagine. Granted, he didn't look like the biblical version of Satan. He resembled an extremely tall Christopher Walken, but more evil and scary with goat eyes and black, curled horns on his head

My nostrils flared, no longer caring about anything but my pajamas. Of course, the reason for my mood might be that I was on the verge of PMS. "Why did you send one of your dogs to drag me down here to have a meeting? Couldn't you have had a nice cup of mocha latte bullshit and meet me with the rest of the humans?"

The "dog" in question chuckled. I tossed a glare in his direction.

Lucifer's face went stony. His voice rumbled as he said, "Don't speak to me in such a manner. I'm not human. I never was. It's best you remember your place before I take it from your cold, dead fingers."

"But—"

"I said do not speak!" he thundered, flames rising behind him and blasting heat across my face.

When I rolled my eyes on habit, his eyes narrowed as he rose from his skeletal throne. The souls trapped in the walls wailed as they thrashed against their torturous confines. They practically skittered away from him as he moved in my direction.

Dread rippled across my skin. He took souls for a living, tortured them for all eternity. Reveled in the anguish like a junkie for his next drug fix. I took a deep breath of stinky air and steeled myself for what was to come. I remained silent, no matter how hard it was to keep my freaking big mouth shut.

His seven-foot tall frame walked around my body and then stopped directly in front of me. "Bend over."

I blinked in confusion as I looked up at him. "What?"

"I'm supposed to kiss your ass, no?" His eyes turned a bright, flaming red like they were made of fire. "You seem to have a problem with authority, and it's about time you learned your lesson about talking back and ignoring your superiors. Raven, while she has leniency due to her father, is trying to keep you out of trouble. I'm starting to believe that's impossible."

Clearing my throat, I said, "But I'm doing an extraordinary job of slaughtering the lesser demons, which you had asked me to do."

His eyebrow rose. "Yes, you are, but you have avoided me for months. In addition, you've seem to come to the belief that all demons are vile, evil creatures. You are *not* to slaughter each one or attempt to. I hired you to expel the ones that escape, not every single being that you see fit."

"But, sir, that's rare to see one on the surface that hasn't escaped."

"Quiet!" he thundered and the tortured souls whimpered.

I remained silent and still. Ol' Luke paced back and forth in front of me, his finger tapping on his chin. He stopped directly in front of me with those creepy, goat-like eyes.

"For some unknown reason, Raven and her father adore you. I cannot fathom why, but without them, I wouldn't have anyone to bring me souls." He tilted his head and sniffed the air before leaning forward to inspect my forehead.

Oh no. The priest. I remained stock-still, hoping he hadn't seen the holy water from the priest's blessing. If he had, I was so fucked. His hot breath flittered over my face, his breath smelling of campfire smoke.

He frowned but straightened as he clenched his fists. "On the other hand, your constant screw-ups and smart mouth is the bane of my existence. Besides your avoidance of me and the help of your reaper friends, we all know how this will end. We won't even go into the good deed you think will save you from my wrath after your death. You're mine, no matter how many times you volunteer at that wretched place. Which will stop immediately, by the way."

My heart stuttered. Nobody knew I volunteered at the shelter, or so I had assumed. How wrong I had been. "I..." What? There was nothing I said that would change his mind. I choked down the rage at his little spies, but I wanted to slaughter them all.

"It. Stops. Now. It would be a shame if the abusers and sexual deviants found the place, along with a few demons. Isn't that right?"

I swallowed. Hard. He hit me right in the feels with that warning.

The Devil smirked, knowing he had me where he wanted me. Then he tilted his head in a terrifying way as if he debated on inviting me to dinner or ripping my soul from my body. I was going with the latter. "You're lucky Raven speaks so highly of you, and that Death also spoke on your behalf. Against my better judgment, I'm going to give you a second chance. You have two months to prove that you're worth staying on Earth among the humans. Sixty days. If you can't show me you're a valuable employee, then you'll be breakfast." He pointed to the writhing wall and the souls screeched as they reached out for me again.

I let out a shaky breath. "Thank you, sir, you won't disappoint you."

"I'm not finished." After a moment of eerie silence, he said, "Raven will still be allowed to be your guardian, or best friend, or whatever she is to you." His mouth blossomed into a spine-chilling smile, his teeth all pointy and sharp. "However, Coren will now be in charge of you and will assist me with your unruly defiance. With whatever means necessary."

"Coren? Who's that?" I asked, my heart thundering behind my ribcage. I wasn't sure if it was in fear or anger. Probably a mix of both.

"Sixty days, Mara. Your time starts at midnight tonight." He waved his hand to dismiss me and ripped one of the souls from the wall. The black mass screeched and clawed its hands along the floor as my boss dragged the poor thing from the room.

The being was nothing but blackness, but it left nail marks against the red brick. I shuddered. This place was the stuff of nightmares.

CHAPTER 9

The only good demon is a dead one.

I turned and ran into the chest of the guy who had dragged me to this wretched place. The annoying but gorgeous demon laughed at me. Then he grabbed my arm and transported me out of there while I cussed and spit ugly words at him.

We landed in front of my tiny apartment complex, luckily without anyone spotting us. I mean, how could I really explain that to Mrs. Spivey who lived upstairs? She'd probably drop dead. Then I'd have to explain her death to Raven and her father. No thank you.

I spun and faced the jerk who had hauled me to hell and back. Literally. "Fine. I'm home now, no thanks to you. You can go back to the underworld."

He shook his head slowly. "Afraid I can't do that, girlie."

"And why not?"

"Allow me to finally introduce myself." He bowed slightly with a mischievous grin. "My name's Coren."

My face blanched and my stomach plummeted. *This* was who I was to spend the next two months with? "But you're a demon."

"You can call me whatever you want," he said with a wink as he righted himself.

"How about dumbass? Does that work for you?"

He narrowed his eyes, but the smile remained pasted on his face. "No, I think not. But while you're screaming under me later, you can scratch any name into my back. I'm not picky."

I tossed my hands up in frustration. "You're going to be a pain in my ass, aren't you?" When he shrugged, I growled, "I don't need your help. I'm fine doing this by myself, thank you very much."

Turning on my heels, I headed to the stairs that led up to my tiny apartment. His footsteps pounded right behind me.

"Well," Coren said, "somehow I doubt that. If you were, I wouldn't be babysitting you."

"Let's just say you can go do whatever havoc you demons do on earth. Live it up while you can."

I shoved the key into my door, unlocked it, and slid inside the door, getting ready to slam it in his face. His hand stopped the door, budged me out of the way, and then he made his way into my apartment.

"Why? So you can try to unsuccessfully kill me again?" He looked around a bit, a frown on his face. "This is where you live?"

I sighed and scrubbed my hand over my face. "Yes. Why?"

"I can't live here. It's too small. Where am I supposed to sleep?"

"Um, how about a hotel? Or on the street? You are *not* staying here," I grunted, tossing my keys on my small, scratched kitchen counter.

He didn't respond but started inspecting my apartment instead. His eyes roamed my romance novels on the bookshelf and he snorted.

With a sigh, I removed a bottle of vodka from the cabinet. Placing a bit of ice in my glass and filling it with the liquor, I chugged the bitter liquid. Pouring another, I took a second shot.

I heard the telltale swish of my sword coming out of its scabbard, and I swung to face him. He held my curved sword up to the light and inspected it with a whistle. "Where did you get this bad boy?"

I stormed up to him and attempted to grab my sword out of his hand, but he lifted it out of my reach. "It was a gift from Raven."

His eyebrows rose. "Do you even know what that is?"

"Duh, a sword, dumbass."

He chuckled. "Thank you, captain obvious. No, do you know what it's made from?"

"I'm assuming steel or something. Why?"

"No, that's not steel. Otherwise, it would weigh a freaking ton." He flipped it over a few times.

"Whatever it is, I don't care. It gets the job done." I finally snatched the sword from his grip. Taking the scabbard from his other hand, I tucked the sword back in the sleeve. "Best you remember that."

He opened his mouth to say something more, but shook his head and said, "I'm shaking in my boots. Speaking of those, I bet my boots would look nice under your bed while you screamed under me."

Letting out a frustrated breath, I opened the closet and tossed a blanket and pillow at him. He caught them easily with one hand.

"You stay in here. Got it? No funny business."

"Whatever you say, *dear*," he replied, his mouth edging into a smirk.

With an exhausted breath, I headed to my bedroom, locked the door, and sat my sword on the dresser near my bed. I never knew when I might have to use it, and I'd gladly stab him if he decided to break my lock for a surprise visit. I wished he wasn't so damn good looking, so damn tempting. And so annoying. This was going to be a rough two months.

*****

The next morning, I had snuck out of my apartment for coffee while Coren snored away on the couch.

The air was crisp as people buzzed around in their business attire and I regretted not brushing my teeth as the barista took my order. Yes, I got Coren a cup of coffee, too. Of course, I ordered it black to match the color of his evil soul.

Cups in hand, I turned around and stopped in surprise. Coren stood there with messy hair, arms tightly across his chest, and a glare that would freeze most people to the core. How had he found me? I went around his intimidating presence and headed out the door.

He caught up with me. "What were you thinking? You left without telling me."

"I wanted coffee. I didn't realize I needed your permission."

"I'm in charge of watching you, and that means twenty-four hours a day."

"Listen jackass," I swerved to face him, "you are not my babysitter. I don't need somebody on my ass all freaking day."

"Um, your boss begs to differ. You will not leave without me. Got it?"

"Don't tell me what to do!" I screamed, and people walking down the sidewalk gave us a wide berth.

Coren growled, "I can order you around all I want! Don't ever think I can't."

"Keep thinking that. That'll be your biggest pitfall." I shoved the coffee into his chest and a bit of the hot liquid spilled out of the lid onto his shirt. He winced but grabbed the coffee. "I thought you'd like this. Go choke on it."

Swirling on my feet, I marched away from him, anger pooling in my veins. My hands shook, my heart thundered. My cheeks burned. Who does this guy think he is?

With the sound of his boots on the sidewalk behind me, I ignored him to the best of my ability. However, each footstep shot my blood pressure higher and higher. By the time we arrived back to my apartment, I believed I'd pass out from rage. I unlocked the door, began to slam it in his face, but he caught it with his palm and then shut it calmly behind him.

"Thank you for the coffee," he muttered.

Instead of giving him a reply, I slammed the bathroom door shut behind me and locked it before starting the shower. I had to get rid of him before I went to volunteer at the shelter today or figure out how to get out of my apartment without him knowing. Could I climb out the bathroom window without breaking my legs? Would he find me again? I couldn't have him shadowing me, especially after the warning about my kind deeds. As the warm water cascaded over my body, I had a thought. What if he could help hide it? Would he?

Only after I shut off the water had I realized I hadn't brought any clothes with me. That meant I'd have to go out in only a skimpy towel. Glancing at the frosted glass window in the bathroom, I realized sneaking out wouldn't work. Not half-naked. Plus, I was on the third floor. Shit.

After successfully tiptoeing out of the bathroom in only a towel, I dressed and walked into my tiny kitchen to find Coren cooking scrambled eggs.

"What's this?" I asked, my stomach rumbling at the smell.

"A thank you for the coffee. I'm sorry. I can be an asshole sometimes. I take my jobs seriously, especially this one."

I frowned. "Why is this one so important?"

Coren was silent for a few minutes. "It's a long story, but I have to be successful when it comes to you. I can't screw up. Not again."

His words caught me off guard, so much so that I took a step back. "What do you mean *again*?"

He looked up from the stove and his caramel-colored eyes penetrated mine. "You're not the only one who has a timeline to prove their worth."

CHAPTER 10

All demons like chaos, right?

After Coren announced that he had a limited time left too, I sat on my bed in deep thought. Was he lying? Maybe. Maybe not.

Most importantly, would it be smart to have him here with the threat of his job looming over him? Why did I care? So many questions ran through my head, but one thing stood out the most; the devil threatened the center with chaos and death. Could I do that to them? Was my help going to hurt those innocent people?

A knock sounded on my doorframe and Coren stood there with two plates of eggs. "What's on your mind?"

I shook my head, so he sat beside me on the bed and handed me a plate and fork. We ate in silence for a few minutes, and finally, with a mouthful of eggs, I grumbled, "I'm supposed to volunteer at the shelter today."

He chewed as he watched me. "I see."

"I can't let the people down. If I go in, I will hate myself if you-know-who found out. If I don't, I will still hate myself."

"Quite a conundrum."

"Big word coming from you," I said back. Sure, I spoke out of frustration, but I was at a loss on what to do.

"And what are you going to do about the *conundrum*?"

"I don't know. You'll just follow me and try to stop me. Or Lucifer will kill them all. Neither situation is something I want to deal with." I stared down at my now empty plate. I felt the tears well up, but I blinked them away. I rarely cried, even when a demon sliced my leg open, but I did over those innocents at the shelter a time or two.

"What if there was a way to keep him from knowing?" Coren asked softly as if he was afraid to say it.

My eyes caught his again. "What are you saying?"

"I could help you, but it comes with a price. Are you willing to pay it?"

"What kind of price are we talking?"

"You'll find out when I collect."

With a deep breath, my heart and head waged a war with each other. Why would he help me? Would the price be worth it? God, help me out here, I begged. No reply came. I had to make this decision on my own and trust a man, or a *demon*, I barely knew.

Finally, after a few minutes of playing with my fork, I nodded. "Deal."

Coren beamed at me. I felt like I had made another deal for my soul.

*****

"Laura, this is Coren. He'll be helping today," I said as I introduced a kindhearted woman with Satan's assistant. God help us all. I was out of my damn mind.

"Nice to meet you," she said as she shook his hand.

I expected lightning to strike, to see a spark of fear behind her eyes, or the wrath of God to rain down on us for standing inside Safety Net. Instead, Laura's cheeks reddened and she glanced at Coren with bashful eyes. Blinking in surprise at her reaction, I observed her as she ogled the good-looking demon she assumed was a normal man.

Shuffling on my feet at the thought of this monster inside of a place of solitude and safety, I glanced around the space before my eyes landed on Coren again. He smiled at Laura, a hint of cockiness fluttering behind those dark eyes. Bringing him here was a mistake.

Then he surprised me by asking, "How can I help today?"

"Well, do you mind doing some activities with the children? They would love to have somebody to play with."

My heart stuttered. Coren. With. Children.

"I'd love to. Just lead the way," he said.

With a big, flirty smile, Laura led him out of the kitchen. Coren glanced at me with a smirk as the door shut and I wanted to hyperventilate.

"I led the wolf to the sheep," I whispered, my hands trembling as I rubbed my face in frustration.

A few moments later, I heard children laughing. Coren laughing. Peeking through the opening between the kitchen and dining room, I spotted him running around with the kids as they played tag. He had a full smile on his face as he dodged a little boy's hand reaching out to "tag" him. I blinked in surprise. He looked like a kid himself as he pretended to hide behind a table.

Coren glanced up and caught me watching him. Retreating in embarrassment, I took a deep breath and tried to remember the reason he was here. The man, no, demon, was my chaperon for less than a month. I bargained something nameless with him to be here, but I'd do it all over again. These people needed me. Laura needed me.

We spent the day apart doing our own separate chores until it was dish duty, and I sighed as Laura showed him back to the kitchen. Both of us worked in silence for a while. I washed, rinsed in the solution, and handed him the clean dishes to dry.

"You don't have to do this, you know," I grumbled as Coren toweled a plate I had washed. He ruined the happiness of my moment, the one time I felt ordinary. I know he hadn't done anything but good today, and he hid that we came here, but my brain's reaction to his presence was defensive.

"I know I don't, but I'm actually enjoying this."

I snorted cynically. "I didn't think you'd like something so honorable."

Coren's hands stopped mid-drying and he frowned at me. "Why?"

"Well, I figured you wouldn't like happiness and hope." Instead of honoring him with a glance, I stared out the window as I scrubbed a cup in the warm, soapy water. "Demons like chaos and agony. Murder and mayhem. This is far from it."

A few uncomfortable seconds passed, but out of the corner of my eye, I noticed Coren's hands shake and his chest lifting in slow, calming breaths. Then I looked at him. His eyes inspected mine as his nostrils flared. He shook his head as if he were frustrated with me.

"These people have seen their fair share of chaos and agony, don't you think? Some even watched loved ones be slaughtered." His hands started moving in erratic, angry motions with his drying task. "They endured insults and judgments because of speculation, heartless words thrown around without guilt. None of this was from demons, Mara. *Humans* can be just as cruel."

With that, he slammed down the plate he was drying and stormed out of the kitchen. I watched him go with my hands dripping soapy water on to my jeans. Was he right? Was I truly as much of a monster by condemning him because of where he came from?

Maybe. Maybe not.

What he did today didn't change my training ingrained from Raven. Why was he any different from the others? Sure, he volunteered without complaint. There was still a question niggling the back of my mind. Was I ready to pay his price for hiding us today, whatever that may be?

CHAPTER 11

Temptation is just another demon to fight.

Coren stood on my balcony, his face bathed in the glow of the setting sun. The sunset illuminated his gorgeous profile, as well as his strong arms and muscled physic.

"Don't stare," I mumbled to myself. "He's off-limits, idiot. You know this."

My hormones didn't care, though. They fired on all pistons as soon as the golden light hit his sharp jaw and dark hair. I swear to God, when I snuck a peek at him playing with those children at the shelter, my ovaries moaned. Traitorous body.

"Don't forget who and what he is, Mara," I muttered and then took a deep breath for strength. Coren was evil. He worked for the Devil. He rose up from hell, his soul dark as coal. I only had to deal with him for two months. I could do this.

The idea of my boss and the amount of time I had left to save my soul sobered my hormones right up. Gone was the temptation of Coren. However, I still felt it rumbling below the surface. I frowned. Emotions and lust had never bothered me before. *Cold is my name, heartless is my game* I thought and then laughed at myself.

"What's so funny?" Coren asked.

Jumping in surprise, I spun to face him with a scowl.

"Ah, so you're back to hating me again I see." He edged closer and trapped me against the counter.

I swallowed.

His arms lifted and my fight or flight instinct kicked in. Then he reached into the cabinet and grabbed a bowl. "I'm hungry. You want some?"

"Want some of what?" I breathed.

He reached above me, his arm barely brushing my hair. He smiled down at me, his mouth close to mine. I just had to move about an inch to kiss him, to feel his body pressed against mine. My heart stuttered. Goosebumps pebbled on my skin. His hand lowered… and he held up a box of Fruity Pebbles in my view.

"Cereal? What did you think I was talking about?"

I opened my mouth to say something, anything at all but snapped it closed. He gave me a wink and moved away from my body to grab the milk from the fridge.

As he poured both of us a bowl of cereal, I told my body to quit being a sap. I didn't do romance, and I sure as hell wasn't interested in a demon. Coren's boss and cohort was the reason I was stuck in a job I hated for the rest of my life. However, my eyes took in his muscles jerking as he put away the box of Fruity Pebbles and milk.

Then my eyes snaked to the calendar with the cute kittens on my fridge. Keeping my soul was uncertain and I had no way of knowing if I'd make it out unscathed.

*****

"Where have you been?" I growled as my best friend materialized in my bedroom.

"I'm sorry. It's been a crazy few days," Raven said, her face a mask of regret. "I've tried a million different ways to talk Luke out of this stupid deal with you, and having Coren here with you. My father even attempted to do the same. I can't help but feel like this is my fault somehow."

Sitting on my bed, I let out a breath and shook my head. "It's not, Raven. None of this was your fault. I got myself into this predicament and I'll find a way to get myself out of it."

"No. You aren't doing this alone. I won't let you. My father won't let you. We love you too much to let you down now."

Blinking in surprise at her confession, I said, "You don't have to do that. I don't know what Lucifer will do to you guys."

"What's he going to do? We bring damaged souls to him for his sick and twisted needs. Without reapers, hell wouldn't exist."

"And neither would heaven."

"Nah, that place won't ever fall, and somebody would take our place to bring souls there. There is too much good in the world, whether you believe it or not. Besides, have you seen how hot angels are?"

I laughed. "I've never heard you say a word about angels before. You didn't tell me they were good looking."

"Yeah, but they are off-limits. I can still watch them and admire their bodies from afar."

We chuckled at that, and then she glanced around my room until her eyes fell on my sword. "It's been a while since I sharpened your blade. The hellfires are the best way to do it. I feel like I have to do something for you."

"I have to hunt demons tonight. With a demon." I groaned. I hadn't thought about it until now. Falling back on my bed, I rubbed my face and held back a scream.

Raven grinned. "I'll have it back to you this evening before the sun even sets. Trust me."

Oh, I trusted her. I didn't trust Coren. What happens if he attacked and I didn't have something to protect myself? On the other hand, I knew Raven wouldn't leave me without protection if she felt I was truly in danger. I nodded. "Okay. My baby is due for some love anyway."

Standing, I grabbed my sword and petted it. As I went to hand it over, Raven's arms came around me in a hug. I remained stiff and unsure. Emotion wasn't something I handled well and her display of affection was abnormal. It made me nervous.

When she finally pulled away, she smirked. "Girl, you have to learn to drop those thick walls around your heart sometimes."

"Emotions are messy and unnecessary." My face was blank, my body rigid. However, I did care for

Raven and her father. A lot. They were the only family I had ever really known. My mother didn't count. She wasn't a model parent, and she was dead.

Grabbing my sword from my outstretched hand, Raven grinned. "I love you too." Then she vanished in a whiff of black smoke, a laugh echoing as she disappeared.

The bedroom door bashed open and Coren marched in with a large kitchen knife, his other hand held out in front of him like he were a wizard casting a spell. I jumped in surprise at the intrusion and gaped at him.

"I felt something fade inside your room," he said, his eyes surveying the area in suspicion. "Are you okay?"

When I didn't answer quickly enough, he threw me behind him and whipped opened my closet doors looking for the intruder.

"Fade? Is that what you guys call it?" When he looked at me for an explanation, I shook my head in frustration. "You're a little slow on your game, moron. Raven poofed in about twenty minutes ago. She just left."

"Raven," he said with a nod. "She's a sneaky little weasel. I should've felt her arrival the moment she faded in."

"She has to be. I don't think she wants to be noticed when she's dragging souls to heaven and hell."

Coren shivered. "Or purgatory."

"I remember that word when I snuck off and went to bible study as a child. Purgatory is a real place?"

"Very real. The tests as they await their fate can be brutal, and in between those tests, there is nothing but dead silence and isolation. It's enough to drive someone mad. I get why people can fear silence."

My eyebrows hit my hairline. "How would you know that?"

His eyes avoided mine. "We need to formulate a plan on the demon hunting tonight. The clock's ticking and I don't want to be caught unprepared."

As he walked out of my bedroom, I followed. "So you're not going to tell me how a demon knows about the perils of purgatory?"

"You really want to know how I know?" he asked and spun around so fast I almost ran into him. With our bodies inches from each other, Coren's eyes narrowed. He leaned his face down, and I thought he might kiss me, but he whispered in my ear instead. "I've observed thousands of persecuted souls that begged for another test. Just one. More. Test."

My eyes widened while the hair rose along the back of my neck. He lifted his head away from my ear and watched my expression. These sixty days were my test. My one test to keep my soul protected for another day. Coren's face appeared cold and calculating like he longed to be back in hell punishing those souls. I shivered though I were inches away from his radiating body heat. However, no matter detached he appeared to be about the souls begging for another chance, I swore I saw pain and regret in the dark depths of his eyes.

A demon with regret? Nah. Impossible.

CHAPTER 12

Demons, monsters, and death oh my!

"Where is Raven?" I demanded as I paced the living room of my tiny apartment.

"If she said she'd be back with your sword before the hunt tonight, she meant it," Coren said, but his words were no reassurance.

I was going to be late, dammit. Not a good way to start a workday with my boss breathing down my neck.

The air quivered and Raven faded in. "Sorry! I'm behind at work. Stubborn old Italian lady who didn't want to leave her secret recipe behind. Another middle-aged businessman who wanted to negotiate his death with me, like it was my choice he ate his weight in greasy foods and suffered a heart attack. Then, of all things," she paused and swallowed, "I had to take a child. I hate taking children. They shouldn't die so young."

Coren and I were silent. Raven spoke about her job occasionally, and her emotions were erratic when children were involved. I wanted to hug her as she blinked back tears. However, this was her job. An inherited job, sure, but people of all ages died. That was the one thing that didn't discriminate. Death was a part of life.

I blinked in shock at my thoughts. Wow. Was I really that jaded and cold-hearted?

Instead of letting my best friend stand in the middle of the room choking back tears, I took a few steps and awkwardly wrapped an arm around her. Patting her back, I said, "There, there. Everything will be okay."

Coren's laughter caught us off guard and we glared at him.

"That was even awkward for me, Mara. You hugged her like she was a prickly cactus."

"I did not," I argued.

"Yeah, you did," Raven said. "But I know you're not good with all this emotional stuff, so that's okay. Even attempting to comfort me meant more than you know. Anyway," she held out my sword, "I wanted to bring this back to you before you were late."

I gently took the sword from her hands and ran my fingers across the beautiful blade. The cool, dark metal hummed as I stroked it and a small smile formed on my lips. My sword always reacted to my touch.

"You're turning me on stroking your sword like that," Coren said. I turned my eyes up to his and he smirked. "If you want to stroke something of mine, I'd let you."

"How about you go fuck yourself?" I responded.

Raven chuckled.

Coren winked. "Only if you help."

"Okay," Raven said, "let's get off the sexual crap and get to work. We have some demons to send to hell."

*****

"I'm starting to think you're bad luck," I told Coren as we made our way through the dance clubs.

"Just because we haven't spotted a demon doesn't mean I'm bad luck," he said as we strolled to our next location.

Raven, Coren, and I had stopped outside of a club called Serpent. I frowned. This place hadn't been here a week ago, and I inspected the red sign hanging above the door. The "S" in serpent was shaped like a snake eating the letter E. My eyes wandered to the line of partygoers hoping to gain entrance to the newest club on the party strip. Something drew my attention to the club, even though my hidden sword vibrated against my back in warning. I adjusted my leather jacket and hair in hopes to keep the weapon concealed from peering eyes.

"Let's go in here," I said and began walking to see if the bouncer would make us wait in line like the rest of the crowd.

Raven grabbed my elbow and stopped me. "Something about this place is giving me a crazy vibe."

"I agree," Coren said. "Let's move to the next club. We'd probably never get in here anyway."

As soon as Raven let go of my arm, I pretended to stroll past the club but swerved in the direction of the bouncer instead. Coren let out a grunt of surprise.

"Mara," Raven warned, but followed me anyway.

"Name?" the bouncer asked. His bright indigo eyes watched me with eerie intensity, but I refused to squirm under his unwavering gaze.

"Mara Argueta."

The bouncer tapped on an iPad with a tanned finger, his gaze still swerving to me occasionally.

"I don't like this," Coren muttered.

After a beep coming from his tablet, the bouncer nodded at the three of us and opened the chain to allow us inside. No questions, no cover charge. The people waiting in line said a few choice words to the bouncer and us, but loud music vibrating through our bodies drowned out their protests. I didn't want to question our unrestricted entrance, but something felt off about it.

The dance club was unlike anything I'd ever seen. Large flaming sconces scattered the walls, and I wasn't too sure if the flames were real or not. A large brick bar accented with wrought iron and glowing candelabras was too our right and a large black marble dance floor to our left. The atmosphere was dark but illuminated enough to see the other patrons and each other.

"This place looks gothic." Coren shook his head. "If I didn't know better, I'd say they were either going for the medieval look, but I think they were trying to make it look like –"

"Hell," Raven finished for him.

Too stunned to respond to either of them, I surveyed the people surrounding us with confusion. The bartenders and servers wore strappy leather that barely covered their private parts and nipples. With weird techno music pounding through hidden speakers, the dancefloor was full of couples intertwined and dancing offbeat.

My sword rattled on my back. Then my skin prickled. Actually, my whole body vibrated with awareness and I swung my wide eyes to Raven and Coren. We had to get out of here. I opened my mouth to speak, however, the DJ said something in Latin and the crowd around us screamed in elation. Misty fog pumped in from somewhere unknown, coating the entire club in seconds.

The mist smelled fruity and I preferred it over the smell of sweaty dancers. A few seconds passed and my vision became hazy. I stumbled and caught myself on Coren's strong arm.

"Guys, what's going on?" I slurred over the loud music but didn't get a response.

When I looked at Raven, I froze. Her eyes were pitch black with no white whatsoever, and she was swaying to the music with a smile. Then I looked up at Coren, who hadn't moved since I'd caught my balance on his arm. He smirked down at me and his eyes were completely white and reflective in the surrounding light.

Shit. I was in trouble. Another spray of mist pumped in and I tried to hold my breath, but I finally had to inhale a second round of whatever they were drugging us with. I reached for Coren, but he wasn't there. Warm hands caressed my waist under my shirt, and the touch sent electrical pulses raging through my body that felt so good I moaned. Coren kept his hand on my waist and came around to stand in front of me. His white eyes took me in and then his mouth met mine. Oh God. I wanted him. Wanted him like fire wanted fuel. Our tongues mingled as we kissed, his hands slinking up my waist between us until he found my breasts.

When his fingers pulled my bra down and stroked across my nipples, my head fell back with another throaty moan as I broke our kiss. Coren's mouth ran along my neck and I opened my eyes to look around us. His hands left my breasts and made their way to my waistline. When he dipped his hand underneath my jeans and panties, I had to hold back the groan from the overwhelming sensations of pleasure. But, as his fingers dipped between my legs, the fog lifted from my brain. Several demons in full form licked each other on the dance floor, and a few others had unabashed sex. A demon and a human were in an embrace to my right, and at first, I thought they were attempting foreplay until I saw it trying to take the human's essence. Raven was to my left with another male demon, her body shifting between her beauty and her skeletal reaper form.

I yanked away from Coren, and he reached out for me again, this time a little too forcefully. "Get off of me," I growled. However, when he kept coming, I punched him across the face.

His brows lowered, those creepy eyes now narrowed in anger. So, I ran. I struggled through the crowds of demons in raptured passion and made my way toward the exit.

"Mara, you know you want me," Coren taunted as he followed.

Finally, I made it outside and past the bouncer, whom I now knew was a demon. I sprinted across the road. Cars honked, tires squealed. I didn't care. I had to get away from Serpent and Coren. Raven could take care of herself, and if she didn't, the dude she was with would be finding himself in hell once she fully transformed.

As I ran on to the sidewalk across from the club, I slammed into a strong, tall masculine body. Arms reached out to catch me from falling back onto the road. I glanced up and my mouth dropped.

"Raven still inside?" Death asked. Dressed in jeans and a tight-fitting black T-shirt, he looked halfway normal. Unless you caught his coal-black eyes.

Looking back, I noticed Coren outside the entrance, shaking his head to clear it.

"Yeah," I said. "Whatever they have pumping in that club drowns out everything."

He sighed. "That's probably the new experimental drug called Serpent's Kiss. Keep your sword handy. I'm not sure what will happen when I walk in there."

I blinked in surprise. Serpent's Kiss? Well, that would explain the name of the club. However, Serpent was a demon club. Holy shit. Who knew? Death stared at me awaiting a response, and I nodded in agreement.

As Raven's father walked across the street, I stared at his ass until I noticed the cars driving right through him. Nobody else saw him but Coren, myself, and the demons. Coren's body went ramrod stiff when he saw Death approaching. They said a few heated words. Death pointed at me. Then, without an ounce of trouble, Death walked through the door of Serpent.

Jogging across the street after the cars slowed, Coren came up to me. When I pulled back in mistrust, he winced. "I'm sorry, Mara."

"You and I, we, I..."

"I know. And I had no clue that would happen, not to both of us." His hand reached up and tucked a stray hair behind my ear. "I don't regret kissing you. I've wanted to do that since the day I first saw you."

I frowned up at him. "You did?"

"Yeah, until you kneed me in the balls. That kind of ruined the mood."

Laughing, I shook my head. "Good thing we stopped before we did something we'd regret in there. Did you know it was a demon club?"

"No. There were no hints, feelings, or anything of what laid inside. They went to great lengths to keep it hidden."

"That's my thought, but something felt off somehow, and my sword vibrated as if it were alive."

Screaming from inside the club had both of us jolting in surprise. Demons in their form ran outside in fear. With Raven slumped over his shoulder, Death quickly dispelled a few of them with a wave of his hand. Now I understood their terror. Death had arrived and he was pissed.

Another escaped his wrath and screeched across the road, right toward us. I slid my sword free, and as soon as the monster came near, I sliced his head off with a quick upsweep of my sword. Death waved his hand and the dead demon vanished from its decapitated state.

The bouncer, a big hulking man, transformed into an ogre of a demon with red oozing scales and mustard yellow eyes. At least eight-foot- tall, he roared and shoved humans and demons aside. The humans didn't see a full-blooded demon because they shouted rude comments to him, but he barreled forward in our direction. Death turned at the commotion, and I observed the struggle on his face for the safety of his daughter, and for mine as well.

As the ogre loped across the road, I planted my feet and held my sword steady. This would be the biggest demon I had ever faced. Coren stood in front of me, his body stock-still and ready for the upcoming fight.

With more quickness than I expected, the demon lifted his big fist and whacked Coren. His body flew in the air like a ragdoll and rested about ten feet away. Swinging my sword, the demon dodged the sharp blade and took a step to the side. I tried to slice his legs next, but a swift kick sent me sliding into the brick building behind us. Pain exploded along my side and I groaned. The creature chuckled, the sound resembling rocks dropped in a metal barrel.

Despite the pain, I rolled out of the way when a large foot stamped down where I'd previously landed. As I moved, I cut the back of its ankle with the sharp, curved blade and watched it stumble and roar. A fist connected with my face and I tasted blood as I sailed through the air and landed in a heap about ten feet away.

The ogre grabbed my neck in his enormous gross fingers, lifting me up into his view. My air supply was instantly squeezed and I struggled against his hold. His damn mouth was so big I could fit inside comfortably, but I knew if he put me inside his gaping maw I wouldn't be comfortable at all. Luckily I still had my sword, but my swings were worthless with his neck so far away.

"Hunter," the ogre said with a gravelly voice. He lowered his head close to mine and narrowed his evil, goat-like eyes at me. "You'll finally get to enjoy hell. We've been waiting for you."

"Fuck... you," I hissed out, barely a whisper with his fingers restricting my air.

With as much strength I had left with little to no oxygen, I took my sword and lifted it. The blade stabbed through his neck and he shuddered at the contact. Then, he roared, his sour breath and spittle hitting me in the face. He yanked me away from my sword, which remained embedded in his skin. I grappled for it, my hands outstretched as the world started to fade from lack of air. The last thing I remembered was feeling his hot breath over my body as he lowered me into his mouth.

*****

"Mara! Wake up," Coren's voice echoed.

Slowly opening my eyes, I groaned. Then the smell hit me. Death and sulfuric stench. I felt drenched and lifted my arm into my view. Yet again, I was covered with demonic slime.

"She's alert, Dad!" Raven yelled.

I winced. "God, do you have to be so loud?"

"God didn't have anything to do with this." She cocked her head with a grin. "Well, maybe he did have some divine intervention in the form of Coren."

Looking at Coren, I noticed he stiffened.

Clearing his throat, he asked, "What are you talking about?"

Raven shook her head. "I saw what you did. How you did it, I'll never know." She looked down at me again. "I wish you could've seen it. Coren woke up from his stupor, saw you about to be eaten, and he climbed that demon like a tree. With supernatural speed, too. Then he finished the job by shoving your sword straight through the demon's throat with a scream unlike anything I had heard before. So freaking awesome."

Sitting up, I wiped some of the goop from my face and arms. I looked at the three figures around me. Coren on edge about something, probably about killing a fellow demon, and then Raven and her father concerned about my wellbeing.

"I know I don't say it enough, but thank you." I meant it. With a grunt to shove away the pain, I stood on wobbly feet. Coren reached out to steady me. "I need to get this gross, nasty shit off me as soon as possible."

Death chuckled. Yes, Death, the Grim Reaper, chuckled. "That's more like the Mara we know and love."

I smirked. Death just said he loved me. Sure, he meant it like a father, and I guess he sort of was. I tilted my head back and laughed. Death was the only father figure I'd ever known, and I thought he was hot. How fucked up was that?

"Are you okay?" Coren asked. "Maybe she has a concussion."

Giggling, Raven said, "Nah. She's okay. I think she's a few keys short of a keyboard, if you know what I mean."

"Hey!"

"What did the demon say to you?" Raven asked. "We couldn't hear from across the street."

The demon had called me hunter, but I wanted to keep that to myself for the moment. I winked instead. "He said I'd taste good. Which doesn't surprise me. I *am* pretty delicious."

Shaking his head with a grin, Death reached for my hand. I placed mine in his. That was a damn mistake. I cried out as my body splintered and a split second later, materialized into my bathroom.

Still dressed in jeans and a T-shirt, albeit covered in some demon blood, Death sighed. "Raven and Coren will be here soon. Spitting mad at me for doing that, I'm sure, but I wanted to get you away from them for a minute."

I eyed him. "Why?"

"I don't trust Coren."

"Looks like we have something in common." I snorted.

"What do you know about him?" Death asked, crossing his arms across his chest.

I frowned at his question. "Not much, really. He hasn't harmed me or threatened to. Why?"

"There's something about him," he said as he began to pace inside my small bathroom. "I asked around to see what any demons would tell me about him, but they were all tight-lipped in fear of repercussions. It has to make me wonder why?"

"Maybe because he's Satan's lapdog?"

"Maybe. But the way he killed that demon..." he trailed off and tilted his head. "They're here. Just be cautious, Mara. Coren may be setting you up to fail. When that time comes, I'll be there to protect you with everything I have." Leaving me with that, he vanished in a whiff of dark smoke that dissipated quickly.

My apartment door creaked open and slammed shut after Raven and Coren entered.

"I told you she's here," Raven argued. "My father wouldn't take off with her and not take her home."

"Why not?"

"Because he's my father, Coren. And he thinks of Mara like his own daughter. He'd never hurt her."

"How do you know? He does take souls for a living," Coren argued.

"How dare you, you insolent jerk," she growled. I felt the air shift, and I knew her anger was going to get the best of her. "I take souls for a living too, in case you forgot."

"Guys," I called out, "I'm in the bathroom. I'll be out as soon as I shower!"

I started the water and started to remove my shirt when Coren threw open the bathroom door and strolled in with his jaw clenched. Raven followed him in with a huff.

"See?" She pointed at me. "I told you she's fine."

Coren opened his mouth to speak, but I cut him off. "Get out! Both of you! I just want to shower."

His hands lifted in surrender, and they both made their way out of the bathroom, closing the door behind them.

Turning the lock on the bathroom door, I sighed because I knew if Coren or Raven really wanted in, they'd bypass the door and appear. I stripped and finally saw myself in the reflection of the mirror after our scuffle tonight. My fingers ran across the deep, purple bruising around my neck, shoulders, and chest. A nasty bruise marred my right cheek. How the beastly asshole didn't crush my windpipe and lungs, I'll never know. How had we stumbled upon a demon club and allowed entrance into said club?

Today's events didn't add up. My life spiraled out of control with each passing day. Not only was I stuck with Coren, who I wasn't sure if I could trust, but I also faced stronger, more advanced demons every time I hunted.

I stepped under the spray of the shower determined to figure out who was behind the recent attacks with advanced demons, and who would want to see me fail. If this didn't stop soon, I had the potential of dying. I was close to it tonight. Death's words echoed in my head, and I wondered if he might be right about Coren.

CHAPTER 13

*Keep your friends close,
but your frenemies closer.*

I woke the next morning feeling sore and fuming.

Raven slept on the couch, her soft snores bringing a slight comfort. For as soft and loving as she was to me, she'd slaughter anyone who meant me real harm.

Coren made coffee in my tiny kitchen, and the sight of him sent both anger and lust screaming through my blood. Dammit. Why did my boss stick me with him? Was it a ploy to distract me from what was actually happening?

He glanced up and frowned. "Oh, Mara. You're injuries look awful. Raven could give you some herbal medicine to speed up your healing."

A brimstone cookie was tempting, but I didn't know if I could handle the taste again. He lifted a hand to my discolored cheek. Anger caused my heartbeat to skyrocket at his soft touch.

"What?" Coren asked. "You're looking at me like you wished I would burst into flames."

"Wouldn't be anything new for you. I've heard it can get hot down there. You know, since you live in *hell*."

He blinked in surprise at my tone. "What's gotten into you?"

"I'm cranky after being practically choked to death. Kiss my ass."

Sure, I made up the excuse, but my mood had a little to do with that too. What I hadn't expected was Coren's arms enveloping me in a gentle hug. My arms remained stiff at my sides, despite my longing to sink into his arms.

"I'm sorry, Mara. I should've been quicker on my feet," he whispered.

As he pulled away, his eyes went to my bruised neck and shoulders visible from my tank top. I swore I saw guilt in those chocolate depths. I wasn't sure if he felt guilty for his betrayal or because he didn't rescue me fast enough. Based on his facial expression, I was going with the latter.

"Can I ask you a question, Coren?"

His eyes met mine as he said, "Anything."

"What are your intentions as my babysitter?"

"I'm not technically your babysit-"

I held up a hand and halted his protest. "Call it what you will, but why should I trust you?"

With a sigh, he turned around and poured a cup of coffee. He added enough sugar to cause a coma. The only sound between us was the clinking of the spoon on the mug as he stirred.

After a few minutes, he said, "I can't blame you for saying that, especially with the circumstances of how you met me. Have I not proven to be trustworthy? Have I pushed you into things you didn't want to do? Did I not help you at the shelter a few days ago?"

"Let's be honest, here." I put my hands on my hips. "I'm a job. A means to an end. I get it, I really do. But if you're the reason I'm facing higher demons and avoiding death yesterday, I'll make sure your life is a living hell. Or join you there after the sixty days and ask Raven and her father to do it for me."

Coren whirled around, his coffee spilling over the edge of the mug. His face lit with anger. "Don't push me, girl. You still owe me a favor, a price you promised to pay."

"Yeah, yeah. We'll see if you ever get to collect." I stormed away, but he caught my arm with supernatural speed and spun me to face him. The move caught me off guard. I had never seen somebody move so fast.

"You have no idea who you're dealing with," he warned.

"You mean *what* I'm dealing with? Yeah, you got that right, asshole. You're a demon. Nothing more." Yanking my arm, I ordered, "Let me go."

He did and I felt his eyes on my back as I marched to my bedroom and slammed the door. We were back to the hatred with hidden sexual tension again. I could take hatred any day of the week, it was the lust I didn't trust.

Tossing myself on my bed, I let out an exhausted breath. I began counting down how many days had passed until my time was up because I'd lost track with all the chaos. My door flew open and I jerked my head up.

Coren marched in, jumped on the mattress, and held my arms above my head. His legs and weight kept my bottom half from moving. His eyes took on a white hue. Unnerved by those creepy eyes, I thrust my head as close to the mattress as possible. His nostrils flared once before he spoke. "Let me tell you something, you audacious woman. I'm not going to let you talk to me like I don't have feelings or any emotions whatsoever. I still hurt and feel pain, no matter what you may think of me."

"Fine," I said. "You said you had two months to prove your worth too, right? Tell me why. Tell me why you think you are so damn special and why I'm so important?"

He hesitated, but still hovered above me. His eyes changed back to normal and moved to my lips. I caught my breath.

"You're not the only one whose soul is in jeopardy, Mara."

"A demon doesn't have a soul, jackass," I spat.

"Are you sure?" He lowered his head and kissed me.

His soft lips moved against mine as our tongues flirted with each other. Coren's removed his legs from over mine and I wrapped my legs around his hips. My body betrayed me as lust took over all sense of right and wrong. My fingers caressed his back and as his mouth moved to my neck, I let out a throaty moan. When his teeth nipped the skin on my collarbone, I wanted to rake my nails down his back.

"Uh, what are you two doing?"

Raven's voice broke us apart and Coren removed himself from my bed faster than I could blink. My cheeks flamed and I winced.

She pointed at Coren, who now stood with a full-blown erection behind his jeans. "If you hurt her, I'll kill you myself. Your soul will never make it back to hell, either. You hear me?"

He held up his hands. "Got it. I didn't mean for that to happen, it just did."

With an apologetic glance in my direction, Coren left me alone with Raven.

"What are you thinking? We can't afford to be sloppy right now. Not with your soul hanging in the balance."

Rubbing my face with my hands, I said, "I know. One minute he was mad at me, the next we were kissing. I don't know how it happened."

"I do. The sexual tension between you two is so thick you could slice it in half." She sat beside me on the bed and patted my arm. "I'm worried about you is all. I can't lose you. You're my best friend, hell, my only friend."

"It won't happen again."

Raven chuckled and shook her head. "Liar."

I groaned in frustration and whispered, "Why am I so attracted to him? I shouldn't be."

"Because sometimes things happen when we least expect them to." She patted my arm again. "Be sure you know what you're doing because I don't know if I can trust Coren yet."

I nodded.

"Get showered and dressed. I'm in the mood for Italian food."

She closed the door to my bedroom and left me to my thoughts. I had kissed Coren – again. This time we were both in our right mind and not drugged. His words from right before the kiss entered my mind again. I had said demons don't have souls. *"Are you sure?"* What had that meant? Was it just a way to get me to kiss him without guilt?

I didn't know. All I knew was that he was unlike any demon I had ever met, and somehow, I had to figure out the truth and to keep it hidden until the knowledge would be useful.

CHAPTER 14

The shadow of death.

Somebody was going to die.

I knew it, Raven knew it, but we didn't know the exact moment the fateful event would happen. Coren, if he knew, hadn't given anything away. He sat at the table eating his fettucine alfredo without a care in the world.

The air vibrated around us, but I suspected the shadowy figure near the kitchen entrance was the reason. I had never asked if Raven could see them, but she had stiffened the moment I had seen it too.

Finally having the courage to ask, I whispered, "What are those things?"

Raven gaped at me but quickly covered up her surprise.

"They're shadows," Coren said between bites. "Some call them angels if they see them before they die, but they aren't. There are rumors they try to steal souls of the departed. That's why Raven's job is so important, besides moving souls to where they go that is."

"You can see them too?" Raven questioned, her eyes darting between the shadow thing and me.

"I've seen them since my mother tricked me," I replied with a shake of my head. "Once I signed that contract, I started seeing them. I assumed they were ghosts."

Coren and Raven glanced at each other.

"What?"

Raven cleared her throat and raked her fingers through her hair. "Um, I've never known a human to actually see them. Unless they're dying, or are an angel or demon, that is."

I shrugged. "Well, technically my soul isn't mine. Who knows why I see them. I wasn't supposed to see you and your father that day either, Raven."

"True."

"What am I missing here?" Coren's eyes narrowed, and I assumed he was feeling left out of a few things.

Keeping my mouth sealed, I scooped some spaghetti into my mouth to keep silent. He didn't need to know my past, or in what manner the Devil possessed my soul. It was none of his business. However, Raven, the little shit, opened her big mouth.

"When Mara was about six, her mother tricked her to sign her soul over to Satan for money. But, when Mara turned sixteen, her mother got the money and died shortly after. Hence where I came into play. To my utter disbelief, this girl," she pointed at me, "saw me and Dad when we showed up for her mother's soul. Long story short, we talked the man downstairs into letting me train her to kill certain demons who slip the veil."

"You were only six?" Coren's expression went from upset to unease in a millisecond.

Lifting my shoulders in nonchalance, I scooped in more spaghetti. Sure, I was a kid and my mother was a bitch. Life goes on, right? If only I hadn't signed that paper, then my life may be much different. Maybe college and a normal job might have found me instead of this. Then again, I wouldn't have Raven seated next to me. Even if she was Death's daughter and took dead souls for a living, she was truly my best friend. And, of course, I wouldn't have Coren here, too. I hated to admit it, but he had grown on me a little bit.

"I'll be right back. If I'm not by the time dinner is over and that dude croaks, I'll meet you at your apartment, Mara." He stood and went to an empty hallway within our view.

In a cloud of white smoke, Coren vanished and left Raven and me in confusion.

I finished chewing my spaghetti and asked, "What was that all about?"

"I have no freaking clue. He's weird." Raven waved her hand in dismissal and began to take a bite of her lasagna. As though the universe knew she'd barely eaten, a man two tables over started choking.

"Shit," she said and dropped her fork on the plate with a clang. "Can't I just get a day off without somebody dying on me?"

"Can't your dad handle it?"

Her eyes swerved to the shadowy figure who had moved from the kitchen and now stood within ten feet of the choking man. A waiter attempted the Heimlich maneuver while his wife screamed for him to help her husband.

"Not while *that* is so close to him. I'll be right back."

She darted down the hallway in the direction of the bathroom. I wanted the waiter to succeed or the emergency personnel to arrive on time. I hated the death of humans. I didn't know the man or his wife, but I wanted him to live. I wanted to believe they were decent human beings that didn't deserve this fate of death and mourning.

I saw Raven out of the corner of my eye as she moved closer in her smoky state that nobody would see but me. Pulling up the hood of her fabled Reaper outfit, she pointed her scythe at the shadow creature. Swearing I heard a curse from the thing, the being retreated from the choking man. Then it turned in my direction and red glowing eyes met mine through the darkness of its shadow. I stiffened as it faded away into nothingness, but the last thing that dissipated were those disturbing blood-red eyes.

My wide gaze swung to watch Raven help the man's soul cross over. I knew whatever that entity was, it now had its sights on me. That could never be good.

*****

"Swing with your body, not your arms, Mara!"

Coren barked instructions at me while we practiced swordsmanship on the roof of my apartment complex. The cool November air didn't keep the sweat from dripping down my back as I attempted to engage him in combat once again.

I thought I had plenty of skill with my sword, but Coren made me feel inadequate. He feigned to the right and expertly blocked my practiced swordsmanship with his own. Thankfully we had chosen practice swords instead of our real ones because I'd be bleeding out on top of my own apartment building. My lungs heaved from exertion and I had a few new bruises to add to my collection.

He said, "You need to be faster and more agile than that."

With a frustrated scream, I came at him again. Whack, whack. The wooden swords clacked against each other as he reflected each one of my strikes. He wasn't even breaking a sweat, the bastard. His fake blade caught my thigh and I grunted in pain.

"If you're going to be fighting higher demons, you need to learn how to move with your sword as though it were a part of your body," he growled and came at me with a ferocity of blows with inhuman speed.

I deflected, rotated, and then cried out as he caught my ribcage the wooden sword. I averted his next attempt, my arms shaking as I held my weapon up to block his own. My teeth gritted as I used all my strength to keep him from overpowering me.

"You give up, yet?" he asked, his mouth curved with mocking smile.

"Never!" I yelled and then twisted on my toes to swing the blade into an arch.

This time I caught Coren on his shoulder and he stumbled back. A mischievous smile lit his face. I'd say he was enjoying the sparring more than he should. Gesturing with his fingers, be beckoned me to attack again. I charged with a guttural scream, our swords smacking together with a click.

"If I had my real sword, you'd be in serious trouble."

"If you say so." His laughter fueled my rage.

We fought each other, and I felt more confident but fatigue crept over my body. We practiced over and over again until I could barely catch my breath. When I tripped over my feet and fell on my ass, I collapsed in utter exhaustion.

Coren reached down to help pull me to my feet. "You're a fighter, I'll give you that. We still have a long way to go."

"Where did you learn all this sword crap?"

"I learned a very long time ago and had an even longer time to train."

I pursed my lips. "That's not really the answer I was looking for."

He lifted his shoulders in a shrug. "Well, you don't have to know everything about me."

"And the same goes for you, too."

With a chuckle, Coren opened the metal door that led us off the roof. He gestured for me to go first, locked the door behind him, and then we filed down the spiraling stairs until we reached the hallway.

Raven leaned against my door and straightened when she saw us. Her eyes raked over me as her nose wrinkled. "Training?"

"What gave it away? This?" I said as I held up the wooden sword. "Or maybe the sweaty, disgusting mess I'm in?"

"A little of both, but I've been waiting for you two. I have some intel."

"Intel?" I questioned, my eyebrows lifting.

"Inside, not here," she mumbled and waited on me to unlock my apartment.

My hands shook as I inserted the key and opened the door. Damn, my fingers and hands ached from our lesson. The apartment door shut behind us after everyone was inside. I desperately longed for a shower, but I turned and waited for Raven to fill us in.

"Apparently Lucifer does want to see you fail, but not for the reasons you may think. I assumed he wanted your soul, but there's something more. Something my father and I can't put our finger on. Do you know if there's something Satan may want?"

My mind instantly went to the shadowy figures I've seen since I signed the contract, and how the last one looked at me. Did it know something I didn't?

Being the stubborn and private person I was, I shook my head. The lie slipped out so easily. "No, I can't think of anything."

I didn't know why I didn't tell Raven, I should've told her everything. That's what friends are for, but I held back. I always held back when I shouldn't, and I trusted Raven to keep me alive.

The room went quiet for a few minutes while I considered what could make Satan go to these lengths for a human. If he wanted souls, he had plenty to choose from. If I knew a way to stop him, I'd do it in a heartbeat. If the Devil got a hold of my soul, there's no telling what he'd do to me.

CHAPTER 15

Don't chase your demons. Run from them.

Raven darted between buildings as I chased her.

Her inhuman speed was the stuff of legends, and she could sneak up behind you while you think she's ahead of you. That's a reaper for you. Luckily, for me, her touch didn't mean death, but for other humans it sure did. Even knowing she'd never guide my soul across the veil of heaven and hell, she still scared the crap out of me from time to time. Like now.

She sprung up in front of me, ten feet tall and screeching like a ghoul. Her beautiful face was now a cracked white skull and behind the empty eye sockets shone red orbs. This was what people feared. This was the fabled Reaper in all its glory. That thing staring down at me with a terrifying face was my best friend.

I closed my eyes as she leaned down near my face. Her frigid breath flittered across my cheek, and as she spoke, I shivered.

"You should know better than fall for my tricks," she said with a deep voice that echoed. "You'd be dead already if it were anyone else."

"Yeah, well, you didn't tell me you'd turn into *that*. You know it creeps me out, Raven."

"And demons that morph into their true form don't?"

"No, because they aren't my best friend. You are."

Raven muttered, "I'm sorry."

Popping my eyes back open, I let out a sigh once I saw she returned to her normal appearance. "I know you and Coren are both preparing me for whatever's coming. I shouldn't have frozen whether it was you or not. It won't happen again."

"Good, because the Devil's coming for you. He'll send his little goons first and will send bigger, badder demons every time. If that doesn't work, he's going to try to drag you to hell himself." She blinked away tears. "I can't lose you."

I nodded. Although she had her second home in hell, I had a feeling if my boss got his way, I'd never see her, her father, or Coren again. As a tear spilled down her cheek, I looked away. Emotions made you weak, right? Yet, here was one of the strongest women I know falling apart because she was afraid of losing me.

My mother's words reverberated through my mind. *"Quit crying, you sniveling little girl. Emotions are a flaw of nature. They'll only make you weak while the world tears you limb from limb. Don't ever show anyone weakness, you hear me?"*

If she had only known how those words, and others she'd spoken to me as a child, would serve me well as a demon hunter. Now, I had caused my friend's tears. Not directly, no, but a reaper was crying for me.

"Do you want a, uh, hug or something?" I asked with my face warped in indecision.

"That would be nice," she cried and then slung her arms around me.

I wrapped mine around her awkwardly and patted her back. As I finally relaxed, something sharp nailed my shoulder. I gasped in surprise at another one of Raven's lessons. Had she poked me with one of her nails on accident? Did her scythe stab me?

Raven pulled back, her eyebrows knitted in concern. "Are you okay?"

I became woozy. My mind went fuzzy as I tried to concentrate on Raven in front of me but her figure blurred. I stumbled on unsteady feet.

"What is going on?" Raven said, her voice going in and out.

"My...m...my...sh...shoul...der."

She spun me around to inspect my back and I began to fall forward, but she caught me. My skin tingled as she yanked something from my skin.

"Son of a bitch!"

"What..." I attempted to speak, but my hazy mind wouldn't work right.

Blinking to try to stay conscious, my vision started to tunnel. I barely felt the world splinter as she faded with me.

*****

Confusion thrummed through me when I woke on the dingy couch from my childhood.

The light from the blaring TV flickered throughout the room. The smell of stale cigarette smoke filtered through my nose. The sounds of a pot rattled in the kitchen. I sat up and rubbed a hand across my face, but the hand was too small to be mine. Squinting down at myself, I saw knobby, skinned up knees and dirty bare feet. Pink, frilly shorts covered my thighs, and I was wearing my favorite yellow SpongeBob shirt.

I was six years old again. Holy shit.

"Mara! Get your ass in here!" my mother called out and I jumped in surprise.

I hadn't heard her voice in ages, and hearing it now, caused both anger and fear. That woman changed my entire existence because of her selfishness. Removing myself from the couch, I headed into the kitchen to see her making dinner with a cigarette hanging from her mouth. The long ash hung precariously from the lit paper and I glanced down at the casserole she prepared expecting to see ashes in it.

"Are you going to help me, girl, or are you going to just stand there like an invalid?"

For the first time in my entire life, I saw my mother through adult eyes. She wore dirty, ripped jeans and a halter-top that showed too much skin. Her body was skinny, sickly so, and her bloodshot eyes stared at me with hatred. Her pupils were too big to simply be drunk. My attention swung to the pill bottle sitting on the counter and things clicked. This woman was not only an alcoholic but addicted to pills, too. That still didn't make up for all the bad she had done to me. I still hated her with every fiber of my being.

Cocking my hip out the best a six-year-old can do, I lifted my eyebrow at her. My voice was childlike to my own ears. "Looks like you're the worthless one, mother. How many pills did you take today?"

Angry bloodshot eyes narrowed. "What did you say to me?"

"You can't control me anymore. You're nothing to me."

Pain slashed across my chin as she slapped me, pitching my small body to the filthy kitchen floor. Looming over me, she took the opening to kick my stomach. I tried to stand through the hurt, but my young body wasn't conditioned like my adult one. Still, my mind was still me and I knew better than to cower from her. That wasn't who I was anymore.

"Is that the best you can do?" I gritted out.

She leaned down close to me, the cigarette still hanging from her lips. The smoke curled up her face and one of her eyes was squinted because of it. She removed the cigarette and let the ashes fall next to me. "Keep pushing me. I brought you into this world, and I'll show you how much pain that's caused me."

"Fuck you," I said and spit at her.

With one hand, she shoved me back down and held me there. She sat on me, pinning my arms with her knees. I bucked and kicked to no avail. Taking a big hit off her cigarette, she blew the smoke in my face as she lowered the smoking ember. I felt the heat from the lit cigarette a moment before she put it out in my cheek. I refused to cry out from the pain, so I bit my tongue so hard I tasted blood. I kept my eyes on hers the entire time. The smell of burning flesh filled the air as my skin extinguished her smoke.

My mother ground the cigarette against the raw skin, attempting to get a reaction out of me. I clenched my teeth to keep silent, swallowing back the blood from biting my tongue.

Pulling another smoke from behind her ear, she lit a second one. "Are you going to be a good girl, now? Or do I have to show you again what happens to bad girls?" My mother puffed the putrid smoke in my face.

"Hate to tell you, mother, but I'm already a bad girl. And it's all because of *you*."

Another slap jerked my head to the side, but I glared up at her again. With a shake of her head, she took a drag to make sure it was nice and hot. This time my neck put out the cigarette. A scream escaped as my neck burned. She threw the butt to the side and grinned.

The grin gave it away.

Her lips edged out too far, her cheeks wrinkling near her cheekbones. This wasn't my mother. This was a demon. And I was trapped in some sort of hallucination with it. This hallucination sure felt real as the monstrosity posing as my mother began to inflict pain.

I waded through my memories of Raven's teachings of demonology, but nothing came to mind. I hated myself for not paying attention.

"What are you?" I demanded.

"I'm your mother, you stupid little bitch," it hissed.

"No, you're not. Even though you're just as sadistic, I know you're demon scum. I demand you to give me your name."

The beast lifted my head a little and then slammed it against the cracked tile. "Never."

I grunted in pain. "So why create this vision? Why not let me be normal so I can fight fair?"

"Because, Mara, this is your reality in hell."

I laughed. "I doubt it, asshole. I'll kill you first."

If I guessed correctly, this demon had pulled my childhood memories with amazing accuracy. I looked around for some sort of weapon. There, under the fridge, was a long-forgotten rusty steak knife.

"Kill me?" The beast lifted its head back as it cackled, which gave me barely enough of an advantage to pull an arm free. "You can't kill me."

My childlike fingers struggled for the knife, barely reaching the handle, but it was enough to move it close enough to grab.

"No," I said as I lifted the knife, "but I can maim you."

I lowered the blade and stabbed its eye. The being screeched and scrambled away, the knife moving with its eye. My mother's body splintered apart, the skin shedding off like a snake. In her place stood a spiny demon with black speckles along its orange, scaly skin. With a wide mouth, the beast attempted to pull the knife out with its long, orange tongue, and then finally succeeded with a yank of square-shaped fingers.

Inimicus.

The name suddenly popped in my head. The sting on my shoulder made sense. This demon had a venomous, barbed weapon, which caused realistic visions. So realistic that you could be trapped in them forever, or die from wounds afflicted in them. Shit.

"Come on Raven," I breathed, and then lifted up my tiny, child feet to kick the demon while he was distracted.

The demon slid across the floor, slamming into the cheap, wooden cabinets with a thud. Letting out a horrendous screech, it slithered out its tongue like a snake and watched me with its one remaining blacked out eye.

"Tsk, tsk. That'll cost you. An eye for an eye, they say."

The vision twisted into my apartment with such accuracy I wondered if the demon had transported me. The scaly beast stood next to me and let out a low chuckle.

"Welcome to hell."

As he disappeared with a swirl of smoke, I jumped in surprise. This didn't look like hell, this looked like home.

Coren walked through the front door and gasped. Dropping a bag he held, he darted forward and wrapped me in his arms. "God, Mara. You scared the daylights out of Raven and me. We couldn't figure out how to wake you up."

"Honestly, I'm not sure if I'm awake now." I pulled away from his arms and shrugged. "You could be an illusion."

Laughing, Coren shook his head. "I'm no illusion. Trust me." He wrapped an arm over my shoulder and led me toward my bedroom. "You must be exhausted. Why don't you sleep while I take care of you?"

I frowned, but I was tired after my ordeal with my fake mother. Why wasn't Raven here? Suspicious, I nodded and let him open the door and help me into the bed. He kissed my forehead, which was so out of character I blinked in surprise.

I opened my mouth to tell whomever this was to fuck off, but Coren's mouth crashed against mine and our teeth clashed. I yanked my head away from his mouth. "What do you think you're doing?"

"What you've always wanted me to do," he replied, his eyes darting between mine.

Without warning, his arms pinned mine against the bed and his legs maneuvered to keep me still. I fought. Hard. But his strength overpowered me. When I heard the telltale sign of a zipper and felt my pants rip with his fingers, my eyes widened. My shirt was torn next and our skin met, but his chest was too hot to be the real Coren. Fight or flight kicked in, and I wasn't a flight type of person.

Because the demon had yet again given me a precise illusion, my sword sat on my nightstand. The blade gleamed in the light. Another weapon with easy reach.

"Why don't you let me have an arm free so I can at least help you out?" I said, my voice sweet an innocent.

Coren's head tilted as he thought about it. Finally, he nodded and allowed my right arm free. I ran my hand through his hair as he leaned down to kiss my neck. I wanted to vomit at a demon touching me this way. My hand followed along his shoulder, then down his arm, and finally on my sword. The handle hummed as I wrapped my fingers around it, the blade begging for demon blood.

I grinned. "Do you know what I think?"

"What, baby?" He lifted his upper body from mine, just enough for a desperate attempt of freeing myself.

I grinned. "See you in hell, asshole."

With surprise on my side, I shoved him off me and swung the sword. The blade slid through his neck with a sickening crunch. Coren's head rolled to the side.

My heart lurched, a surprising reaction that I'd contemplate later. Until the body transformed back into the Inimicus without a head, I stared at Coren's body in a teary-eyed stupor.

When a bright light hit my eyes, I screamed. This time I knew I was back when I woke inside Death's apartment in the real hell. I had killed an Inimicus demon in one of its fabled delusions. A feat, according to Raven in her past lessons, was nearly impossible. Yep, I had just awesomed all over the damn place.

"Are you okay?" Death asked, his handsome face peering down at me.

"I think so," I whispered, and saw Raven and Coren hovering next to him.

Raven sat next to me on the black leather couch while she blinked back tears. "I didn't know if we'd be able to save you or not. How did you wake up?"

My eyes swung to Coren. The image of Coren's decapitation from my vision made me want to cry. The vision from the demon was too real and I swallowed back the sadness that welled inside of me. Had I begun to develop feelings for him?

Clearing my throat, I said, "I killed it."

Coren puckered his brow. "You killed an Inimicus inside its own illusion?"

"Yep. I sure did." I sat up.

The world tilted for a bit and Raven reached out to steady me. I shook my head, letting her know I needed to do this on my own. She bit her lip as she watched me struggle to gain my bearings. Coren kept his hand out in case I tumbled forward, or off the couch.

"How is that possible?" Coren asked. "How did you kill it?"

I avoided Coren's gaze. I couldn't look at him. Not with that illusion stuck in my head.

Death shrugged his shoulders. "Anything is possible, Coren. You should know that more than any of us."

My eyebrows rose. "What is that supposed to mean?"

"Nothing. I was here watching over you is all." Coren kept his eyes on me to avoid him, but I had a feeling Death knew something about him that Raven and I didn't.

Chapter 16

Find comfort in the chaos.

"Where's Coren?"

"I snuck away from him this morning, but you can bet he'll be here in," I checked the time on my cell phone, "about two minutes."

Laura's eyebrows rose. "You have to sneak away from him? Is he abusing you?"

With a sigh, I wished I could've said yes. He'd never lift a hand in anger. I began to doubt my judgment skills lately. "No, it isn't like that. I needed a few minutes away from him. He's driving me crazy."

"How so?"

"Well," I glanced at the door to make sure we didn't have any eavesdroppers, "he knows how to push all my buttons. He's constantly around, either yelling at the TV or making me food. Then he's good looking, but I can't do anything about it. Not a damn thing."

Laura wiggled her eyebrows. "He is a gorgeous hunk of man beef, huh?"

"Man beef?" Wrinkling my nose at her choice of words, I said, "I don't know about that."

"But you do think he's handsome?"

"Of course. You'd have to be blind not to see how hot he is."

A deep voice resonated in the kitchen. "You think I'm hot?"

I froze. Shit. Not even two minutes had passed, but Coren had arrived.

Laura winked at me and I gave her my best I-hate-you-so-much-right-now glare. She had goaded me as soon as she saw him walk through the door. I was going to make her pay for that by giving her dish duty today. As she left the room with a sly grin, I didn't think she cared.

Not wanting to look at Coren or answer his question, I glanced around the utilitarian kitchen wishing I'd spot a bottle of tequila, but it was a useless endeavor. SafetyNet banned alcohol from the premises.

"Mara," Coren said, drawing out my name, "are you going to answer me?"

Finally turning to face him, I said, "What would you like to help with today? I won't be doing dishes, so I'll probably be serving or helping with the kids."

"You snuck off without me again. That's dangerous."

"I can take care of myself,"

"What about Laura? And the people staying here? Can they take care of themselves if a horde of demons show up?"

Damn. He knew how to hit me in the feels. But he was right. I had put these people and Laura in jeopardy by my actions.

"Who is going to save them from you?" I countered, my voice a bare whisper.

He lowered his voice and took a step in my direction. "Maybe they aren't the ones needing saved from me. Maybe I'm protecting them from *you*."

"I'm not the one who–"

"First, you have a contract on your soul. Second, you hunt demons for a living. Finally, you have Lucifer after your ass, and he'd love to see you land on it. No matter how violent and ruthless, no matter how many people die from his anger."

I gaped at him. "I'm just trying to help."

He took another step closer. "What do you think would've happened if I hadn't arrived and masked you being here? Could you live with the consequences?"

I opened my mouth to respond and closed it with a snap.

"These innocent humans would've been ripped to shreds and dragged through the pits of hell. What kind of a monster risks the lives of people they want to help?"

My eyes stung as they watered. Tears accumulated along my eyelids. I looked up at the tiled ceiling as I willed the unwanted emotion away. I felt like an asshole, an utter failure as a person. I had risked the lives of so many people who wanted a fresh start, a new life past abuse and chaos. I had nearly introduced turmoil beyond what they had ever experienced in life.

Turning on my toes, I spun away from Coren and went out the back door of the kitchen. I shivered from the cool air and wrapped my arms around my waist as I inspected the parking lot covered in dried leaves. I took a few deep breaths to calm my thundering heart and blinked away the tears. The door opened and closed behind me, and a warm jacket that smelled like sandalwood and citrus covered my shoulders.

"I know I shouldn't have said it like that," Coren said, his hands still sitting on my shoulders over his leather jacket. "I'm sorry. I didn't know how to get through to you."

I took a deep breath. "I should've known better, but sometimes I act without thinking. That's how I got in this predicament with you and my boss. Sometimes it's hard to realize you're the reason for the bad when your heart is in the right place."

"Sometimes you can try to do the right thing, but it ends up being the wrong one instead. That doesn't make you a bad person, Mara. You're only human."

"Human," I snorted. "I'm not sure if there's any humanity left inside me."

"Yes," he turned me to face him, "there is. You slaughter demons to save humans, not because you like to kill them because they're evil. You are a good person in a bad situation."

We stared at each other; Coren's face a mask of compassion and understanding. The back door squealed on its hinges and we turned.

Laura asked, "Are you guys heading home?"

With a sigh in resignation, I looked back up to Coren. "This is the one place I feel normal. I can do the dishes, help people, and do mundane chores. I'm asking for your help. Please."

There was a moment or two of hesitation before Coren said, "We'll be in shortly, Laura."

She went back inside, the door creaking behind her.

As I walked toward the door, with Coren behind me, he whispered, "You still owe me, Mara. Don't forget that."

So we were back to that. His favor. The one he could collect at any time. I let out a grunt of annoyance, which sounded more like a growl.

He chuckled.

*****

After the shift, we stopped at my coffee haven. I ordered my usual and sat at the back corner booth with my back against the wall. The cool metal of the chair felt good against my tender muscles and I let out a breath. Mopping sucked, but I hadn't complained one bit. Coren's black coffee was up in no time and he sat across from me.

I drank a few sips before I set the coffee on the copper table. "So, are you going to tell me what this favor will be?"

His eyes twinkled over the mug. "I don't even know what it'll be just yet. When the time comes, I'll let you know."

"Are you going to give me more than a moment's notice?"

"I wish I could say I will, but I don't know."

I shook my head. "You don't know much, do you?"

"Well, do you know everything you'll need from Raven, even if it's weeks or months in advance?"

He had stumped me, so I shrugged.

"That's what I thought." He smirked and took a drink of his steaming mug.

"I don't like owing people. Even if it's Raven or her father." I took another sip of mocha goodness.

"Speaking of those two, mind telling me how you met them?"

"When I signed the contract, I could see things here and there. Mostly out of the corner of my eye, but the closer I got to my sixteenth birthday, I noticed two beings hovering near the apartment. I chalked it up to what I saw after I signed with the big bad, but then my mother died. Her soul was ripped from her body. I saw it happen. To the shock of everyone involved, I spoke to Raven and her father that day. That's about it."

"I doubt it's that simple, Raven." Coren tipped his cup in my direction with his eyebrows raised.

"Well, that's the watered-down version. I'd rather not relive my life before her death, especially after it was relived with the Immicus demon." I shuddered when I remembered the other illusion, and then my heart constricted, as Coren's dark gaze bored into mine. I imaged his face spinning away after I sliced his neck. I knew it wasn't real, but the image floated in my memory like smoke in the wind.

His head tilted as he watched me. "Are you okay?"

I blinked a few times to clear the image scorched into my mind and nodded. "Yeah. Just bad memories. Memories I'd rather forget."

Hoping for a change of conversation, I almost jumped for joy as Coren said, "I'm sorry you had to see all that again. Anyway, what are the plans for tonight? More demon hunting?"

I looked at the time on my phone. "Of course. But I have a few hours to take a nap."

"You can nap after all this caffeine?"

"I can nap even if I have only been up for an hour. Let's go."

Coren shook his head, and we both left the building after returning our mugs to the counter.

I did get my nap, even if it was only for an hour. I thanked my lucky stars that Coren let me sleep without interruption. I felt a presence in my bedroom and creaked an eye open. A scream escaped and I stumbled out of bed onto the hard floor.

Coren busted into the room, his eyes taking the creepy white hue. He spotted me on the floor and Raven snickering at me.

"Why did you scream?" she asked, her voice still tinged with laughter.

"Because your damn face was like an inch away from mine! Why would you do that?!"

She threw her hands in the air. "I wanted to make sure you were breathing!"

"You two are going to be the death of me," Coren grumbled. He left my bedroom, slamming the door behind him.

Once I threw on a pair of sweatpants and climbed back under the covers, I gave Raven my best I'm-going-to-kill-you stare. "Where have you been?"

She sighed and sat on the bed. "Dad and I have been busy protecting your ass. Something is going on with Ol' Luke, and we can't figure out what his angle is with you. Not yet, anyway."

I softened immediately. "You two don't have to do that. I can take care of myself, you know."

"Yes," Raven said, "but you're our family. And family takes care of each other, even if they might lose their soul."

Staring at the ceiling, I puffed out a breath from my lips. For the second time that day, my heart constricted behind my cage of ribs. Usually, that cage held my heart in an emotionless prison, which is where I liked it to be. Lately, the enclosure cracked just enough to let little slivers of emotions seep through. At first it was for Raven and her father, and now after the deception with the demon, those fissures started opening for Coren.

"Did you hear me?"

I turned my attention back to Raven. "You and your father mean so much to me, and I don't say this enough, or *ever*, but I do love you two. You both put your life on the line for me all the time, and if that isn't love, I don't know what is."

Raven's eyes widened. "You're scaring me. You don't plan on doing something stupid do you?"

"When do I not?" I said with a laugh.

She slung her arm around me. "At least this time you have several people on your side and you won't be doing stupid stuff alone."

Leaning my head on her shoulder, I chuckled. "We'll see about that."

Chapter 17

Two steps from hell, don't ring the bell.

"You stupid asshole!" I screamed at the scaly demon slithering down an alley.

For a snake-like creature with only two front arms, the sucker was fast. I was already out of breath, and I cursed Coren under my breath. His idea was to stay out of the way and let me do my job to let Lucifer think he hadn't helped me when I sent this hideous thing back. Demons, according to Coren, lived off gossip. I guess there was nothing to do on the lower levels of hell except blab their mouths, and Satan would know instantly if I had help.

My boots slid on the wet concrete as I rounded the corner next to an abandoned laundry mat. I was going to have to tackle the demon if I was ever going to catch it or be smarter than running around buildings for the past ten minutes.

Finally, without a second thought, I flung my sword and watched it sail through the air. Luck was on my side as it slid through the tail of the beast. A deafening shriek filled the night air and I winced at the sound, but I rounded the demon.

"You will not sssseee the earth for long, my sssweeet girl," the demon hissed through a forked tongue.

Its breath was putrid, the teeth yellowed with age. Small breasts protruded from its chest, and the creature's face resembled a human, albeit mottled with avocado-colored scales and scabs. Snake-like eyes the color of Cheetos stared at me with disgust.

"Oh really? Says who?" I questioned, trying to get some gossip out of the snaky shithead before I sent it packing.

"Lucifer." Only the pronunciation sounded like Lusssssifer.

"And how does he think he'll get me there? I won't give up without a fight."

"Trickery and bribessss."

"Kill the Lamia," Coren said from beside me.

Looking up in surprise, I saw him lean against a brick wall like he were bored. He picked his nails and disregarded the demon currently staked to the ground with my sword.

"Pleasse," the Lamia begged Coren, "let me enjoy one night on earth."

He looked at the demon now, his eyebrows raised. "And if I allow it, what information will you give me?"

"Anything. Pleasssssse."

"Why is Lucifer desperate to get Mara's soul?"

I blinked in surprise. Coren didn't make idle conversation with the demon. Point for him.

"I don't know…"

In a lightning-quick movement, Coren removed my sword from the tail and rammed it through the Lamia's right shoulder. It screeched in agony.

He leaned close enough for the Lamia's snake tongue to dart out and flick against his chin. "I'm not going to ask again."

"We've only heard rumorsss, but we aren't sssure if it'ss the truth. But we've heard it'ss because of her abilitiessss after she sssigned the contact."

"And what abilities are those?" Coren asked, and when the Lamia didn't answer, he flicked the sword handle, causing the sword to painfully dance against the scaly skin.

With a cry of pain, the Lamie groaned out, "Being able to see the shadowsss."

Coren's eyes darted to mine for a quick second and then back to the demon. "And why would that be a big deal to him?"

"Becaussse she can talk to them."

He waved his hand at the Lamia in dismissal. "Finish it."

"Nooo!" it cried.

I noticed Raven arrive in my peripheral. I took the sword out of the Lamia's shoulder with a sickening crunch of bone. With as much strength as I could muster, I swiped the blade through its neck. In a matter of seconds, Raven and the demon disappeared.

Pressing my back against the brick wall behind me, I let out an exhausted breath.

Coren rested next to me. "When were you going to tell me you could talk to shadows?"

"I didn't know I could. I never tried because I was scared of them," I replied with a shrug. "Until that day at the restaurant when the guy died, I never had one really notice me until then."

"Do you know what this means, Mara?"

Shaking my head, I looked up at him with a raised eyebrow.

"It means that if Lucifer is scared about your abilities with shadows, then we may have found his weakness."

"Shadow beings are his weakness? This is the same guy that has a screaming wall of souls. Surely it can't be that simple."

"Nothing is ever simple. Somehow, the shadows are the key. Let's keep this between us for now. I don't want to freak out Raven or Death if the Lamia lied."

I snorted. "A deceitful demon? Say it isn't so."

A shadow figure hovered near the chain-link fence. He had watched the entire scene unfold with the Lamia, and happened to be the same entity from the restaurant. His glowing red eyes scrutinized me with interest, and I had no idea if he already knew what the Lamia had said, or if he had uncovered I could speak to him.

"There's a shadow here," Coren whispered. "I fell its presence, but I can't see it."

"There is?" I asked, hating myself for lying.

"Maybe we should keep moving and try to see if the Lamia told the truth later."

My eyes swerved to the shadow and then back to Coren. "Okay. I'm exhausted anyway. Do you mind if I use the restroom in the diner before we leave?"

"Sure," he said and walked me to the door the next block over and leaned against the side to keep watch. We weren't in the best neighborhood.

Since the being had followed us, I tilted my head ever so slightly at the shadow to let it know I was going inside if they wanted to make contact. As I rounded the corner to the restrooms, I met the ruby red eyes of a gorgeous half-naked male outside to the women's restroom.

He was no longer a shadowy figure, but a full-blown man. A very, very nice looking man, too. His chest was wide, and his stomach displayed sinewy muscle. My eyes traveled down his chest, to the "V" at his hips. Thank God he had jeans on, or I may have gotten an eyeful. Doubt I would've minded.

Mussed blond hair touched the tip of ears, and his squared jaw was free of stubble. I swallowed. The only time I had ever seen anyone this handsome was Coren. If Coren was an Adonis, this guy was sin.

"Hello, Mara," he said, his voice slightly accented. "My name is Lor."

"What do you want?" I asked, unsure how it was possible I saw him as a human now. Plus, I was wary of any being who dripped raw sexuality. Coren included.

"For you to keep your soul."

I stood stunned. My soul, the one thing I hadn't technically owned since I was about six years old and I wanted it back. Nobody said it was possible, but this shadow spoke with such conviction I wanted to believe it.

Coren's voice broke our surroundings, and I looked behind me to see him greeting the cashier. When I looked back at Lor, he was gone.

After I finally did my business, I followed Coren wordlessly back to Raven's car. We decided riding together was the best for now, and if one of us ended up covered in demon slime, the other could fade us both back. Of course, that meant me coming along for a spiritual Uber ride. Humans weren't meant to fade in and out. It hurt like a son of a bitch.

"I have a question," I finally said as we reached Raven's car.

Coren turned to face me. "Sure. Go ahead."

"Are shadows people, or were they ever people at one point in time?"

"I'm not sure. Some legends say they're from another dimension. Others say their aliens or spirits of elders, and some say they are rogue entities released from voodoo rituals. Maybe they are ghosts of some sort. The gossip is they steal souls of the recently departed. Who knows? All I know is that heaven and hell won't speak much about it when it comes to them."

My eyebrows quirked. "Do you know many people in Heaven? I assumed they didn't associate with demons."

His lips twitched. "Who said I was a demon?"

"You work for the devil. Duh."

"Think what you want about me, Mara. All I know is that I will move heaven and hell to save you from Lucifer's menacing plan"

The cage around my heart slid open a bit more. "Thanks, Coren. I mean it."

He slung an arm around my shoulder as we walked back to the car. We walked in comfortable silence, and I enjoyed the comfort of his embrace. I felt safe for once. Until another demon strolled out in front of us. This one looked like a burly cage fighter with muscles bulging behind his jeans and a black T-shirt. He was easy on the eyes, but his huge neck and beefy body were too much.

The guy cracked his knuckles as he stared at us with eyes as black as a moonless night.

"Another demon starting trouble, and this one seems to be on steroids." I pulled my sword from my sheath. "What happened to your neck? Did your shoulders eat it because of roid rage?"

"Well, well," the hulking dude said, his voice so deep that my skin chilled. "Fancy seeing you here."

"Mara is under my protection, Zagan," Coren warned, pushing me behind him as if I was some vulnerable female.

I stepped around to his side, my hands wrapped around the hilt of my blade. Even though I had a feeling this muscular demon would stomp me into the ground, I planted my feet in preparation for a fight.

"Tsk. Tsk." Zagan shook his head. "You're not supposed to care about your ward, Coren. That could be dangerous for you."

I blinked in surprise. "He doesn't care about me."

At the same time, Coren growled, "I'll show you how dangerous I can truly be."

Chancing a glance at Coren, I frowned before looking back at Zagan. He hadn't denied the caring thing, but then again, he was currently facing a potential foe. Anyone in his position had to show his threats were serious.

Zagan smiled at me, and his teeth were straight and as white as copy paper. "I'm not here to battle...*yet*. I'm here to send a warning. If you so much as interfere with a demon hunt again, I'll be back. Gossip runs as thick as blood back home."

"I did what I had to. Don't question my method and I won't question your loyalty." Coren folded his arms across his chest.

"I'm just doing my job, Coren. Nothing more."

The hulk of a man fell to the ground and I started toward him until Coren stopped me.

"He's fine. Just passed out. He'll wake up in five minutes tops."

My hands met my hips as I narrowed my eyes at Coren. "Who in the hell was that?"

His chocolate eyes watched me. "An old friend."

"Thanks for clearing that up," I retorted. "Was that what he looks like?"

"That's not his body."

"What?! Are you telling me he possessed that bodybuilder?" And here I had assumed possessions were as rare as red diamonds.

"Commandeered," he corrected.

I rolled my eyes. "That's just a fancy word for a possession."

"Actually, no. Zagar borrows bodies and gives them back. The people wake up with a slight hangover and are fine. A full possession means the soul is combined with a demon and could die after the demon leaves. Totally different."

"Isn't Zagar a demon?"

"Not really," he hedged.

Anger rippled through me. "You're full of answers aren't you?" When he only stared at me, I hissed, "You can fuck yourself."

Sick of half-truths, I stormed off, my long legs striding a good distance away from Coren. He didn't follow. Hadn't I held the truth from him as well? Lor had made contact, and I had a feeling he would again.

What if I saved my soul and Coren left? Had I wanted him to leave? While at first the man gave the impression of a horny, vile demon, he had started to leak into my heart. I mean, I still believed demons were revolting creatures, but Coren was unlike the others. He was kind, smart, and had fighting skills like mad. Who would've thought I would begin to have feelings for a demon?

My feet slowed and I took a deep breath of the cool night air. The street light cast an orange glow across my pale skin as I turned to look for Coren. I studied the abandoned streets and alleys. He was gone.

CHAPTER 18

Theater of illusion.

My apartment was as silent as a grave.

I had gotten used to Coren's presence in the short time frame he'd been here. Raven hadn't returned after I killed the lamia, either. For so long I'd lived like a recluse, afraid to get close to anyone in fear of discomfort and pain.

My childhood had instilled that in me, and if I had cried, whined, or even displayed happiness, my mother rewarded me with animosity. Actually, she shouldn't have had a child in the first place, but here I was in all my messed up glory. Maybe I had become a fighter because of her. Maybe my will to live was in spite of my upbringing.

"You look deep in thought."

I spun and faced the shadow from earlier. "What are you doing in my apartment?"

His baritone voice seemed to echo in my tiny space. "Our conversation was cut short earlier. And I wanted to see you again."

My head tilted as I took him in. Dressed in a black button-down and dark jeans, he appeared to be ready for a night on the town, not a conversation with a demon hunter in her apartment. The only thing that gave away that he wasn't truly human was his scarlet eyes. The color was so shocking against his pale skin.

"You don't drink blood, do you?"

His face twisted. "What kind of question is that? Of course not."

"Fine. Can I ask you a few questions about what you are, then?"

He tilted his head in agreement. The movement was so old fashioned that it was out of place in the modern world.

"How do you spell your name? Is it like lore as in a tradition or myth?"

"No, it's spelled L-o-r. Different meaning, but I guess I'm a myth to many." He shrugged.

"Are you even human?"

"Don't I look human?" His hands gestured to his body.

"Yes, except for your eyes. Looks can be deceiving, buddy. Even salt looks like sugar, but the two are not the same."

"Don't most people like salty, sweet treats? Consider me a, what's it called?" His brows puckered as he tried to come up with a word. "Salted caramel."

My nose crinkled at his analogy. "What?"

"I was born among humanity, but that's where things get complex. My race belonged to another realm, but I happened to be born on Earth. The other shadows were not born here, however. They come from the other plane of existence called Perdita. The devil sent his spawn to take over my homeland. The few that escaped went to my birthplace to flee an awful fate of slavery and death."

My eyes went heavenward wondering how God could allow an entire race to suffer the wrath of a power-hungry, evil ruler. Then again, maybe he was the reason I could speak to Lor in the first place. I looked back into Lor's eerie eyes. "I'm sorry about your home. I can't imagine losing your entire world to the likes of my boss."

His lips parted in surprise. "Your boss? You *work* for that monstrosity?"

"Against my will," I said, holding up two hands in surrender. "When he tricked me into signing away my soul and my new job was the only way Raven and her father could keep me here on Earth. Why do you think I kill demons?"

"Did you ever wonder," his eyes flared, "why Satan would allow a human to kill his kin?"

His kin? Who used that term these days? Apparently, an old ass shadow did. "Because they slip the veil and wreak havoc and death."

Lor laughed, the sound deep and throaty. "Is that what he told you?"

"Yes. That's what he also told Raven and Death."

"Ah, the reapers. You all believed him. A satanic entity known to trick all manner of beings for their souls?"

When he put it like that, I hesitated to respond and bit my lip instead. I thought about what he said the first time I saw him in the flesh. "If that's the case, then how do you expect to save my soul?"

"Now that's something for another day, my dear…"

My door locks clicked as they slid open. Lor went full-on shadow and blended into the darkness of my hallway.

Coren entered the room, his eyes finding me in an instant. Without a word, his long, strong legs carried him across my small living room. He cupped my face and kissed me. I let him. His lips lit a fire under my skin, a hot passionate spark of sensuality that pooled in my abdomen.

When he ended the kiss, I opened my eyes to see him staring down at me with hooded lids. His eyes weren't dark brown. They were more of a coffee color flaked with hints of gold and orange. His hands left my face, caressed my shoulders, and then stopped at my waist.

"I'm sorry. I tend to lose my mind when it comes to you," he whispered.

Lor chuckled from the hallway and I attempted to keep my face impassive. Had Coren heard him?

Coren stiffened. Crap on a cracker.

"Show yourself," he ordered, his grip tightening on my hips.

"Coren," I warned, but his eyes went straight to the hallway.

I followed his gaze, my heart pounding in my ears.

With an air of confidence and arrogance, Lor stepped out of the shadows in full form.

"Lor, Coren." I made introductions. "Coren, meet Lor. A shadow I recently met."

Coren's hands wrapped around me. I wasn't sure if it was for protection or to show Lor I was his. I guessed it was the possession thing, which infuriated me. Using my hands for expertly placed thrust, I pushed out of Coren's arms. He growled and attempted to reach for me again.

"No," I said. "I don't want you to mark your territory. I'm not anyone's property."

"Well, technically, you're Lucifer's," Lor stated.

With a wince, I looked at Lor. He leaned against the wall outside of the hallway, his arms across his chest.

"Listen, asshole," Coren snarled, "she will not be going to hell."

Lor inspected a nail before he finally spoke. "Agreed."

Coren relaxed for a moment and watched Lor like he would with a deadly snake. He cleared his throat. "What?"

"I concur. Hell wouldn't be kind to her, and without her soul, she'd be nothing but his concubine."

Coren's eyes flashed in anger and his jaw ticked.

After a few minutes trying to figure out what the hell a concubine was, I inhaled sharply when it sunk in. "Oh hell no. That son of a bitch will not lay a finger on me."

"You won't have a choice, Mara," Lor replied softly. "You'll be beaten into submission over time until there's nothing left but a hollow shell of who you are now."

Dread settled over me. My eyes roamed to my calendar and to the red marks counting down the days left. Fifty-seven days to figure out a way to stay here.

"I won't let that happen. I don't care if I have to die to keep her alive."

I looked up at him in surprise, but he didn't look at me. He kept his eyes on Lor.

Lor nodded. "Good. My brethren and I are formulating a plan to save her. We may have the key to all that, but you keep her safe until then. We'll be watching until she needs us."

"Stalker," I joked. I was little creeped out at a bunch of shadows watching me.

The edge of his lip tilted upward. "Until next time, beautiful." Lor faded from the room.

As he dissipated completely, Coren swore under his breath. "You need to watch out for him and his friends. We know nothing of shadow people, and they may be after your soul as well. I'm not sure if I can trust him."

"Sometimes I wonder the same thing about you."

Coren's nostrils flared. "How could you not trust me? I've done everything I could to keep you safe, along with hiding your ass SafetyNet."

He was right. My mouth tends to blurt out the first thing on my mind without a filter. I opened my mouth to tell him "Not without a price, right?" but we were interrupted.

Raven poofed into my living room. We both turned to face her in surprise.

"Sorry, guys. I've been knee-deep in dead bodies," she said.

I grimaced. Raven wasn't technically knee-deep in piles of human remains but instead overloaded with souls to transport. Still, I pictured her standing in her cherry heels amongst a butt load of bodies. The visual caused a shudder to ripple through me.

She continued, "Mara, I didn't mean to be so absent lately. That's not a good friend. Actually, it's a crappy one and I apologize. But, I brought you a surprise to sort of make up for it."

Raven held up a white paper bag with a smirk. My mouth watered because I knew exactly what she clasped in her hand. Cookies, but not just any cookies. These babies were from Heaven Scent Bakery. Yeah, yeah. The name wasn't lost on me, but they made the best cookies on the planet.

With a grabbing gesture, I said, "Gimme. I forgive you. You could run me over with your car and bring me those and I would forgive you."

Smirking, she placed the bag in my hand. The sweet aroma of freshly baked goods floated out of the bag and I opened the bag without a second thought. Placing one of the peanut butter cookies in my mouth, I groaned.

"I wish she did that with me."

Raven chuckled. "Roll her eyes back like that in an orgasm?"

"Hey," I said with a mouthful of peanut butter gooeyness, "I did not make that face."

"Yes, you did," she said. "I mean, those cookies are the bomb. I can't blame you. I ate a half dozen earlier."

"What's the big deal?" Coren questioned, reaching into my bag to snatch a chocolate chip. He was lucky I hadn't bit his fingers off. I tried to seize the cookie back, but he shoved the entire thing in his mouth before I could. I gave him my best death glare. How dare he steel one of my cookies?

Once he finished, he said, "Those are great. I get it now. I'm surprised my eyes didn't roll back, too."

Raven shifted on her feet. "Another reason I'm here is there are rumors circulating about Coren helping you slaughter demons. Lucifer is not happy. Don't be surprised if you see him make a surprise appearance soon."

Snorting, I rolled my eyes. "Like that surprises me. He'll come up with whatever excuse he needs to threaten my soul. Lor said something about –"

She held up a hand. "Wait. Spell it."

"W-A-I-T."

"Lor's name, dork." Raven rolled her eyes.

"L-O-R."

She bit her lip. I clenched my hand into a fist, afraid I was going to find out that another being wanted my soul. You know, since it was apparently so shiny and made of precious metals or something.

"Lor. Why does that sound familiar?" Raven pondered, her pale face crinkled in thought.

"He's a shadow that has the hots for Mara," Coren ground out.

"He so does not."

She tapped her chin. "One minute. I'll be right back."

With a swirl of black mist, Raven popped out of the room.

"What the fuck?" I gave Coren a puzzled look.

He shrugged. "Hell if I know."

How in the world had Raven known Lor's name? He was a shadow, a being from another realm that happened to be born on this one. A man who believed he knew how to save my soul.

With a cloud of smoke, Raven appeared holding an old parchment paper. The swirly handwriting was barely visible from age, but she read the writing with ease. "The chosen one, at the hands of lor, shadow, and angel, will ruin the world of evil. The chosen can end all malice with the sickle. They can and will be strengthened by a suiter, an ally, and death."

Coren perked up. "What is this?"

"An old prophecy," Raven said. "My father assumed it was me because of the world sickle. He read it to me several times over the years, and we recently looked over it again. That's why it was so fresh on my mind. Lor is spelled differently, so I assumed it was how they wrote it in ancient times. Now I know better. And sickle could mean a sword, too. I think this is about Mara, not me."

"Bullshit." I laughed. "I'm not some chosen one. I'm simply a person without a soul."

"What if saving your soul means ridding the world of some of the evil?" Raven questioned.

I ran a hand over my face. "Why does everything always have to be a pain in my ass?"

"Because," Coren shrugged, "that's life."

He was right. Life was a son of a bitch, or at least mine started that way from the time I popped out of my mother's womb. Things escalated from there. Abuse, reapers, demons, and the devil. Oh my!

I let out a frustrated breath and thought about Lor's conversation. "Have you two ever wondered why the demons are slipping the veil and I was chosen to hunt them?"

Raven pursed her lips. Coren's eyebrows rose and he looked at his feet. The only sound in the room was my clock ticking from the wall. I observed Coren. His dark eyes narrowed and he cursed under his breath.

"I never thought he could be so devious," Coren muttered.

"You had no idea Satan could be devious? I mean, the dude has wanted my soul for a long time. Almost killed us all for it." I sat on the couch and crossed my legs. They remained standing.

Coren took in a deep breath. "Yes, but why would he go to this much trouble? Surely your soul has to be worth so much more than we all know. But why?"

"Because I'm freaking awesome?" They ignored me.

Raven nodded in agreement. "I want to know the answer to that, too."

"The lamia said it was because I could speak and control shadows." I lifted a shoulder. "Lor made an appearance after he watched the entire thing with the snake thing."

"He watched us?" Coren raked a hand through his dark locks. "I felt a shadow near, but I hadn't paid any mind to him. Now I feel like I should have."

After a second or two, I asked Raven to read the prophecy again. She did.

"An angel? Like from heaven?" I asked with a sour expression.

Sure, I knew angels existed, but I'd yet to meet one. I mean, my soul was marked for the devil, the supposed dark angel banished from heaven. I'm sure I wasn't a fan of the man upstairs.

Raven read it over one more time. "I'm not sure. Maybe this person's name is Angel. I mean, Lor is here."

Coren looked down at the paper in Raven's hands. "Do you know anyone named Angel?"

"No, I don't think so. I could ask Laura if anyone came in with the name Angel recently, I guess."

"But what if it means a real angel?" Raven shook the parchment. "That would give you a good chance at saving your soul. We deliver souls to one area of heaven with only one angel on duty at a time. We can't even talk to anyone there to sway their decision in your favor. My dad and I are doing everything we can. Even with the pull we have in hell, Lucifer tends to say one thing, but changes his mind once we're gone. "

"He's a master manipulator," I said matter of fact. "The guy rules hell after all. Can't you stop bringing him souls as leverage?"

She cringed. "We can't."

"Why not?"

"Let's just say it's a part of our DNA."

I opened my mouth to push her into answering me, but Coren spoke. "Raven and her father have a spiritual obligation. Their lives depend on it. Quitting their jobs isn't an option."

She mouthed thank you to him and a flicker of annoyance drifted through me. I knew if Raven hadn't wanted me to know something, I wouldn't until she was ready. We'd been friends long enough, and if I pressed her, she'd only get angry and poof off to wherever she goes to sulk.

The irritation still was there. I swallowed it back for now. "I can't quit either, so I get it. My obligation is forced. Either way, the last word in that prophecy. You know, the *death* thing."

Raven's head cocked to the side. "That either means my father or the afterlife. These types of things have a way of twisting words. My father believed it was about me until you mentioned Lor. Prophecy isn't inevitable, Mara. We all create our own paths."

She was right. I refused to let prophecy or fate define me. My life was my own, and no one else could determine my destination. Well, except for where my soul was concerned. I wasn't giving that part of me up without a fight. I straightened with a new resolve.

After Raven gave me a tight hug, one I gladly returned, Coren walked her out the door and into the hallway. They shut the door behind them, and I had a sneaking suspicion they were going to try to come up with a plan. I took in a deep breath, enjoying the moment of total quiet. For once, I was alone inside my own apartment.

With a chuckle, I slid the locks closed on my door with a resounding click. I headed to get sour cream and onion chips, ready to enjoy a bit of peace and quiet. I knew it wouldn't last. Once Coren noticed I had locked him out, he'd lecture me about the dangers of being alone. I shook my head at his paranoia as I opened the bag for the crispy goodness.

Hadn't I thought my apartment was too quiet? Now I wanted silence. As I shoved a chip into my mouth, I headed into the living room.

That's when the sound of a throaty snarl came from my balcony.

CHAPTER 19

Even the best of men cast shadows.

My head slowly turned to the third story balcony, and my eyes widened when I saw the demon perched on the railing.

The beast's knees were bent the opposite directions, like some sort of demented, strong ass bird. With sharp obsidian teeth, it growled at me again. Drool dripped from its lower lip and I met the evil glare of bright yellow eyes. I took a few steps toward my sword. Black smoke swirled around its burgundy skin as it moved to watch me. Huge obsidian bat-like wings protruded from its back.

My sword was on the other side of the couch, and I attempted to make slow methodical steps in that direction. Once I finally reached my baby, I went to grab it. The sound of claws grating against the glass sent my heart to lurching into my throat.

I slid my sword free and faced the monstrosity. Thin black fingers slid the door open, long claws screeching on the glass. The putrid smell of sulfur floated on the breeze and inside the living room. The beast made a clicking noise similar to the Predator movies. In fact, the face resembled the movies as well.

"Bring it on, you ugly son of a bitch," I taunted.

In one leap, the monster crashed against my couch, claws raking an inch from my face. I rolled out of the way, and the large wings scratched against my ceiling as it followed my movement. Then, as if the demon expected me to charge, we crashed together in the middle of my living room. My sword stabbed its shoulder, barely missing where a human heart would be. The creature didn't even flinch when my blade sunk into the dark skin. *Shit.*

With a hard kick, I was able to free myself enough to roll away. The hideous creature stood and expanded its wings to their full terrifying length. This time I flung my blade and it sliced through red skin near the stomach area. The thing tugged it out and threw it to the side. The metal clattered against the floor and I slid for it, but I was too late. I was on my back and fighting to keep my face from being chewed on.

Pounding sounded against my door, and I cried out, "I'm a little busy!"

I knew it was Coren, but I didn't have a second to worry about him. Right now, my main concern was keeping this demon's teeth from sinking into my face. Claws dug into my arms. The agony of them biting through my skin was so intense I had to bite my tongue to keep from screaming. Hot drool dripped on my face, and I wanted nothing else than to wipe it away but couldn't.

Teeth gnashed at my face again, this time about a half-inch away from my nose. My sword was too far away to grab, and the weight on top of me left me no option but to keep the demon from killing me. I was so fucked.

Black smoke drifted down from the demon to swirl around me. The smoke seeped along my body in cold tendrils and the demon's gaze moved from my face to look over my head. I struggled to breathe through the thickness of evil coating me. Coldness seeped through my body and I shivered.

When it clicked in what I assumed was a warning, the beast was ripped from my body in one tug. Since its claws still dug into my arms, I let out a screech of pain as they shredded through my flesh.

I reached for my sword, only to realize it was still several feet away. After two attempts and slipping in my own blood, I removed myself from the floor barley in time to see Lor twist the demon's head. It fell with a sickening thud. Coren retrieved my sword and sliced off the demon's wings in one swift movement.

Without the help of Raven, we all watched the demon's soul, or essence or whatever, sail back out my open balcony door. I assumed Raven or her father would take care of that mess. Still, there was a seven-foot-tall demon, wings and all, dead on my trashed living room floor.

I let out a frustrated breath. "How the fuck am I supposed to get rid of a demon's body from my apartment? It's not like I can toss it in the dumpster."

"Mara," Coren breathed as he rushed forward.

Lor disappeared into my kitchen as Coren inspected my arms. Adrenaline does amazing things to the body. I hadn't paid attention to my shredded skin and blood dripping down my forearms and over my fingers in rivulets. When the adrenaline finally fades, that's when shock kicks in. I stared down at my tattered arms in confusion, my heart pulsing in my ears.

"She's really pale," Lor said, returning with some towels.

A quiver rippled over me, but I couldn't stop staring at the blood. I frowned. What happened? Why was I bleeding?

"Get her a blanket," Coren snapped. He pressed the towels over my arms.

Warmth enveloped me and I felt weightless. "This is nice," I whispered. "I like floating."

"She's in shock," Lor stated from somewhere around me. "We have to get her to a hospital."

"And tell them what?" Coren questioned, his voice gruff with both concern and anger. "She's lost a lot of damn blood!"

A few seconds later, glass shattered. The sound echoed through my head like we were in a cave.

"Problem solved. She fell through the balcony door. Get her to a hospital. I'll take care of the body."

"What's going on? Why is there blood everywhere and an *âme damnée* on the floor?" Raven sweet voice broke through my cloudiness. "Oh my God! Mara!"

"Hi, Raven! So glad you could…" Bright stars swarmed in my vision. I blinked a few times to clear them, but tunnel vision took over next.

"She's going to need a blood transfusion, Coren. Get your ass moving before she dies from blood loss!" Lor's biting tone was the last thing I remembered.

*****

The beeping sound grated on my nerves. My eyes felt heavy, and I struggled to open them. I instantly regretted it.

Bright lights blinded me and I groaned.

The sound of a chair creaking caught my attention. "She's waking up."

"Mara?" Raven said, her hand clasping mine.

"Do you think it'll work?" Coren asked.

I squinted my eyes open and saw Raven, Death, Lor, and Coren standing around me. I was on a bed with white sheets. Clean sterile walls surrounded me, and I looked around to see a monitor next to the bed and an IV under a clear bandage on my hand.

Lor nodded. "It should. We'll know when we pull those bandages off."

"What..." I croaked. Raven handed me a cup and I drank a sip of water gingerly. "What will work?"

"Lor applied a salve to your arms." Raven squeezed my hand. "He says you should already be healed and there won't be any poison left in your system."

"Somebody tried to poison me?" I shook my head in an attempt to remember what had happened to my arms. I lifted the one with the IV and saw white bandages from my wrists up to my shoulders. Then it clicked. A winged demon tried to kill me...

"How long have I been out?" I let my arm drop.

Coren raked a hand through his dark locks. "Three days. Three long days."

The breath caught in my throat. "Three days?! I have to get back to work before my sixty days are up."

I tried to sit up and Death gently pushed me back down. "Relax. You still have some time."

I looked at Coren, but he looked away. I said, "But I lost three days and I can't waste any time because –"

"We think we may know how to protect you," Lor interrupted.

"I think it's a stupid idea," Coren muttered.

With a sigh, I looked at each person in the room before landing back on Lor. "How?"

"Angels, my dear. Shadows can't do much until we know the specifics of your contract, which we are working on. Death and Raven have been working feverishly to find that as well. Coren has been trying his best to keep you out of trouble. I think this is going to get worse after you were nearly killed."

"I have been having that almost being killed problem lately." I snorted.

"Let's see if the wounds are healed," Coren stated, his jaw flexing a few times. "Then we'll find out if you can be trusted, Lor."

Lor raised his chin. "I'm still deciding if you can be as well."

My eyes rolled so hard I'm surprised I didn't see the back of my skull. "Guys, get these bandages off and this IV out of my arm. I want to get out of here."

With his jaw set, Coren grabbed a pair of surgical scissors from the table next to a sink. He handed them to Death, who began cutting away the bandages from my right arm. When he began to peel back the gauze and bandages, he let out a shaky breath.

"Flawless skin," he said, closing in eyes in what must have been relief. With my other visitors peering over his shoulder, he looked up at me. "I'm sorry you have to deal with a corrupt man who isn't afraid of killing you to get what he wants."

"He isn't a man," Coren growled. "No man would kill an innocent woman."

"Lucifer was never a man." Lor shook his head. "But he would kill her without regret if he could control her. That's what he's wanted all along. To rule over her. She'd make an extraordinary demon."

"Yeah, well, he can kiss my ass." I winced when the scissors caught some of my arm hair as Death cut the rest of the bandage away. "I won't be one of his slaves."

Lor's scarlet eyes gazed at me. "My sweet girl, aren't you already?"

"He's got control over me. That's different."

"Aren't slaves controlled?"

"Would you shut your mouth, Lor," Coren barked. "Mara is not a slave."

Lor opened his mouth, but Death pointed at him with the surgical scissors. "If I hear another word about slavery and Mara today, I will drag your soul around with me for all eternity."

His mouth clicked shut, but I hadn't missed how his nostrils flared once.

Death continued to cut the rest of the bandage away. I stared at my arm in wonder. My skin was perfect. There was no hint of the damage the demon had done. No scars, no scratches, nothing. "Thank you, Lor. I don't know what I would've done if I wasn't able to use my sword again."

He gave me a wink and then faded into a shadow and left. Coren's shoulders relaxed, Death let out a soft breath, and Raven closed her eyes for a minute. Their relief in Lor's exit was palpable, but why? He'd done nothing but help me when I needed it the most.

Raven's father started cutting the wrap on the other arm, so I said, "Lor has been nothing but kind to me, he assisted Coren with my attacker yesterday, and made a salve for my arms that left me unscarred. So why are you all nervous around him? Hasn't he proven himself?"

The only sound was the metal scraping of the scissors in response. I looked at Coren, who stared back at me with a blank expression. Of course, Death focused on cutting my bandages. When my eyes narrowed on Raven for a minute, she caved.

"Because we were under the impression they stole the souls of the living. I don't know if that's true, but if it is, Dad and I wonder if he wants yours for himself."

I tossed up my unbandage arm up in frustration and let it drop back on the bed with a thump. "You all need to get along. At least until I can figure out how to get my soul back. Once that's taken care of, then you can all strangle each other."

"She's right," Coren said, his eyes still pasted on me. "Mara is my number one priority. She's all that matters. I will stop at nothing to free her, even if it kills me in the process."

Death stopped cutting halfway up my arm. His eyebrows rose as he looked at Coren. Raven sat back in the chair and drew in a sharp breath.

I looked around clueless. "What?"

"You realize how dangerous this is for both of you?" Death asked and then continued cutting my dressing.

Coren gave a quick nod. "Yes. But you have my word that I'll protect her with my own life if I have to."

With a frustrated sigh, I looked at both of them. "What's dangerous? Why?"

Letting out a slow breath, Death said, "When the time is right, you'll know. It's not my place, *mi cielito*."

Mi cielito. Raven had said it meant "my sky" or "my heaven" but I never asked her father the meaning. He hadn't used the nickname in a long time, not since I had trained with Raven as a teen. That meant whatever they were hiding was going to bite me in the ass. Right in the butt cheeks with sharp, annoying teeth made out of regret and ruin.

While I knew Death and Coren had hidden something from me, I understood the reason. Sometimes things spoken aloud could lead to fear of damnation, often if the words had unknown consequences. Whatever they held behind tight lips might cause more repercussions than endorsements.

Raven bit her lip and grabbed my free hand. She tried to write something on my palm with her middle finger as the pen. I frowned because I couldn't figure out her code, and I sucked at guessing words like that. Trying for the third time, she pursed her lips and "wrote" slower. L. O. Pause. V. Another pause. E. Then she looked at Coren quickly and back at me, twice.

Fuck. Holy fucking shit.

My face must have shown absolute panic because Death said, "Did I cut you?"

I shook my head quickly, and he finished and pulled the bandage away. My eyes swung to Coren for a second, and he tilted his head as my cheeks flamed as hot as a Las Vegas sidewalk. Sure, I had heard that demon from the other day mention he cared for me, but I figured he had goaded Coren for the sake of being evil. Now that Raven had spelled the word on my palm, and Death had obviously noticed something too, I felt unsure about myself.

Did Coren really love me, or was it a ruse to distract me? I didn't know and didn't know if I cared. Okay, I lied. I cared about staying alive, and I cared about him. But was he a recovered demon or a devious one?

"Let's break you out of here," Coren said.

I nodded, but I avoided his gaze like a criminal avoiding his parole officer. I felt his stare like a fiery brand, but I focused on the feeling of my skin prickling as Raven grabbed my arm to transport me out of the hospital.

As soon as we both arrived in my living room, I stared in shock. The sliding door to the balcony had cardboard where the glass should be and glass peppered my hardwood floor. Huge puddles of blood shone on my floor, and a lot of it, too. The blood pooled in the spot the demon had pinned my body, some smears that I had slipped in trying to get up, and then they dripped along my house similar to paint splatters on a canvas. I itched my arms as I remembered the claws carving through my flesh. The demon was long gone, and I presumed Death had taken care of it.

Raven rubbed my back in a friendly gesture. "We'll get this cleaned up for you, okay?"

I nodded but continued to stare at my drying blood, the glass, and my overturned, clawed couch. Finally, I asked, "What's an amdonny?"

She blinked at me in confusion and then nodded. "Oh, you mean *âme damnée*. The word is pronounced Ahm Dah-ney. I don't know if you want to know what that thing is." When I gave her my best death stare, she sighed. "Okay, maybe I don't really want to tell you what they are. The real question is why one was sent to your apartment."

"Tell me what they are, Raven."

Looking over my trashed apartment, she nodded slowly. "They're a damned soul. Or, in other words, a person who's soul belonged to the devil. He collected their debt and turned them into that thing.

But they rarely escape hell, as your boss keeps a tight leash on them."

Blinking in disbelief, I scratched at my arms again. "Is that... is that what I would become if... if I don't save my soul?"

"No, I don't think so. No matter what, we're not going to let him take you, Mara. We'll save you. You know that."

"If you can't, is it possible I become one of those winged assholes?"

When she didn't answer, I looked at her. Raven's face appeared crumbled in defeat. That had been my answer. Somehow, someway, I was going to stop the devil from trying to kill me and trying to take my soul in the process. My boss wanted me dead and his reasons was beyond me. So what if I talked to shadows, so what if I hunted demons? I refused to give up and every demon he sent my way would die a slow, painful death from now until eternity.

"I want to practice my sword skills and defense against deadly demons. I think I need it now more than ever."

"I think that's a fabulous idea," Coren said from behind us.

I hadn't heard him arrive, but I swung around to face him. Then I turned my attention to Death. "Will you all teach me different ways to defend myself?"

"Of course." Death nodded. "Once you're rested."

"I rested for three days," I countered, but Death shook his head.

Letting out a puff of air from between my lips, I turned and headed to the bathroom to shower.

*****

While the repair crew worked on my balcony door, I relaxed on the bed and read a book.

Coren, Raven, and Death took care of me the entire day, and I'm sure they were the ones doing a lot of the cleanup, mostly because I didn't want to see the mess anymore. I think if I saw my blood staining the floor again, I'd have to move for good.

Lor popped in with pizza and breadsticks. I hadn't known pizza could survive a fade, but here I was, eating another breadstick. I chuckled I'd have to remember that for Raven and Coren in the future.

Moving the paper plate to the side, I plopped the book down on my bed as I sat up. I was antsy. My back hurt from laying on my bed the entire day and I itched to stretch my legs. The hammering and vacuuming had stopped over an hour ago, but the smell of bleach was still strong. I assumed it was safe to come out of my bedroom.

I slowly opened the door, went down the hall, and peeked outside. I let out a sigh of relief when there was no blood. The floor was pristine and the replaced glass to the balcony revealed the normal landscape. Sure, I had no replacement couch yet, but I'd get one eventually. Still, I stood unmoving right at the threshold to the living room.

I couldn't help but feel violated. A demonic creature had entered my apartment and ruined my arms and my couch with its razor-sharp claws. My small home was supposed to be sacred, free from the evils on the outside. Yet, one came in and left its tarnished mark on the place.

Coren came out of the kitchen and noticed me frozen in place. "Are you okay?"

Being the strong person I was, I wanted to lie to him, to tell him everything was fine. "No. I'm not."

He strolled over and wrapped me in his strong arms. "I'm sorry. What can I do to make it better?"

"Just hold me for a minute." I enfolded my arms around his muscular waist and leaned my head on his chest.

We held each other, the only sound our soft breathing and Coren's heartbeat in my ear. As he pulled away, he searched my eyes for something.

Holding out a hand, he said, "Take a step forward past the hallway. I won't let anything happen to you."

"Neither will we," Raven said softly.

Noticing Raven and Death standing near the front door, my chin rose an inch. All I had seen in that moment was Coren, and I hadn't turned to Raven or her father for reassurance. Guilt sparked to life as I gave Raven a weak smile. I took Coren's hand in mine.

Taking one big step into the room, I let out a shaky breath. I took another, and another, until I was standing in front of my balcony window looking out the evening glow of the city. The sound of claws grating against glass filtered through my memory, but I shut it out. Three people who cared about me stood directly behind me with strength and support, and that outshone any bad memories at the moment.

"Is it time for my training now?" I questioned quietly.

Death cleared his throat. "Are you sure you're ready?"

I turned to face my friends and straightened. "Yes."

"Okay." Death produced his scythe out of thin air. "To the roof?"

CHAPTER 20

Don't fear the reaper.

Death circled me in the fading yellow light from the city around us. His cloak fluttered in the breeze as he whirled his scythe in his hand.

"Charge me," he demanded.

I hesitated, because, well, this was Death. *The* Grim Reaper. One nick of his scythe would send me straight to hell. No stops at "go" on my way down.

With a deep breath, I twirled my sword in return, never taking my eyes off him. I knew he'd never hurt me, but I was outmatched like I had brought a spoon to a knife fight.

Without a warning, Death took a step forward and swung his blade. I held up my sword and blocked his an instant before he would've sliced my head clean off. The metal clanged and reverberated through my shoulders. My arms shook, and he used his weight to push me back a few feet. I'm strong for a woman, sure, but his brute strength alone would beat me down. I lifted my knee and hit him right in the balls. Grunting, he fell forward and I used that momentum to punch him in the nose.

"Son of a bitch," he muttered, still bent over. He stepped back to lift his free hand to his nose because the other hand was still holding his weapon.

Instead of letting Death overpower me again, I took that opportunity to swing my blade and stopped short of his throat.

He smiled, but his eyes were squinted in what I assumed was pain. "Good girl."

I beamed at him and turned around to wink at Raven. I had bested Death, and I let go of my sword similar to a mic drop. Pain exploded along my scalp as I flew backward and was flipped upside down by my hair. In about a second flat, I landed on my back with a blade pressed against my sternum.

He had produced a wicked-looking dagger and pushed the metal tip of the weapon against my skin. "*Never* trust a demon. *Never* turn your back on your enemy."

Wincing at the pinch of my skin on his blade, I scoffed. "Did you pull my fucking hair?"

Removing the metal from my chest, he shrugged. "Evil doesn't play fair, *mi cielito*."

My nickname again, the one he rarely used. Apparently, I'd hear it often now. Death extended a hand and I took it. He helped me to my feet, only to knock me right back down on my ass with a swipe of his leg.

Letting out a sigh, I waited until he extended his hand again. I yanked his hand with all my strength and I pushed my feet into his solar plexus. He toppled over my head but landed on his feet easily. I barely heard his feet scrape in a counter-attack when I rolled out of the way. A metal ping hit the ground next to me and pebbles from the asphalt roof peppered my face. I rolled to a standing position, barely missing his blade for the second time.

Death kept coming, his skills beyond anything I'd ever seen. He moved fast, but efficient. His cloak swirled in the wind, the hood flapping around his handsome face. With a smile, he took a few steps in my direction.

Lifting my sword, I deflected blow after blow, each attack ringing with a metal hiss. My arms shook, and my fingers throbbed from the vibration each time the sharp metal connected. The next time he swung, I ducked and rammed my shoulder into his stomach. We toppled, but I landed on top of him this time, my sword aimed at his Adam's apple.

"Is it my turn yet?" Raven asked.

Death smirked and grabbed my blade gently in his fingers to move it from his throat. "Play nice with her."

I rolled my eyes and stood. I knew Raven wouldn't hold back, not that Death had. Stretching my arms with my sword, I readied myself.

She handed her sickle over to her father. Raven pointed to my hand. "No sword this time. You use it as a crutch."

"Are you serious?"

"Yep. As serious as the dead."

Her father walked over to take the sword, but my hands on the hilt tensed. He held his hand out. "Let it go, Mara. You can do this without your blade. I have faith in you."

His black eyes were tender and full of understanding. I had a feeling he didn't like giving up his scythe any more than I wanted to give up my sword. But I knew he could kick ass without either of the two. I nodded once and handed it over to him.

When I turned to face Raven, I spread my legs and stretched my shoulders. I had to do this, not only for my own pride but to prove to them that I wasn't helpless.

Raven bounced on her feet like a seasoned fighter, her hands up for a boxing match. After a few seconds of intimidation and her stupid bouncing, she winked at me and faded, only leaving a wisp of black smoke in her wake.

"Cheater!"

"So are demons," Raven whispered in my ear from behind me.

When I spun around, she was gone again "How can I fight you when I can't see you!"

"Figure it out," she murmured from behind me.

"Asshole!" I screamed, my blood steaming at her trickery.

I swung my fists blindly, and of course, hit nothing but air. Coren caught my attention with a snap of his fingers. He pointed to his eyes, ears, and nose. I frowned. See no evil, hear no evil, smell no evil? I finally got his point and my mouth opened in surprise. I would've never thought of this method on my own because most of the time I used brute force instead of brains. This was something I had to learn since the higher demons were able to fade in and out easily.

"Boooo," Raven singsonged next to me before she vanished.

I took a deep breath to focus on my senses. The faint smell of sulfur from the underworld, the soft swish of her clothes, and the small tendrils of smoke as she moved. As I focused, I began to anticipate her appearance. First to the right, then to the left. Finally in front of me.

Pulling my fist back, I smashed it right into her face.

She instantly became visible, dropped to her knees, and let out a groan. "You punch…like…a bitch."

Grinning, I helped her to her feet. She stood and punched me square in the jaw. I flew back a few feet, landing on my back. The air was knocked out of me, but she wasted no time transforming into her reaper form.

A skeletal hand reached down, but I rolled out of the way and jumped to my feet. I still struggled to breathe a bit, and I dodged her attacks to the best of my ability. I had no idea what she had planned next, but I wasn't waiting to find out.

"I give!" I cried out as I spun out of the way of her grip again.

"No," she growled, her voice deep and creepy.

"Fine," I said reluctantly.

Raven anticipated my next step and snatched me up by the throat. My feet dangled as I struggled for air. Panic set in and my eyes went wide as I looked to her father and Coren for help. Death was holding Coren back, his voice low and unintelligible.

"Use your head," Raven said. "Let go of the panic."

So nice of her to offer pointers while she choked me. I stopped fighting her hold and thought of a way to get out of the situation. She was a reaper, a collector of death. What could I do to stop her? Raven was at least seven feet tall at this point.

I started swaying my legs until I was able to put my booted feet against her chest. Stars twinkled in my vision, but my right leg connected with her arm repeatedly until there was a snap. She dropped me and I once again landed on my ass. This time from several feet in the air.

Letting out a groan, I observed her transform back into her light-haired beauty. Only this time she cradled her arm and bit her lip in what I assumed was pain.

"Shit." She winced. "That's going to take a while to heal. Good job."

"I'm sorry, Raven."

"Don't worry about it. You had no other option and I want you to fight dirty."

I took a deep breath, mostly to refill my lungs some more. "I know."

"Let's take a break for a few minutes," Death said, finally coming forward to inspect his daughter's arm.

Still spread out on my back, I breathed in and out in an attempt to get oxygen back to my brain. Sweat beaded along my hairline, and I wiped it away.

"Are you okay?" Coren sat next to me. He looked up at Raven and back at me. "She took it a little too far."

Wiping my brow again, I said, "No, she didn't. Raven wanted to teach me how to get out of an attack with a stronger demon, especially if I lose my weapon. She's right, you know. I do use my sword like a crutch."

Coren shook his head. "Your sword is... special. I've never seen one as unique as yours. It's who you are, a part of you. Don't ever think it won't protect you when you needed it the most."

I frowned. "My sword is special and unique? What makes it that way?"

Coren appeared to struggle for words, but Death interrupted whatever he might say. "Okay, are you ready to get started again?"

"Are you ready for me?" Coren smirked.

That devilish smirk almost sent me over the edge of oblivion, but I reigned it back. Barely.

"Is that an innuendo?" I asked, my voice breathy and rough.

He winked and helped me up from the asphalt roof. "Give her the sword back, please."

Death did. He and Raven leaned up against the brick wall near the exit to watch us.

I took a few steps away, knowing I had been outmatched all night. Coren was a high demon. A very high demon. Maybe even one of the highest I'd ever met. My eyes roamed over him, pausing at his crotch before I met his eyes. I had wondered what he had in his pants. *Shit. Stop thinking about his crotch and sex* I chided myself.

Coren moved forward, not a weapon in sight. He rolled his neck and stretched his arms.

"Are we doing this without swords?"

Popping each one of his fingers, he replied, "Keep your sword. I don't need one."

"If you say so."

Raven laughed and Death shushed her. Coren stared at me, his gaze unwavering. He gave me a "come here" motion with his fingers. Of course, my mind went dirty with the two-finger gesture. What I wouldn't give to have his–

Coren's eyes blazed like he knew exactly what I was thinking. *Ignore it, Mara. Ignore his amazing body, his beautiful face.*

I darted forward with my blade lifted, but he used my momentum against me. With a shriek of surprise on my part, Coren tossed me up and over him. I landed on my feet and spun to counter him. Every time I attempted to best him with my sword, he outmaneuvered me, either by catching the wrist that held my weapon or by knocking me flat on my backside. Fucker was good at this. It infuriated me.

With a swift move, I lifted my leg to kick him in the face, but he caught my leg and spun me in some sort of karate move you'd only see in the movies. I landed flat on my back and he took that moment to grab my ankle and drag me across the roof. Using my nails, I tried to stop his motion, tried to get free.

Raven yelled, "You have a leg free. Use it!"

Death hushed her.

Using her advice, I kicked him with my free foot anywhere I made contact. His wrist, his hand, his stomach. But it was the back of his knee that was the winning ticket. He collapsed and let go of me. I scrambled away and gained my footing again.

The next time I went to attack, he twisted my wrist and pulled me to him. Our mouths were only inches apart. His strong body pressed against me and one of his strong arms enfolded around me. With my sword trapped between us, he leaned forward so our lips were a mere centimeter from touching. So close, but so far away.

"You're no match for me," he whispered. "If I was really evil, I'd take you in front of everyone."

My rage burned, but so did the heat low in my abdomen. The thought of him taking me on the rooftop caused my synapsis to fire at a rapid pace, even if he meant killing me. All I thought about was his mouth on mine.

I closed my eyes and let my head fall back. "Take me. Right here, right now."

I wanted him to ravage my body, but I wanted to prove a point more.

Coren hesitated, his breath fanning my neck. A few seconds passed and he finally took a step back and released me, which is all I had needed. I lifted my fist and gave him an uppercut right to the jaw. He stumbled back in shock and I stopped my sword an inch before his jugular.

I grinned. "*Never* trust a woman. You're lucky I kicked your knee instead of your balls."

In a quick movement, his legs swept mine out from under me and I landed on my backside for the millionth time tonight. He pounced on top of me, holding my sword above my head with his wrist on mine. His head lowered to my ear.

"You're lucky we have an audience," he murmured. "Fighting with you turns me on."

Clapping interrupted us, and Coren removed his body from mine. I closed my eyes in frustration. Both at losing the matches and for wanting Coren as badly as I did. It seemed we were like-minded and sparring with each other was an aphrodisiac.

While I bested each of them in a moment, they also would've killed me if they weren't my friends. What would happen if I ended up in hell as Satan's pawn? Or like the ugly beast with wings that showed up at my apartment. Nobody would want me then, not even Coren.

"Well, love, you gave it your best."

Lor's voice caused my eyes to pop open in surprise. He helped me from the ground with a gentle hand. Coren's gaze was anything but friendly, and Raven and her father had their arms crossed as they glared at Lor.

I smiled at him. "Still not good enough, though."

"You'll get better with practice. I'm willing to offer my help as well. If you'd like to practice with me, that is." His crimson eyes held a hint of mischief. "I know the perfect place."

Tilting my head in curiosity, I said, "What do you want in return?"

"Nothing."

"No," Coren stated. "I'm not going to let you take advantage of Mara, no matter your intentions. She's not going anywhere with you."

My gaze zipped to Coren for a split second. Hadn't he said I owed him a favor when he decided to collect? His double standard was laughable. Lor offered me some training without anything in return. I needed as many combat skills as necessary. Even better, my decision was a big "up yours" to Coren for telling me what I could or couldn't do.

I nodded once. Lor grinned. As quick as a snakebite, he snatched my arm. I let out a groan as the pain crested from the upcoming relocation. Coren grappled for me as my body vanished, but I assumed they only grasped air as we faded away from the rooftop.

CHAPTER 21

Shadows aren't always in the light.

Lor caught me from falling when we arrived at our destination.

Mountains illuminated by the setting sun filled my view to the left, and rock formations surrounded the house below the edge of the cliff. I blinked to adjust to the darkening atmosphere. The air was cool and crisp, barely an ounce of humidity.

"Where are we?" I asked, turning around to see not only the gorgeous view, but a large adobe style house.

"That is the Garden of the Gods," he answered as he pointed to all the red rocks from our view of the house. I gave him a quizzical look, so he continued as he pointed to the mountains. "Those are the rocky mountains. We're in Colorado."

"Colorado?!" I blinked and stumbled back in shock. He whipped out a hand and kept me from toppling to the rocks below.

Sure, Raven, Death, and Coren faded me in and out inside our town, and the longest destination was hell. I assumed hell was a straight shot south. Colorado was over a thousand miles away from home and we had traveled in a blink of an eye.

I began to realize how powerful Lor really was. But was he powerful enough to save my soul? That was the million-dollar question.

"Lor?" A man's voice came from the house. "Is that you?"

"Yes, Vex," Lor answered. "We're out here."

"We?" a female asked. Her voice was lilted and as sweet as sugar.

Tilting my head, I took in their shadows from the large picture window facing the mountains behind us. Curiosity piqued my interest, but I refused to let it show. I reached for my sword, but it wasn't there. I patted my sheath attached to my belt, feeling both naked and underprepared for what was to come.

The man and woman made their way in our direction. Lor nodded in their direction. "That's Char and her husband Vex. Fable and Zen should be along shortly."

I snorted. "Great names. Did you all pick them out at random from a dictionary?"

Lor glared at me but didn't honor me with a reply. Our couple from the house had arrived. They eyed me warily. Char was tall and strong, her pixy face hiding her true age. Her coppery red hair framed her chin in a bob. Vex with black hair with a wisp of ashen hair near his ears. His face was strong and sharp, but he had nary a wrinkle.

"Who are you?" Vex questioned, his arm on his wife. Although both their eyes were red, they were a darker crimson than Lor's blood red ones.

Of course, I realized Vex was holding his wife back, not protecting her. I glanced up at Lor, who shrugged and gestured with his hand for me to say something.

"Hi. I'm Mara Argueta." For some reason, I wanted to curtsy but figured that would be too smartassy. Instead, I held out my right hand.

Char looked down at my hand, back up to my face, and cautiously shook my hand. "Nice to finally meet you. You're not what we expected."

Opening my mouth to say something rude, Lor snatched my free hand and squeezed it in warning. He said, "While her died hair and tattooed skin may fool you, she's as quick as a whip and her mouth is even faster. You'll have to forgive her if she says something that offends."

Vex waved a hand. "You forget Zen is as rude as they come. We're used to it."

"Sounds like Zen and I will get along just fine," I muttered, and then seeing Char's eyebrows raise, I cleared my throat. "For his mouth, that is."

Lor slapped his forehead.

"No, not that his mouth and mine will get along, but that I'll like his mouth." Now it was my turn to slap my forehead. "Let's try this again. I'm a natural smartass. It'll be nice to be around another person without a filter."

Char let a smile blossom across her lips. "I know what you meant. I like to see people falter over their words. It shows character."

Lor laughed and grabbed my hand in his. I froze at the contact. His hand was soft but strong and felt strangely good in mine. Unlike Coren, there was no sexual attraction with Lor. He was like a brother and that was okay with me. Lord knows I didn't need two men fighting for my cold, dead heart. I barely handled Coren.

I smiled up at Lor and squeezed his hand in return. "Thanks," I breathed.

He gave a quick nod. Addressing Vex, he nodded to me. "Our girl here needs some training. While her…," he made a face, "friends have helped her with combat, I thought it might be good to support her mentally."

With a wicked smile, Vex rubbed his hands together. "I always love a good game. Been way too long."

His wife winked at me. "Are you sure about this? These guys are pretty competitive."

Well, I wasn't ready, but Lor had brought me to Colorado after all. Might as well take advantage of it. I nodded, patting my belt for my sword again.

"You don't need it," Lor whispered. "You'll get it back when I take you home."

Two more figures emerged from the house; both of whom I assumed were Zen and Fable. A tall, lithe blonde woman followed a muscular man with light brown hair. They seemed to move in harmony, their footfalls barely audible. Of all the shadows surrounding me, I suspected these two were the killers. Their movements were too quiet, too perfect not to be. Yet, no weapons were visible amongst their tight clothing.

Lor made introductions. "Mara, this is Zen and Fable. Guys, this is Mara"

Zen, the man, looked me up and down. His eyes were so red they glowed. "The demon hunter? This can't be real. She's nothing special and she has no muscle mass."

"Well, muscles from steroids like yours usually mean a small dick, so don't judge me until you know me," I retorted back.

Fable tilted her head back with a laugh. She slapped Zen's shoulder. "I think you have met your match."

Char chuckled and swept her hand across the view in front of us. "We're going hunting. You two in?"

Swallowing hard, I tried to ignore her use of the word *hunt*. Lor's hand tightened in reassurance.

"Who are we hunting?" Zen asked, his eyes still on me.

"I assume we're going to play a game with Mara. Isn't that right?" Fable waggled her eyebrows, her ruby eyes twinkling in excitement.

"Yes, but we are only trying to give her some mental stress. Our girl has been hunted by some big bads lately, and I want to make sure she can rely on her brain as much as her sword," Lor said.

Char frowned. "Oh, you poor girl. Lor told me the devil has been trying to take your body and soul. It's not right. We won't let that happen, darling. We're going to save you."

I wanted to scream and asked them how. How they believed they could when Death himself couldn't. I wanted to punch something in frustration. Instead, I took a deep breath and nodded.

Fable rubbed her hands together. "Are we going to do this? We haven't played this game in ages. I'm getting antsy here."

Zen kept his eyes on me, his mouth edging into a smirk. "I'm looking forward to it."

"Capture the flag, then. I'll go out and set the flags. When I return, we'll start." Vex blinked out as he vanished, but I saw a hint of his shadow as he left.

Lor shook his head once, so subtle I almost missed it. I crinkled my brows in confusion, but he had witnessed me watch Vex leave. They hadn't known I could see them in their form. This little power would come in handy tonight.

"So," Zen asked, "how did you become a human demon hunter?"

I gave him a once over. "My mother sold my soul, she died, and I guess I had nothing better to do as a teenager."

He scoffed. "A teenager? Who trained you?"

With a knowing smile, I answered him. "The grim reaper and his daughter."

Char let out a low whistle. "Thanks for telling us that little tidbit, Lor. That changes things quite a bit."

"Well, if I had known I would have." Lor's red eyes practically blazed as he narrowed his eyes in my direction.

I shrugged. "You never asked. Why do you think Death, Raven, and Coren were practicing with me tonight? For shits and giggles?"

"You're impossible," Lor grumbled.

"So people tell me."

Vex returned and the first thing I noticed was his shadow and glowing eyes. He appeared next to Char. "There are two flags set up, each with their own color. Are we drawing for teams?"

"I'm on my own," I answered.

Lor shook his head. "I'm going with Mara. The rest of you can decide what you want to do."

"Two against four? That hardly seems fair." Fable raked a hand through her hair as she looked over the surroundings.

"Please," Lor said, "I can take you all on in a spirited game of capture the flag by myself."

"Only this time you'll have a slow human with you." Zen laughed. "Sucker."

"I'll guard their flag," Fable stated.

Zen twitched in surprise. "Darling, we've never been on separate teams."

"Well, you've been nothing but an asshole to Mara, so this is payback for being a dick."

After a few tense minutes, Vex took out a small map and showed the two locations where each flag was located. The blue flag, which was mine, was located close to Sentinel Rock. The red flag, the one I was supposed to steal, was near something called the Cathedral Rock.

I had never been to Colorado, let alone try to figure out landmarks at night. My belly somersaulted as I looked over the landscape so unlike home. Did they have bears and mountain lions here?

"You ready?" Lor asked, patting me on the shoulder.

Startled, I realized everyone had already made their way to their starting points. Lor and I were the only ones lagging behind.

I nodded and took a deep breath.

As Lor led me down into the now-closed Garden of the Gods Park, I squinted my eyes to see our surroundings in the glow of the full moon.

"Don't be too nervous. My friends can be...what's the word?" Lor paused. "Eccentric."

"They're not family?" I questioned as the ground crunched under our feet.

He shook his head slowly, his gaze looking down at the ground.

My heart ached for him. There were only a few that escaped to Earth's plane of existence. If he had no family left, that meant they had died by the hands of the man who paid me a weekly check. My stomach roiled at the thought.

After a few seconds of silence, I said, "Sometimes friends are family. Blood doesn't matter when you have people who love you. Look at me. My family is Raven and Death. They have always been there for me, and I'm only human."

Lor nodded. "And what of Coren?"

"Coren is..." I sighed. "I don't know."

"Whatever you decide with him, be sure to guard your heart. I'm not sure if he has evil intentions where you're concerned."

"Why doesn't anyone trust Coren?" I asked, tossing my arms up in frustration.

"The same reason your friends don't trust me." He guided us around a mound of rocks. "Because they don't know what I'm capable of. I'm an enigma."

"Coren's a demon, so I'm-"

He cut me off with a hand. "Are you absolutely certain he's a demon?"

I frowned. Coren had never said he was one, and he'd made me question the same. But how had he worked for the Devil if he wasn't? I looked up at Lor's face. "He lives in hell. Who else would live in hell besides a demon?"

Lor took my hand and helped me over a rock formation to look over our surroundings. "Many creatures live in hell, my dear."

I opened my mouth to ask what other beings lived there, but Lor held a finger to his lips. He gestured to our right, and I strained in the moonlight to see who or what was there.

"You go to the left and I'll go to the right. We'll meet back up at the road there," he whispered as he pointed to the road below us.

The road seemed so far away, but by the time I had nodded, he was gone. As I walked as quietly as I could, my eyes scanned all over to look for any signs of darkness among the glimmering light.

I crouched low behind some shrubbery to scope out the area. A hazy shadow materialized a few feet away. Their ruby eyes glowed in my direction and I held my breath. I reached for my sword and cursed myself when I came up empty-handed. Lor had taken it, which forced me to use my wit to outsmart a pack of shadows. Sadly, the only wit I had was a smart mouth.

"Come out, come out, wherever you are," Zen taunted.

His voice was disturbing in the dark and sent shivers up my spine. I held as still as possible, my breath shallow. Zen hadn't known I saw him, and he stayed in his obscure form as a means to outsmart me.

I took a step back. A branch cracked under the heel of my shoe and Zen's gaze whipped in my direction.

"Fuck," I muttered and took off at a dead run. The road loomed about twenty yards away, but I felt his presence closing in. I wasn't fast enough.

His footsteps pounded behind me in the same cadence as my heart. Then it dawned on me. Zen had no idea I saw him as a shadow. If I wasn't out of breath from exertion, I might have laughed.

I stopped in an instant and crouched low to the ground. He was running so quickly that he couldn't stop, and as soon as he ran into me, I flipped him over my back. Once he landed on the hard ground, I pounced and used my body weight to hold his shadowed legs and arms in place.

He tried to squirm free but froze. "Holy shit. You can see us."

I smirked. "Surprise!"

Lor appeared beside us and looked down at his friend. "Surprise indeed. Hello, Zen."

Once I removed my hold, he shoved me off him and stood to face Lor. "You knew this the entire time. You could've warned us."

"Now where's the fun in that?" He held his finger to his lips. "No telling secrets until the game is over, only locations. You know the rules."

Zen growled low in his throat, but he nodded in agreement.

"Is he out of the game now?" I questioned, my gaze traveling over the landscape.

"For the most part, but he can help the others on his team if they see him. He just can't move from this location." Lor grinned. "The little demon hunter has a lot of skills, Zen. Don't judge a person by their outward appearance. If Mara had her sword with her, you'd be dead instead of out of the game."

Pride swelled within me. Lor believed in what I could do. I beamed at him and said, "Damn right."

"You bested me. I have to respect you for it," Zen said, his voice clipped. "But you still have two others to defeat. Vex and Char are a force of nature. Good luck."

When we left Zen on his own, I asked, "Are we going to be able to beat Vex and Char?"

"Oh yes." Lor chuckled. "The rest may think they are unbeatable, but I have a secret weapon."

"Me?"

He nodded. "Of course. They can't hide from me, but they'll try to slip by you without a second thought. They'll be sorely disappointed."

I couldn't help but smile. Self-doubt crept in like a fog lately, especially with powerful demons attempting to kill me. If it hadn't been for Coren and Lor with the winged beasty, I would've died. However, Lor acted like we had a chance to win this game because of me.

"I'm going shadow, but you go around those tall red formations there. We'll be coming around the back of the rock where our flag is located."

"Um, I don't know this place. You'll have to show me what to look for."

With a few points of his fingers, Lor explained where I needed to go to meet him. He explained it with such ease I knew where I needed to maneuver without tripping over a rock, or worse, falling off one.

The cooler temperatures felt great, but the thinner air caused me to breathe harder. There was some traffic noise from the highway somewhere near the park, but other than the glittering lights from the closest town keeping me company, the night was peaceful. Thankfully, the moon provided enough light to progress without many problems. If you didn't count when I tripped over a bush. Twice.

When I noticed the massive landmark Lor had mentioned, I went to the left as quietly as I could. Red glowing eyes hovered in front of Cathedral Rock. What I assumed was a glow stick illuminated the blue flag, and I had to fight the temptation to steal it right then. Lor had asked me to learn mental strength, so I kept to my path.

"Little demon hunter, all alone." Char's voice came from my immediate left.

Because I was focused on our flag, I had failed to notice Char gaining momentum on the other side.

Her form flew by me and taunted me as she laughed. I stood still, focusing my attention on the blur of shadow as she came at me again. This time, Char was close. I lowered to the ground and kicked my leg out at the perfect moment, and she toppled onto her stomach. I jumped and landed on her back, holding her arms above her.

"Little shadow, all alone," I whispered, playing on her words.

She sputtered, most likely spitting out dirt from her mouth.

Smiling, I removed myself from her form and stood. She rolled over and looked up at me. I said, "Mums the word. Remember the rules, Char."

"You sneaky girl." She propped herself up by the elbows and tilted her head. "How in the world can you see us as shadows?"

I lifted a shoulder. "I wish I knew."

Char's eyes lit, glowing even brighter in the dark surrounding us. "Go get your flag, Mara."

I nodded and left her, knowing she couldn't move after her capture.

As promised, Lor waited on me behind the rock formation.

"What took you so long?" he whispered.

With a grin, I whispered, "I took Char out of the game."

He laughed, his voice echoing across the space of rocks and sparse shrubbery. "They have no one left to capture our flag. Vex has no idea all of his teammates have been captured."

"How do we get to our flag with him so close?"

"We both go in opposite directions. You to the left, and me to the right. While Vex is busy with me, you'll steal the flag."

"You sure this will work?"

He nodded. "Oh, I'm sure."

Taking a deep breath, I rolled my shoulders to remove the tension. "So, on the count of three?"

"One."

"Two."

Lor winked. "Three!"

We ran in opposite directions, neither of us looking back. I darted around shrubbery and rounded Chimney rock. Lor and Vex were at a standoff, each of them in full shadow and attempting to best each other. Lor, however, hadn't even glanced in my direction, and I assumed he didn't want to give away my location.

The blue flag was about ten feet above the ground, the pole balanced on Chimney Rock. I'd have to do a quick climb and a long jump to reach it. After taking a deep breath, I ran. When I jumped up on the rock, Vex turned in my direction.

"Go! Go!" Lor shouted.

Vex turned and reached for me, his hands barely reaching my calf, but I had jumped. His hand caught air as mine caught the flag. I landed on my feet and held the flag above my head. Letting out a scream of happiness, I strolled over to Lor and threw my arms around him in celebration.

Vex sucked in a breath.

Looking at Lor, I realized he was still a shadow. The glow stick attached to the flag was visible straight through him. I hadn't cared. I was so damn happy I had won.

When I finally stopped hugging my friend, I looked at Vex and said, "Yeah, yeah. I can see you guys."

"Let's get back to the house," Lor stated. "I assume the rest of the gang is tired of the same scenery by now."

"I'll round them up," Vex said and disappeared as he took off.

Glancing up at the stars, I wondered what time it was. "I bet my friends are worried sick about me. I should be heading back home."

Lor shook his head. "Not until we rub in the fact that my friends were bested by a human."

"Okay." I smirked. "Gloating first, then you take me back."

"Deal."

CHAPTER 22

Dance with the devil.

Coren stood in front of me with his arms across his chest, his breath heaving in what I assumed was anger.

"Do you realize how worried we all were?" he asked.

With an eye roll, I snorted. "Please. Spare me the lecture. I knew what I was doing."

"And yet you seem to forget that Satan wants to kill you and steal your soul."

I took a step forward until I was nose to nose with him. "I was well protected with Lor and his friends. You all act like I can't take care of myself and make my own decisions."

His eyes moved to my lips. "I know you can take care of yourself, but you're also ill-equipped to deal with higher demons."

"Like you?"

A sad smile lined his lips. "If you truly believe that's all I am."

"I don't know what to believe anymore," I breathed. Then I leaned up on my tiptoes and pressed my mouth against his.

Even if I was mad as hell that he planned to lecture me about disappearing with Lor, I forgot how handsome he was. At that moment, I wanted nothing more than to kiss him and feel his body against mine.

As we kissed, Coren's arms slipped around my waist and he pulled me against him. His fingers caressed my lower back under my shirt, and little shocks of pleasure rippled through me. I moaned and his arms tightened.

A throat cleared. We looked up to see Death leaning against the wall with his eyebrow raised.

My cheeks burned as I pulled away from Coren, and I avoided Death's eye contact. But I said, "Nice timing. Am I grounded for being caught with a boy?"

"Always the smart mouth," Death said with a sigh. "Raven was searching hell and Earth for you. I'm here because I wanted to make sure you're okay."

"Why wouldn't I be?" I asked with a frown. "I was with Lor."

"That's exactly why we're worried." Coren scrubbed a hand across his face. "He fades you out of there quicker than any of us can move, and then you come back hours later. Where were you?"

I hesitated for a moment. "Colorado."

Coren's Adam's apple bobbed as he swallowed. "You're joking, right?"

"Why is Lor taking me to Colorado any different than either of you taking me to hell?"

Coren opened his mouth to speak, but Death beat him to it. "Hell is on a different plane of existence. It's the land of the dead, so to speak. It's a quick jump to a different reality, but jumping somebody across half the country is another feat. None of us could do what Lor did tonight."

"None of you?" My eyebrows hit my hairline. I knew Lor was powerful, but this brought his ability to a completely new level.

Death shook his head slowly. "None."

"That's another reason not to trust him. He could take you to someplace to be slaughtered," Coren said, his voice barbed with annoyance.

I barked out a laugh and headed to my small kitchen. "If he wanted me dead, I would be dead. Same goes for all of you, too."

Raven's voice floated in from the living room. She must have faded in a second ago. "She's right. Lor could've killed her at any time. We have bigger problems. Lucifer asked Mara for another meeting."

The blood froze in my veins and I stopped in my tracks. By some miracle, I still managed to appear deadpan by the news.

"When do we have to leave?" Death questioned.

"About two minutes ago, but he's meeting us at the coffee shop down the street." She shuffled on her feet. "I don't like this."

"I don't either," Coren murmured. "But we have to be prepared and she's not going in there alone with him."

Death nodded. "That's something I think we can all agree on."

A few minutes later, we all made our way down the sidewalk as a unified force. I walked in front, Raven and Coren on either side of me, and Death behind me. I even thought I felt Lor somewhere close by.

The nerves inside me rattled my heartbeat, and I had to take a few deep breaths. Although my guts were a mess of nerves, I kept my face impassive and cold. I had no other choice because Satan preyed on the weak. My sword vibrated against my back and I looked up.

My boss smirked when he saw us. "Well, well. Look at all of you protecting what's mine."

"I'm not yours," I growled.

"Your signature says otherwise. Now, let's get some coffee and have a nice chat shall we?"

Raven put her hand on my shoulder to reassure me that they would protect me if things went south. If the Devil was involved, things would definitely end badly.

He placed an order and sat at a small table with two chairs. Once I received my Frappuccino, he gestured for me to sit across from him. I hesitated until I realized my friends had sat on either side of us. I slowly lowered myself into the chair and took a sip of my drink.

"What do you want?" I asked, plopping my cup down on the table.

He stirred the piping hot coffee. "Is that any way to speak to your superior?"

"We all know I don't deal well with management. You're no different, except you smell like ground up assholes."

Raven covered her mouth with a hand. I wasn't sure if it was to keep from laughing or because she was shocked. I'm betting it was both.

He turned his attention to Coren. "Why haven't you been giving me status updates on her progress?"

"We've been a little busy lately," he answered calmly. His expression gave away his anger, though. "I'm sure you knew about the high ranking demons wandering our realm."

Lucifer's black eyes practically twinkled. "I've heard rumors of such things."

I snorted and his attention turned to me. "So why am I so important that you'd risk sending them after me?"

"I never said I sent them."

"Okay." I rolled my eyes. "But you still didn't answer the question."

"I want what's mine. If it wasn't for Death and Raven's meddling, I'd already have you." His hands fisted on the table.

Twisting my cup in between the two of us, I said, "I'm beyond thankful for them. Otherwise, I'd be one of your tortured souls in your wall, right?"

His eyes bored into mine. "No, I have other plans for you, Mara."

"Ah. And what plans are those? It's my soul, so I'd like to know what you plan on doing with it."

"That's none of your concern. It's not technically your soul, anyway."

A shadow passed behind Lucifer. I knew I had felt Lor lurking around outside, but hadn't realized he had made his way inside. He gestured to himself and then pointed to me.

"Is it because I can see shadows?"

"You can see them?" My boss's eyebrows rose.

"See, that's the thing. When you and my mother tricked me as a child, you left a huge oversight in my contract. That's on you." I gave him an evil smirk. "You see, you didn't care about me or my abusive mother. Well, until after I was of age and she was long gone. You fucked up, didn't you?"

"I never make mistakes, my dear girl." Satan shoved his untouched coffee away.

I laughed, and then went serious as my hand slammed the table between us. "Don't test me. I'm not in the mood. You gave me this ridiculous time limit, and for what? To try to figure out how to kill me?"

He leaned forward with a nefarious grin. "If I wanted you dead, you would be dead." His hand gestured to my friends. "And them, too."

"I'm done. This meeting is nothing but a waste of time." I stood and Lucifer snatched my arm.

The fires of hell flicked up my wrist, burning my skin. I groaned in pain but held his gaze. My friends stood to protect me, but I shook my head at them. I wanted to hear what this coldhearted jerk had to say.

"I could rip the soul from your body right here and nobody could do a thing about it," he hissed. "I'm being generous by allowing you to stay here for a while longer." His arm tightened as he pulled me forward and he whispered so low I barely heard him.

"Just a little tug is all it would take. For you *or* your friends. "

"Fuck you," I growled. "You can kiss my-"

The shadow behind me surprised us both. Her arms wrapped around me and barely tapped the Devil's fingers. She severed the contact between Lucifer and me with a simple touch. The heat faded away in an instant and her cool hands wrapped around the same wrist my boss had grabbed. I let out a sigh of relief at the cooling sensation.

Shaking out his hand as if the touch hurt him, Lucifer looked around. "Shadow, show yourself."

I smiled. "Which one would you like to see?"

Sure, there were only three of them right now, but he hadn't known that. My eyes darted to my friends for a second, and they seemed relieved that Fable had saved me. I doubted they knew it was Fable and not Lor, or if they knew how many were in the room with us.

I did. Lor stood behind Lucifer, Fable still had her arms wrapped around me in a protective stance, and Zen stood next to Lucifer. Zen held so much fury it vibrated the air around me. While I hadn't spotted Char or Vex, I assumed they waited out of reach in case we needed them.

Lucifer's eyes narrowed. "We'll resume this another time, Mara. Don't forget what I said about how easy it would be."

In front of everyone in the room, humans included, he faded back to hell. All that he left behind was black smoke rising to the ceiling.

Fable slipped away from me.

"What a damn coward," I muttered.

Coren stood with my friends to check on me but froze mid-stand. I frowned at their reaction.

"I think the term pussy fits better," Fable said as she strolled in from the hallway near the restrooms.

Zen and Lor soon followed behind her. I mouthed, "Thank you" to them for not appearing out of thin air in front of a couple of humans left in the coffee shop. I was lucky they didn't freak the fuck out when Ol' Luke disappeared.

"Who are you two?" Raven finally asked.

Coren stood next to me. "Yeah, I'd like to know that myself."

Death, on the other hand, tilted his head as he stared at Fable. "I know you. How do I know you?"

"I met you long ago when you were a reaper in training. I was sent to deliver a message."

With a frown, Death said, "But that was well over a millennia ago." His eyes widened as he gasped. "The prophecy. That was you?"

"What!?" Raven cried, her shocked gaze landing on Fable as well.

"I didn't write it, but I was tasked with its delivery. The scroll was supposed to go to William the Conqueror, but I knew he'd use it for war and power. Then I saw you helping a sick woman cross, and I knew what I had to do. The rest is history." She winked at me.

I blinked a few times in shock. "How old are you people?"

Death shrugged. "I'm roughly fifteen-hundred years old. Raven is two hundred. I have no clue on the rest of them, but I have a suspicion they are old."

My eyes swung to Fable. "You?"

"You never ask a lady her true age," she answered, her nose rising with pride.

"Please. She's about a thousand years old." Zen scoffed. "Same with me. Lor is the baby. What are you, Lor? About eight hundred now?"

He tilted his head in agreement.

Sitting down in my chair, I took a deep breath as I stared down at the grain in the hardwood of the table. I fingered the smoothed knot under the polished wood. These people around me were old enough to see the most amazing and terrifying events in history. And here I was, barely a blip in their lifespans. Why did I matter so much? After all these years, why me?

"Coren, how old are you?" Raven asked, the curiosity in her voice causing me to look up.

"I'd rather not say," he hedged. Coren glanced at me, his eyes unreadable. "You ready to go hunting? The sun is almost set."

I knew a change of subject when I saw it, but I'd press him for his age later. Maybe he'd be more comfortable in private. My eyes swerved to his crotch, and then I cursed myself for thinking of the word private. Cheeks burning, I headed in the direction of the exit. The rest of the gang, shadows included, were quick to catch up.

*****

Once we were back to my tiny apartment, I said goodbye to Fable, Zen, and Lor for the time being and headed into my kitchen for some wine.

I rarely drank, but I needed it after dealing with the nightmare of a boss. Sure, there are many horrible bosses out there, and people may believe their jobs are hell. But my boss is from hell, and I may end up there before my shift was over. So there was that.

Coren was currently on my balcony with the phone pressed to his ear, and Raven leaned up against my kitchen counter.

She let out a breath. "I'm sorry you couldn't have a normal life."

"It is what it is." I handed her a solo cup of wine. Her eyebrows rose at the plastic cup in her hand. "What? I don't like to do the dishes."

"Still, you should've been able to go to college, have kids, and maybe meet a man to marry."

"Isn't that backward? Shouldn't I meet a man first and then have kids?"

"Well, you don't necessarily need a man to have children. That's what sperm banks are for."

I made a face. "Yeah, there's always that. I never expected a husband or children. From a young age, I knew my life was fucked."

Raven took a sip of wine and her voice resonated inside the cup. "I'm sorry you didn't have a good childhood."

"Me too." I lifted the plastic to my lips to take a swig but lowered it. "I'm sorry I'm a sucky friend and never asked. What happened to your mother?"

"She died shortly after I was born, or so I was told. I have to guess it was tuberculosis given the year of my birth."

"Wait." I held up a hand. "Your mother was *human*?"

She shrugged. "I'm not sure. I don't know how that would work, especially with me being a reaper and all. My dad won't talk about her. He changes the subject every time I ask."

"I'm sorry. I wish you knew more about your mother."

"It's not like it would change the outcome if I had. I would still be a reaper, and she would still be dead if she were really human."

Nodding, I understood what she meant. Her mother would've been long dead. Raven was about two hundred years old, and nobody I knew had lived that long. Well, except for my friends who were supernatural beings. I stared at Raven while she scrolled through her phone. What would happen to her once I died? Sadness overwhelmed me at the possibility of her being alone again. Her or her father would have to bring my soul to hell unless they pulled a miracle and I ended up in heaven. The likelihood of that outcome would be as common as a unicorn trotting down the sidewalk.

My eyes swerved to the balcony to see Coren stretching in the setting sun. His sinewy biceps flexed at the movement and I observed the shadows between his muscles and skin from the fading sunlight. Heat rose low in my abdomen as he turned his sharp jaw and full lips in the reddish glow. He would either destroy me or save me. Perhaps both.

What happened when I had to choose between my life or the death of my friends? While the rest of the group had been so preoccupied with saving me from Lucifer, those whispered words echoed in my subconscious again. *Just a little tug is all it would take. For you or your friends.*

I looked down at the scratched linoleum floor of my kitchen. Anger seared through me because Lucifer threatened those close to me. He knew what I'd choose if it meant saving my friends. I'd die for them without a second thought.

CHAPTER 23

Don't go breakin' my cold, black heart.

The sword throbbed against my back.

Without a doubt, there was a demon inside the place. I swung the double doors open like I was an outlaw in an old western. What I did not expect was the doors bouncing back and slamming me in the shoulders as I took a step forward. So much for a badass entry.

All heads turned in my direction. If the music had screeched to a halt, I would've crawled under a table to die of embarrassment. Thankfully, it had not. I pushed the doors more carefully this time and entered the Silver & Ale Pub. After a few seconds, the patrons resumed their drinking and eating as if the wooden doors hadn't just pummeled somebody.

"Smooth," Coren said coming up beside me.

"Shut up," I growled, and then slid up to the bar. "An old fashioned please."

"And you?" the bartender asked Coren. His red beard and green eyes implied an Irish lineage, but the hint of an Irish accent lilting his voice sealed the deal.

"Black 'n black."

Coren paid for our drinks and we watched the bartender while he made them. After he slid them in front of us with a coaster, Coren waited until he walked away and put a couple hundred-dollar bill in the tip jar. His expression said exactly what I was thinking. *Some insurance in case we break something. Or the demon does.*

I surveyed the area as I took a sip of my drink. The small pub was a shotgun-style building from the historic downtown area. It was narrow and long with hardwood floors as far as the eye could see. While this type of architecture was popular in its heyday, it made pursuing a demon extremely difficult.

I heaved a sigh. "My sword vibrated before we even came inside. Maybe we passed one on the street?"

He shook his head slowly. "No, there's one here. I can feel it."

"You can feel them? Is it a part of your demon makeup?" *Why hadn't he told me that little bit of information?*

His gaze shifted away and he scanned the crowd. "Do you see anything suspicious?"

Crossing my arms, I stared him down. "Why do you always seem to distract me or ignore me when you let information slip? It's annoying."

A smirk lifted his lips. "Yeah, well, you're about to slip out of your low cut shirt. Not that I would mind, but it's distracting."

Adjusting the shirt, I huffed at not only the truth of his statement but the fact that he had yet again changed the subject. I ignored it for now, only because we had a beast to find.

"You think your muscles aren't distracting?"

His gaze swung to mine. "Is that so? I can show you the whole package later ton—"

A bloodcurdling scream rent the air and I jumped up from the barstool. We had to fight through the panicked people running from an unknown threat. I lost Coren in the melee. I made it to the back hallway near the restrooms first and I slid to a stop in shock. A beautiful blond woman leaned against the wall, her clothes half torn and displaying most of her naked skin. Her head was thrown back at an odd angle. She screamed again and her blood vessels popped out all over her body.

I finally spotted Coren a few feet away from me. The color had drained from his face as he stared.

Pulling my sword free, I searched the vicinity for the vile beast, unsure which way the attack may come from. "Where's the demon?! Coren! Do you see it anywhere?!"

"It's in her," he said, his voice so low I barely heard him.

"You're kidding, right? Tell me you're kidding." I backed up a step when the woman's tongue ran over her teeth with a wicked smile.

Coren took a deep breath. "It's in her, Mara."

"A *full* possession? That's impossible. Death has only witnessed one, and he's lived for over a thousand years."

I wanted to look at him, but I was scared to look away from the poor girl. Her blue eyes had turned as black as tar. She seized and dropped her head as she sagged against the wall.

"What do we do?" I held my sword out in front of me, but I don't think I could kill a human, possessed or not. Sure, I'd killed demons looking like a human, but never a human with a demon inside of them.

He had remained quiet, and I resisted the urge to glare at him for being useless.

She tensed and Coren finally found his vocal cords. "Get ready. You get the demon's name and I'll try to save her. "

I nodded, trying not to think about the other scenario.

Her head rose slowly, methodically, until her dark eyes found me. Her voice was weird because two people were speaking at once. Her normal voice of a woman, and a deeper, more sinister voice. "You've been a bad girl, hunter. Tsk, tsk."

"Who are you?" I questioned, my voice strong despite wanting to vomit.

"This vessel?" The woman's hand motioned to her body. "Her name is inconsequential."

I took a step and pointed my blade forward. "No, you stupid monster. I want to know the name of the pathetic asshole that couldn't face me without taking the body of an innocent woman."

The laugh with double voices caused the hair to rise on the back of my neck. I had watched scary movies as a teen; I had even watched the exorcism ones. Still, nothing, no movie, no story, could ever prepare me for what I witnessed now.

She tilted her head at a peculiar angle and took two steps in my direction. "Would you like me to take you over instead? It would be so easy."

"Name!" I ordered.

I spotted Coren coming around the back of her, unsure of what he had planned.

"Names are power." It smiled with black saliva covered teeth, but it was crooked and misshapen on the girl's face.

"Ugh. Another cryptic demon. Surprise, surprise." I rolled my eyes in exasperation.

Raven chose that moment to pop in next to me. Her eyes rounded as she took in the scene.

The girl licked her lips, her tongue snaking out as far as it could possibly go, and her jaw cracked with the movement. Black slobber covered her lips.

"Noooo. This can't be real." My best friend blinked a few times. "Please, with all that is holy, tell me that woman doesn't currently have a demon taking up residence inside her."

Shifting on my feet, I winced. "Uh…"

"Reaper," the possessed woman whispered.

"Oh my God. Her voice is even the stuff of nightmares." Raven shivered.

Nodding, but bringing my attention back to the woman, I said, "You mean the two people talking at one time? Yep." I narrowed my eyes and turned my attention to our target. "I won't ask again, demon. What's your name?"

The thing, no woman, took another step in my direction. I assumed this particular evil entity had never walked in stilettos, but it picked it up fast. Her legs weren't as wobbly as before. Now it took a measured step again, the high heels clicking on the hardwood floor.

"You're so pretty, Mara Jone Argueta. I'll enjoy playing with you in hell." A hand reached for me, it's clawed human hand inches away.

"What are you waiting for? Kill it!" Raven cried, her eyes wide.

"She's still human, no matter what's on the inside. I can't do it."

I froze as the demon's eyes twinkled in the low lights of the pub. Another step in my direction and it would be on me. Why couldn't I kill it? This demon didn't care about human life, mine included. All it cared about was destroying me, and I pussed out because I cared too much about life.

With another creepy cackle, the demon whispered, "Just one tug is all it would take."

The breath left my lungs and my chest tightened. "What did you say?"

Before it could lay a finger on me, Coren grabbed the woman and whispered in her ear. She screeched, clawed, and began screaming a language I had never heard of in my life. The dialect sounded ancient, that much I knew. Then, to my utter shock, Coren replied. In the same language.

Raven grabbed my arm, her fingernails pressing against my forearm. Each time the woman and demon screamed, her nails dug further into my skin.

"Arde in regnum phasmatis!" the demon shrieked and then burst into maniacal laughter.

I watched the next horrific act playing out in slow motion. With a sickening crunch, Coren snapped the woman's neck. Her head twisted around and she slumped near my boots, her empty blue eyes staring up at me.

*****

"I completely understand why you killed her, but you should've at least tried to restrain the woman," Death said. "We could've interrogated the demon inside of her."

I looked at the three people surrounding me. I wasn't sure how long I'd be in a daze after what happened, but none of them detected I had started paying attention. They had moved me to a padded bench inside the pub, which was eerily empty and silent.

"I already feel guilty for killing, okay? Don't make this harder." Coren rubbed a hand over his face.

Raven placed a hand on her father's forearm. "Dad, there wasn't anything Coren could do. I've never seen anything like it. This wasn't the work of a low demon possession."

"Did you get a name?"

Raven and Coren both shook their heads.

He gave a curt nod and he gestured to me, "She's going to be pissed off beyond control. Don't be surprised if she doesn't start swinging."

I chuckled and all heads swiveled to me. "I'll at least give you a warning before I start punching people. Okay, maybe only a half a second warning first."

Looking around, I noticed the woman's body had disappeared, and I thanked the Lord for that. Anger bubbled inside of me at the death of the woman. I turned my fury on the man that broke her neck.

"You!" I glared at Coren. "How *dare* you take a life? Just when I thought you had redeemed yourself of your demonic ways, you go and do that?!"

"Mara, I can explain." His fingers touched my hand.

I yanked it away. "Don't touch me."

"Please let me tell you why."

"You killed the woman in cold blood. That's what happened. You could've saved her. You could've done anything else."

He reached for me again, but I scooted away from his touch. "Don't. I don't want another demon to touch me again."

Coren opened his mouth to speak, but he thought better of it after a quick glance at Raven and Death.

With a scoff, I removed myself from the padded seat and stormed to the door. "I'm outta here."

"Mara, wait!" Coren called after me.

"Burn in hell," I snapped. I pretended I hadn't noticed the hurt and shock on his face.

As I strode down the sidewalk, I wondered why I believed Coren was capable of good things. Why he got under my skin and lit a fire nobody else had. I still felt guilty for telling him off and for leaving the pub.

Emotions were messy business. There were no rules, no set of guidelines where your heart was concerned. Physical pain I handled surprisingly well, but these invisible, unrelenting feelings about Coren seemed unmeasurable.

I stopped suddenly, my boots sliding to a stop on the concrete. I might be falling for Coren. A demon hunter was falling in love with her prey, the one being she was supposed to hate. *Son of a bitch.* I had to walk away now before we both did something we'd regret. With new determination, I took a few deep breaths of the cool night air. I had to become an emotionless, cold-hearted girl again. There wasn't room for love in my heart, or in my chaotic life.

I had two things to focus on. I had to hunt demons without mercy, and I had to keep my fucking soul before Lucifer finally murders me or takes it by force. That meant that I had to figure out a way to stop Satan before he stopped me.

What was the opposite of hell? Heaven, of course.

I needed to locate an angel.

CHAPTER 24

God, are you there? It's me, Mara.

The limestone Catholic structure seemed empty. I craned my neck to see the large steeple jutting into the morning sky.

Our Lady of Angels Cathedral was the same church in which I saved the priest and received my blessing. A stained glass angel had arms outstretched. The next one had both hands holding some green leafy things. Both had a yellow halo surrounding their heads.

"Are you sure you don't want me to go in with you?" Raven asked, her head tilted up to see the steeple as well.

I shook my head. "No. I'm good."

"Why a cathedral? Couldn't you find answers from one of us?"

"Maybe I'm looking for a little bit of forgiveness, too."

Raven was oblivious to my plan until we had arrived. We both knew I would be safe inside, but she hesitated.

"Are you sure this is a good idea?"

"I'm sure. I'll just stay away from the holy water." I laughed and patted her on the shoulder.

She didn't find it funny.

I made my way across the street to the entrance of the cathedral. The heavy wooden doors were unlocked and they squealed on their metal joints when I opened them. When they slammed behind me, I jumped.

Slowly making my way up the small staircase that led to the sanctuary, I paused at the two bowls with water and a sponge. What would happen if I touched it? I carefully touched the sponge and felt the cool wetness of the holy water. I remembered old movies where they touched their forehead with it, so I parroted what I remembered from them and waited. I hadn't burst into flames and I let out a breath I didn't know I held.

My eyes swung over the wooden pews and stained glass. On one side, there were images of a man with a cross, which I only knew was Jesus from bible study when I had snuck there with a friend. The alter at the front of the space rose from the floor and I slowly made my way to it.

Candles illuminated each side, their red glow beautiful with the different colors streaming in from the stained glass. Hues of red, blue, yellow, and indigo filtered in and over the wooden seating. A stone table sat on top of the raised space, and what I assumed was a bible sat open on top. I hadn't understood a lot of the symbolism, and I blamed my upbringing for that. My mother didn't attend a church of any kind. Which made sense if you really thought about it. No true Christian would ever sell their daughter to the devil.

When I was about a foot from the alter, a man's voice caused me to start.

"May I help you?"

I swung around and saw the same priest from the street. He wore a simple shirt and pants with the white collar announcing his priesthood.

"I was wondering if you could answer some questions."

He nodded and gestured to the first pew. "Of course."

Sitting, I swallowed the nerves that bubbled up my throat. My gazes flitted around the space, unsure what to do now that I was here.

"Would you like another blessing?"

This time I swung my view back to him. His graying hair, kind blue eyes, and gentle smile made me feel oddly comforted. "I doubt it would help, but you're welcome to. The reason I'm here is to ask about angels."

Tilting his head, he eyed me curiously. "Why wouldn't it help you? All souls deserve to be forgiven in this and their past life. I could tell you our confessional hours, or you could always make an appointment with me."

Shaking my head, I cleared my throat. "I'm here more on a personal matter. No confession needed."

"Of course. What would you like to know about angels?"

"If I needed to find one, how would I do such a thing?"

The priest blinked. "Find one? I'm not sure what you mean."

"I need to know if it's possible to find an angel in the flesh. I'm in danger, and I think an angel may be the only way to right a wrong."

"My dear child, angels reside in heaven at the side of our heavenly father, and the only way to speak to them is through prayer."

Somehow, I knew this was an impossible task. I stood. "Thanks for your time. I should probably go."

The pew creaked as he stood as well. "I'd like to bless you again. If you don't mind."

Again. So he had remembered me. Not being one to object to a man of God, I nodded. I needed all the help I could get.

He made a cross with his hands in front of me and said, "Heavenly Father, your infinite love for us has chosen a blessed angel in heaven and appointed him our guide during this earthly pilgrimage. Accept our thanks for so great a blessing. Grant that we may experience the assistance of our holy protector in all our necessities. And you, holy, loving angel and guide, watch over us with all the tenderness of your angelic heart. Keep us always on the way that leads to heaven, and cease not to pray for us until we have attained our final destiny, eternal salvation. Amen."

I shifted uncomfortably once he finished. I appreciated his blessing, but anxiety crept in. "Thanks," I mumbled and then started to leave.

As I made my way to the exit, one of the stained glass windows caught my attention and I slowed to a stop.

An angel stood dressed in silver armor. With a sword held over his head, he stood on a green beast.

A helmet adorned his head, and I spotted the dark hair, dark eyes, and the sharp chiseled jaw I knew all too well. I shook my head, deciding I was tired and hallucinating. There is no way in hell that angel looked like Coren. I was losing my damn mind.

I practically ran from the church, jumping when the bells rang above me.

"Everything okay?" Raven asked, her brows puckered at my reaction to the bells.

"Yeah. I swore I saw a stained glass in there that resembled Coren." I laughed at the audacity. "I think I need to sleep. Or have an expresso and about a dozen donuts."

"Could you imagine Coren on a stained glass in all his glory?"

"No, he's a demon, duh. I'm surprised you think that about him."

"Look, I may bring the dead to heaven or hell, but I'm not dead myself. I know a hot guy when I see one."

I snickered, and then linked my arms with hers as we crossed to the donut shop. "I think we both need a sugar high."

"I think you need to get laid. Obviously, you're seeing Coren everywhere."

I groaned. "I do not need to get laid. And certainly not by Coren."

She winked and then beamed at me. "Whatever you say."

*****

When I entered the apartment, Coren was sitting on the couch. He removed himself from the couch when he saw me.

"Where did you go?" Coren questioned, his voice tight.

"To the donut shop with Raven," I replied. I set a donut box on the coffee table. "Why?"

"You didn't tell me where you were going."

"I didn't think I had to. You're not my babysitter." I tried to get around him.

He moved to block me. The irritation practically pulsated off him. "Actually, I am. You can't take off without telling me."

My brows furrowed in annoyance. I gritted out, "Don't you dare tell me what I can and can't do."

"What are you going to do about it if I do?" His body edged forward until we were toe to toe.

"Make your life hell on Earth."

"I see." He strode forward and I stepped back until my back pressed against the kitchen counter. He placed his palms on either side of me, caging me in. "Are you sure?"

My heart thudded. Damn it. I wanted to hate him, I really did. But his body was so close the heat between us intensified.

Coren lowered his head and licked along my lips. I inhaled sharply. The contact of his tongue on my mouth lit a fire straight to my core. I wanted to moan, but I held it back. Barely.

He smirked. "Even when you're pissed, you still want me."

"I don't want you." My lungs heaved at the close proximity of his body pressed against mine. His lips were so close that I could pucker my own and kiss him.

"You're a horrible liar."

"How could I want Satan's lapdog?"

With his head slightly tilted, he studied me for a moment. "I could say the same about you, too."

Although I hated to admit it, that stung. The hurt of his words radiated inside my heart for a few seconds before rage took its place. I shoved him away from me so hard he stumbled back in surprise. I pointed to the door. "I want you to leave. Now."

"I'm afraid I can't do that." Coren shook his head slowly. "I care about you too much to leave you alone right now."

I closed my eyes. "Why? Why do you care about me?"

"Why?" He scoffed. "Because you're amazing, smart, and funny. You try to act like you're emotionless, but we both know you're not. You're beautiful, both for your appearance and because of your no filter honesty. You never cease to amaze me with your bravery to face anything, anyone, without fear. That's why."

Biting my lip, I took a deep breath in and out through my nose. Damn Coren for waking up emotions I hid so damn well for most of my life. I had my mind made up to be detached and cold again, but then he went and said that. I opened my eyes and asked the one thing I'd been avoiding since the Irish pub. "What happened with Leanne Markums, the possessed woman?"

His body flinched at her name, but he collected himself enough to speak. "The thing had already damaged her heart and brain and had poisoned her from the inside out. That was the reason for the black saliva. She would never survive the exorcism, so I thought making it quick was better than a painful death. I should've told you when I noticed it, but I was afraid the monster would've taken you over next. Especially if it touched your skin. The fingers were so close to you. I had to act fast. While the woman was innocent, the thing inside of her was not."

Surely Coren was mistaken. Demon possessions were as rare as a white giraffe. Well, except for Zagan. But Coren said he had just "commandeered" the body, not possessed it.

"What kind of a demon could do that to a person?"

He let out a slow breath before he answered. "There's only one that comes to mind, and he's no demon."

"What kind of entity could take over a human and kill them without mercy if not a demon?"

"An angel, but this being fell a very, very long time ago."

"Who?" I asked, dreading the answer. According to my classes with Raven, many angels had fallen from heaven and were now part of hell.

Coren looked me dead in the eyes and said, "Lucifer."

The blood drained from my face as I remembered the whispered words from the possession, the same ones Ol' Luke said at the coffee shop. *Just one tug is all it would take.*

Chapter 25

If I can't bend heaven, I will raise hell.

I swung my sword with more fury than necessary. The demon barely had a chance to react to my presence.

Black blood spurted through the air and landed at my feet. I watched as the body fell with a thud. For the first time in my life, I reveled in it. Before Raven had a chance to collect the body, I kicked the orange skin of its abdomen repeatedly. I screamed and kicked it again for good measure. My lungs heaved in both exertion and rage.

Coren and Raven stood with their mouths agape but kept their respective distance, which is what they had done most of the night.

Finally, Raven said, "What's wrong with you? That's the third one you've slaughtered like that."

Glaring at them both, I gritted my teeth and kept walking down the street. I was pissed at myself for feeling so gullible all of these years. I had believed Lucifer wanted me to do a job, to save humanity by murdering demons on Earth. How stupid I had been. Lor was right all along. The devil hadn't cared about humanity, my life, or anyone but his own. That prick was a trophy hunter of souls. The poor, innocent woman was merely one more he could hang on his wall with pride.

I'd take out these revolting creatures until I collapsed. Tonight was for Leanne. A life taken without remorse from an asshole of a boss, a man I pictured slaughtering with each swing of my blade.

When we rounded the corner to where the Serpent bar used to be, I paused to look up at the now dark sign.

"Don't even think about it," Coren warned, his voice tinged with anger.

My eyes roamed the dark windows. No sound echoed from the shut doors, no door attendant guarded the entrance. "I doubt the place is still open, anyway. Would they be so stupid after Death went on a demon killing spree?"

"Yes, they would." Raven laughed. "Greed and pride are the downfall of demons and the fall of a lot of angels back in the day. That and lust."

Snorting, I turned from the entrance of the club. "You could say the same about a few of the humans, too. It seems nobody is immune."

"True," she said. "But where do you think humans were introduced to such things?"

I lifted a shoulder and continued walking down the street. Besides the demons we had slaughtered, the sidewalks weren't crowded. Usually, partygoers perused the streets at all hours of the night, no matter if it was a Tuesday.

Anger still flirted along my veins, each beat of my heart begging for blood. For revenge. Not that I minded. Sure, I'd have to replace my jeans and possibly my new boots, but that came with the territory.

"Want to tell me what's bothering you?" Raven asked, her voice a bare whisper.

"No." I shook my head.

"She's pissed about the possessed woman," Coren said.

If a glare could kill him, mine would've done it. My nostrils flared once and I clenched my jaw.

Raven sighed. "You had no choice, Coren."

My sword vibrated in my grip, and I turned down Main Street.

Coren sighed. "I know that. You know that. Mara doesn't."

With a sharp twist of my heel, I headed in the direction of the train station near the corner of Main and Center streets. My sword pulsated against my fingers and palm, telling me whatever we were going to encounter was going to be bad. Very, very bad. I didn't care.

"I know she can see a lot of things, but not the supernatural world like us." Raven stopped short. "Why are we at the old train station?"

"That's what I'd like to know, too." I held up my sword as it reverberating with a ring of metal.

"Oh shit," Raven said.

*****

The old train station was vacant. What remained was a ruined shell of its original glory. The roof sagged occasionally, and the windows were missing. The smell of rotting wood and metal floated on the night air.

There were no lights because some vandal had busted them out. Glass littered the gravel lot, the shattered pieces shimmering in the moonlight. The rusted railway was in disrepair. A half of a century had passed since they carried citizens in and out of town.

Despite the creepy atmosphere, there was an absence of sound. Something had absorbed the sound of our footsteps and the busy highway within a few blocks of here.

"I don't like this," Raven whispered, but it sounded oddly muffled.

"Me either," I said, "but we have to find out what's here."

"Your reckless anger is going to get us killed tonight," Coren growled.

I used my pinky and itched my right ear in case I had somehow gotten an ear infection. Our voices were muffled and quiet. I expected them to echo against the buildings around us, but they were eerily soundless.

"Shut up," I told Coren, but I wasn't sure if he heard me or not.

Through the weird silence, the sound of rocks clattering was as clear as day. We all froze, unsure what was going to greet us in a matter of minutes.

Horror. That's what met us.

The demon walked like a spider, its knees and arms bent at the wrong angle and its head hung about six inches too low in its neck. Mottled gray skin covered its exterior, pulled straight from a zombie apocalypse movie. And the thing smelled just as bad, too.

"Hunter," the demon said, its voice cracking as if it hadn't spoken in years.

"Raven, what is that ugly thing?"

She didn't answer so I chanced a glance in her direction. She stared straight ahead at the demon. So had Coren. They were alert and ready to fight, but they hadn't heard me. Whatever this thing was, it could mess with sound and use it against us.

Clack clack. The rocks skittered again, and when I turned back, the ugly beast was within two feet of me. Holy shitballs.

I held my sword in my hands and took a deep breath, instantly regretting it. The demon smelled like death, the sickly, sweet smell causing me to hold back a gag.

"What do you want?" I asked.

Milky eyes blinked at me and its mouth moved a few times before it said, "Why your boyfriend, of course. He'd make a tasty treat, and then I'd feast on you. Suck the marrow from your bones."

"Fuck you, you ugly son of a bitch. I'll kill you before you're able to think about laying a hand on any of us. You have no idea what you're dealing with."

"Ah, but I do." The laugh that escaped sounded more like squeaky gears. "I don't think you do. Blind little hunter."

"I'll show you blind." I moved quickly forward, shoved my sword into its skull, and twisted.

The demon fell and convulsed. Pale eyes circled to look up at me, and then at Coren. "Blindness comes in all forms, bitch."

Sound rushed back, slamming into us at warp speed. The sudden hearing ability was deafening and confusing all at once. Dizziness hit me as I heard horns honking, the clicking of the gas pumps a block away, and a rodent skittering from somewhere to my left. I fell to my knees and came face to face with the demon's cloudy gaze. Putrid breath hit me as the zombie spider thing smiled.

A sickening crunch that sounded as loud as a car crash caught my attention. I covered my ears and watched as Raven twisted the demon's head from its body.

As she held the dead demon's head in her right hand, the previously loud noises were bearable. I took in a deep breath of relief.

"What in the world is that thing?" I asked to no one in particular.

Raven grabbed the soul of the creature, and the black mass clawed at her face. She squeezed its neck and said, "That is a sound eater. A coldara. As uncommon as they are ugly."

As she disappeared to take the demon soul to wherever they go, I finally gazed at Coren. He shook off his disorientation quicker than I had. He picked up my sword off the ground and handed it to me.

"Thanks," I muttered.

One whiff of the sword later and I wanted to find something to wash off the coldara's blood. I finally vomited. Right on Coren's boots.

He jumped back in shock, but I'll give him props for not gagging or vomiting when I puked on him.

"I'm so sorry." I winced at the splatters on his jeans. Then I dry heaved.

Coren looked down at the mess and winced. "I think we should go change, or find a place to wash up. I can't go around with vomit the rest of the night."

"Why don't you fade to my apartment," I said and held out my sword with a gag, "and rinse this off while you're at it."

"Fine," he replied and snatched the sword out of my grip. He faded away a moment later, leaving only a wisp of smoke.

"Now that was hilarious," a deep voice said from beside me.

I started and then gave Lor an evil stare. "You watched the whole thing and didn't help?"

Lor chuckled "No, my darling, I only saw the part where you heaved your guts on Coren's shoes."

Taking a deep cleansing breath, I wiped off my mouth. "Yeah, not my proudest moment."

"What is that putrid smell?" He scrunched up his face and covered his mouth and nose with his hand.

"My puke?" I asked, half-joking because I knew he smelled the long gone coldara. When he deadpanned, I said, "That smell is a coldara. Scary as shit and smells like death."

"No, Death smells like sandalwood and ash. That thing smells like decomposed body parts."

I rolled my eyes. "Okay, so not Death himself, but death as in the dead."

"Tomato Tamato," he said, using the old cliché of the different pronunciations of words. His body revolved around as he inspected the train station. "Sad to see this place in such disrepair. I bet the gold inlays and beautiful artwork inside is long gone. I wish you could've seen it."

"I keep forgetting you're old."

His red eyes swung to mine. "Darling, I'm not old. I'm experienced." He winked. "In every way imaginable."

"Are you hitting on me?" I asked with a wink.

"He better not be. I'll rip his heart from his chest," Coren said, his voice murderous.

"Ah, good to see jealousy is alive and well. She is beautiful," Lor gave a wicked smile and his red eyes glowed as he stared at Coren, "but Mara is my friend, nothing more."

"If you even lay a finger on her-"

"Coren, shut up," I barked. "I'm not yours to threaten Lor with, so being jealous only makes you look like an asshole."

While it was slightly flattering, possessiveness only pissed me off. Jealousy with anger only said Coren hadn't trusted me, not that we were in any sort of relationship. If I wanted to hang out with Lor, then there shouldn't be a problem with it. Lor was my friend, a handsome one, sure, but only a friend.

"Mara, a man only wants sex and," Coren started but I held up a hand to stop him.

"Watch who you put in that man category, Coren. Lest you put yourself in the same." I turned on my heel and away from Lor and Coren.

They continued to stare each other down, and I turned the corner on Main and in the direction of a coffee shop.

"Men," I grumbled.

"Yes, men are the bane of our existence." A man leaned against a bakery's brick wall. His blonde hair rimmed his ears, his nose said roman God, and his body curved with muscles behind his fitted shirt. He inspected his nails and then looked at me. At least I think he looked at me. He hid his eyes behind dark sunglasses. "But they make good soldiers when necessary."

I reached for my sword, only to realize Coren still had it. *Stupid, stupid, stupid.* "Who are you?"

He followed my hand in search of my sword and smiled. "I'm not here to hurt you. I'm here to enlighten you." He took a step forward. "My name is Aralim."

I inspected his dark jeans, blue T-shirt, and his gorgeous face. While he hadn't appeared threatening. Panda bears didn't either, but they'd rip you to shreds if you get too close. Aralim might be deadly.

My chin lifted, and I spread my feet in anticipation of a potential fight.

His eyebrow quirked at my stance. "Some demons can be angels, some angels can be demons. Always remember the highest waterfall has more than one leap."

"What in the fuck does that even mean?"

"Mara?" Coren's voice came from close by.

I looked back at Aralim but he was gone. Simply vanished into thin air. No smoke left in his absence. Was he a ghost? A figment of my imagination?

"Over here," I called out, my eyes searching the surroundings for the mysterious visitor. If another creature popped up to give me a "warning", I was going to scream.

"Everything okay?" he asked, handing over my sword.

Taking it from his hands, I tucked it into my belt sheath. I refused to mention the stranger because there was no use in worrying him. "Peachy. Where did Lor go?"

Coren rolled his eyes. "He'll meet us at your apartment tomorrow evening. The sun is coming up and we all need some rest."

I nodded and looked over the area, including the rooftops. I'd have to ask Raven what demon wouldn't smell like the stench of hell. Aralim had smelled like lilacs and honey. If I saw him again, I'd ask what kind of cologne he used because Raven and I would buy stock in the shit.

Once we arrived back at my apartment, Coren pulled a few ingredients out of my pantry.

I observed him pour some sort of mix in a bowl. "When did you have time to buy groceries?"

"They have a thing called the internet and you can get groceries delivered." Coren shook his head as he added milk. "It's quite amazing, actually. I wish we had this when you had to hunt for food."

"I tend to forget how old you are. At least if the apocalypse happens, you'll be able to hunt for our food."

He stopped his mixing and frowned. "Don't joke about that. It's not funny."

Holding my hands up in surrender, I said, "Sorry. I didn't realize joking about something impossible would be a sore subject."

"What makes you think it's impossible?" He poured the mixture in a hot pan.

"The myth is just something used to scare us all."

Flipping the pancakes, he bit his lip but remained quiet. Too quiet.

"What? Do you know something I don't know?"

He cleared his throat and tapped the spatula on the counter twice. "The apocalypse is highly possible. Actually, it could be closer than you could even imagine. One mistake, one wrong move, and the world would become a war zone in an instant."

"Be realistic. The world already has war and famine. Sure, we could potentially have another world war or possibly another depression era."

"What would you say if one person could cause the entire thing?" Coren removed the pancakes and added more mixture to the pan.

"Is that what they told you in hell?" I snorted. "Because last I checked, the place was filled with gossips and liars."

"Not exactly." He placed a plate of steaming pancakes in front of me. Then dug in the cabinet for syrup.

My eyebrow rose in annoyance. "You're always good at evading your time in hell, aren't you?"

He poured syrup on his pancakes until they resembled sticky soup. "I find that being evasive keeps them guessing."

After he held the bottle up, I took the syrup from him. "You could say it's withholding the truth, too. Being deceptive isn't always a good thing."

"Maybe. Maybe not," he said and took a bite of his breakfast. He chewed and shrugged. "Deception isn't always a lie. Sometimes it's keeping things concealed for protection of those around us. Do you think you'd like to know everything that Raven and Death face with each deceased?"

I shuddered. "Hell no. I'd have nightmares forever."

Coren held up his fork and made a checkmark in the air while he chewed.

His breakfast was close to being done and I'd yet to take a bite. We finished our plates in comfortable silence. The sun was up and exhaustion caused me to slide my half-eaten plate away. I wanted to watch some television and fall asleep, but Coren slept on the couch.

He seemed to understand what I wanted and said, "You can watch television until you fall asleep. I'll sleep on the floor."

I shook my head. "No, you can sleep on the couch as long as you don't touch me. You can recline back and I'll scrunch up. I'll be out in no time, anyway."

Nerves quivered through me. Being this close to Coren in an intimate setting wasn't something I'd experienced since I'd began my demon-hunting career. But, it was only a couch, not a bed. I took a deep breath and curled up on one side of the couch, Coren on the other. I turned on an older sitcom and watched as long as I could before my eyes

CHAPTER 26

*No one expects an angel
to set the world on fire.*

I snuggled closer against the warmth, a strong
heartbeat a lullaby against my ear. Strong arms
wrapped around me and pulled me closer.

The comfort of being embraced...wait.

My eyes snapped open and I took in my
surroundings. The television now played an
unknown movie. My sleep-riddled brain hadn't
caught up to my predicament. All I knew was that I
was comfortable and warm on the couch. Until I
looked down and saw an arm around my waist.

"Good morning," Coren said, his voice muffled
against my back.

I blinked a few times, trying to comprehend why
I was on the couch. I rolled over and stared at Coren
in confusion. He nuzzled against my neck, his warm
breath fanning across my skin. His hair was mussed
from sleep, and sometime during our sleep session,
he'd lost his shirt and slept in only jeans. Not only
that, but my shirt had ridden up and his hand
caressed my bare stomach.

"What happened to you staying on your side of
the couch?" I asked.

"I did."

"Then why are we…" I couldn't say cuddled. It wasn't in my vocabulary.

His mouth curved into a sexy grin. "Actually, you were the one that moved. I bet you weren't asleep five minutes before you flipped around and laid your head in my lap. Not that I mind. This is nice."

I tried to get up, but Coren pulled me back down. "What are you doing?"

His hand lowered to my beltline. "Just a few more minutes?"

I opened my mouth to protest, but his fingers made their way to the front of my panties and I inhaled a sharp breath. When he flirted with each side of where I now wanted his fingers, my hips bucked on their own accord.

Coren's mouth kissed my neck as he brushed a finger against my clit and then went lower. He dipped inside of me and then back again. When he began to spend attention to my clit, I groaned as my legs spreading to allow him better access.

His hardness pressed against my leg, and I snuck my hand in his jeans to wrap my hand around him. He hissed in a breath as my hand caressed his erection. Heat blossomed low in my belly, spreading to where his finger played.

I turned my head and kissed him. Our tongues mingled, and I groaned in his mouth, which only spurred him on more. My hand quickened around him, and his lungs heaved along with mine. His mouth moved to my ear, his tongue licking along the outer lobe.

Like a fire slowly spreading, the orgasm rocketed through me. I screamed out something unintelligible.

Coren shuddered. "Fuck."

Wetness coated my fingers as he came. We both breathed in puffs of air as we came down from our climax. Sweat beaded along my brow, but I didn't have the strength to wipe it away just yet.

He reached behind him and grabbed his shirt from the back of the couch. "Wipe your hands on this for now. I'll help clean up as soon as I catch my breath."

Cleaning my hands with his shirt, I chuckled.

His head tilted as he studied me. "What?"

"An orgasm is a great way to wake up." I winked.

Laughing, Coren gave me a quick kiss and then removed himself to take care of the mess I helped him make.

This felt normal, this felt human. While I never imagined I'd sleep with Coren's arms around me, I had no idea I'd allow him to touch me so intimately. Yet, it felt right in some weird way.

I sat up from the couch and smiled in satisfied bliss. He had redeemed himself from the front he put on when I met him. Coren may be a demon, but his heart was anything but evil. My smile fell when I realized Lucifer would kill Coren if he knew I cared for him. I glanced at the bathroom as the water shut off. I'd have to make sure my boss never, ever found out about whatever was going on between Coren and me.

Footsteps in the living room caused me to look up. "What's wrong?" he asked.

I looked at him and took in every feature, every muscle, his honeyed eyes, and his presence in my apartment. I had no clue how long he'd be here, or how long it would take my boss to kill us both.

I gave him my best fake smile possible. "Nothing. Thinking about how much time I have left."

Coren sat beside me on the couch and kissed the top of my head. "I won't let anything happen to you. I'd risk my life if it meant you'd get your soul back."

I closed my eyes. That's exactly what I was afraid he'd say.

*****

Night had fallen and demons had risen in droves.

My sword vibrated so much over warnings that my fingers were becoming numb. Lucifer was testing us tonight. At first, there was small gremlin creatures with moving teeth, then a goat-like being with two heads, and now we had killed an ezzamuth, the beast resembled a spiny tree, complete with bark skin.

I rested against the wall with my sword, my hand dripping green, murky blood.

Raven rushed in and looked about as haggard as I felt. "What shit is this night?"

"Fuck if I know." I shrugged.

She took off with her prey and I glanced at Coren. He held a long sword in his left hand and observed our surroundings. I had no idea where he'd gotten his sword, but it was deadly. The handle's dark metal wrapped around his hand and the double-edged blade was razor-sharp. I watched it cut through a demon as if was made of butter and not scales.

Blood splattered his skin in an array of colors, testimony of the multitude of demons we had executed together. His sinewy muscles flexed with each movement, and with the lethal sword in his hand, he resembled a roman warrior. A sexy warrior at that.

"Quit looking at me like that," he said.

"Like what?" I surveyed the street instead of gawking at him.

Coren placed his fingers under my chin and moved my face to look at his. His lips met mine for a steamy kiss. When he pulled away, he smirked. "I can't be distracted and do my job at the same time."

"Tsk, tsk." A rasping voice said from behind us.

We both reacted in an instant, but my sword pushed into the demon's throat first. This one appeared humanoid with eyes the color of tangerines. Black hair cascaded down its back. Despite the odd mouth and weird colored eyes, if you glanced at it you'd think this was a person.

"You've been a bad girl." It laughed with multiple rows of teeth like a shark.

"I thought you might have had a dick for a tongue, but you only have teeth."

"I don't think I'm the one that had a dick in their mouth. Right, hunter? " The demon turned its attention to Coren for a quick moment before looking at me again. "I bet my liege would love to know what his bitch has been up to."

My heart stuttered once. Demons loved gossip, and it would be a matter of hours before my boss knew about the two of us. Once he did, we'd be dead in a matter of minutes. Or I'd get to watch Coren die, or vice versa.

"Do you think we'd let you get a chance to tell him?" Coren asked, his voice low and dangerous. "There are ways to keep you from opening your big, ugly mouth."

The demon raised his chin in defiance. "Once I'm back in hell, you can't stop me."

I kept my sword steady, but I knew the demon was right. Once Raven brought his soul back, he'd blab. I opened my mouth to say something but snapped it shut as I looked at Coren.

Coren's smile was evil. His expression was malicious and vile, all of which caught me off guard. I had never seen wicked cruelty on his face before. This was the demon side of Coren, and that part of him craved chaos and death.

He stepped around me quickly and whispered in the demon's ear. If a demon could pale, this one had. Pure fear crossed its face as it turned to run. Coren snatched it up by the hair and rammed his sword through the demon's back. He whispered in its ear again, and I strained to hear what he had said. The only word I caught was "almawt-u" before Coren twisted his sword and the demon went limp.

He yanked his sword out of the now dead demon and its body fell with a sickening thud.

The whole situation reminded me of the possessed woman from the bar, only this was a full-on demon. Yet, Coren hadn't decapitated this one, and that's the true way to send one back to hell. Right?

I waited for Raven to show. Glancing around us, I frowned.

"She's not coming," Coren said. "I couldn't risk the dagdriman spreading our secret."

I swallowed and turned around to face him. "Don't you have to decapitate them?"

"If you want to send them back to hell, yes."

"Wait." I glanced around him to the demon, but it wasn't there anymore. Demons don't vanish into thin air unless they fade in and out, that is. I knew without a doubt that one had died and dead demons can't fade. As Coren predicted, Raven hadn't shown. "It's gone. What did you do to it?"

"The best way to describe what I did is I expelled the demon." Coren shrugged. "Sort of like an exorcism."

"How in the fuck can you expel a demon, when the thing is an actual demon?" I shook my head in disbelief. "And how, as a demon yourself, can you do that?"

"Let's say somebody from a divine background taught me everything I know." He winked. "But the beasty won't be running back to Lucifer any time soon. We have to be more careful now."

I blinked. Be more careful? We'd kissed in public twice, once under drugs, and touched each other for the first time this evening. I swiveled on my heel and left him standing confused.

He caught up to me and we walked beside each other in silence. While I had feelings for Coren, I couldn't risk either of our lives. Not now, not when we were so close to finding a way to save my life.

"What are you thinking?" Coren asked.

We rounded the corner to Elm Street. "I'm thinking about getting revenge."

"You know," Coren replied, "I think Confucius said 'Before you embark on a journey of revenge, dig two graves.' We should both take caution with those words or we could all be dead before the time is up."

I nodded. Sure, vengeance may seem like a fool's errand, but I was going to lose my soul anyway. Why not go down swinging?

*****

We had walked for about four blocks when the hair on my arms rose. The air felt thick and unpleasant.

I swiveled around in alarm, scanning our surroundings. Whatever was near was powerful.

"Are you okay?"

My eyes narrowed at Coren. "Can you not feel that?"

"Feel what?"

My sword rattled so hard against my back it practically rang. This wasn't good.

Pulling my sword free, I pivoted to observe everything. The streets were empty, as this neighborhood was free of bars and nightclubs. Then I saw him.

My blade vibrated in my hand again, and with a dead run, I headed in the direction of an alley across the street. I heard Coren's feet pounding steps behind me, but I ignored them for the moment.

A man stood in the alleyway, his chest heaving. He was shirtless but had jeans hanging low on his hips. A poor woman laid at his feet, blood pooling below her.

"You piece of shit," I said, causing the man to turn in my direction.

His eyes were flamingo pink with black streaks throughout. They were so unique it surprised me and I stumbled to a stop. Recognition dawned. My mouth gaped as I stared at Aralim.

Smirking, he nodded in greeting. "Wondered when you'd show up."

"Well, I'm here." I twisted the sword around with one hand. "What are you going to do about it?"

"Nothing." His gaze darted Coren, and then back to me. "I'm ready for my fate."

Blinking in shock, I froze but still held my blade at the ready. "You're ready to go back to hell?"

"Who said I was going to hell?" He smirked. "Always the jury, judge, and executioner."

"Whatever. You're nothing but a spineless asshole." Twisting my sword around again, I stepped closer to him.

He turned his attention to Coren. "Is she always like that?"

"Always," Coren answered.

This time, I looked at Coren. I used my sword to point to the man. "You know him?"

He shook his head. "No, but I know a fallen when I see one."

I wouldn't have been more stunned if lightning had struck my ass. Why hadn't I felt this much power from him when I met him yesterday? With a sigh, I looked back at the fallen angel. "For killing the woman, I have no choice to send you wherever you end up. And I'm angry enough to make it as painful as possible."

When he didn't answer, I stalked forward ready to slice him from limb to limb.

"Don't touch him," Coren warned.

I ignored Coren and kept my attention on the fallen angel in front of me.

"I didn't kill her, but do as you wish." Aralim held his arms straight out on each side and his gaze held mine. "I'm ready and tired of this life. I thought I was bored in heaven, but I was alone for centuries in hell."

I ignored his being alone comment, because who cared? He fell and went to hell on his own. "Who killed her then?" I asked as I was within a few feet of him.

"Mara, don't. You can't kill him." Coren said, but I disregarded him. I saw him move to be closer to me out of the corner of my eye.

Wings unfolded from the Aralim's back seemingly from nowhere, and they caused me to pause as I took them in. Beautiful feathers the color of snow spread out behind him. Each feather was a different shade of white, and they practically glowed in the lamplight from a nearby post. Aralim was magnificent and enchanting. I bet he could have any woman he wanted on Earth. Maybe that's why he fell.

His wings shifted a bit. "I didn't kill her. That was the demon on the roof. He's waiting for you."

Without looking up, I snorted. "Why should I believe you? You're no better than a demon."

"True. I've done awful things, seen awful things. But that demon? He's strong and he knows we're here. It's a trap."

"So you set up this trap?"

He shook his head slowly. "No. You did."

I frowned at his words. How can I set up my own trap? When Aralim chuckled, anger welled inside of me and overflowed like it had a life of its own. Fire burned through me, each breath a raging inferno.

With a warrior scream, I ran forward and swung with all my might.

"Mara! No!" Coren yelled and reached for me. It was too late.

Aralim never moved. He stared at me with those pink eyes, his wings spread out behind him. He didn't even flinch as I swung my blade. The only thing he said before my sword hit home was, "Broken wings can still fly."

As his body fell to the ground, gold blood splattered me in the face. I stared at his fallen form, his wings bent underneath him. His golden blood glistened in the low light and it was a beautiful as Aralim was. I let out an exhausted breath as reality hit. I had killed an angel. A fallen one, yes, but an angel nonetheless.

I turned to Coren to ask him about repercussions but a bright, blinding light blasted through the alley. I flew back against the brick as if a bomb had detonated. My head slammed into it with a *whack* and the rough exterior grated against my skin.

Coren quickly covered my body with his. His arms tucked my head against his chest. I squeezed my eyes closed when my hair whipped against my face, and because of the stars in my vision from my skull bashing against the wall.

"Don't move!" he shouted over the chaos.

Hurricane-force winds had erupted in the small alley. Metal creaked and groaned. Something large fell to our right and debris slammed against the brick with a boom. Glass clanged as windows exploded. Coren grunted as something hard smacked into him, but he refused to let me go.

"Are you okay!" I shouted, but he didn't respond.

The warmth of his embrace did little to calm my rapid thoughts. Was Coren hurt? How fast did demons heal? What were the repercussions of killing a fallen angel? Especially one that may be one of Lucifer's soldiers.

The wind around us went from a roar to whistling through the alley. Dust and rubble peppered my skin. Coren's arms tightened and he used his hands to block as much dirt debris from hitting my face.

When it finally died down about two minutes later, Coren pulled away to inspect every inch of my body. "Are you okay?"

Looking over myself as well, I nodded. "Yeah, I think so. Just a nasty headache." I inspected his body, too. "Are you okay? There was a lot of debris flying –"

Blood blossomed under his ribs and his ripped shirt exposed a deep gash on his right side. I stared at it in alarm and pressed my hand against the wound to staunch the blood flow. The blood still streamed down from his ribs to his jeans. *How had he held me so calmly with the injury?*

"How are we going to explain the damage? The alley and street looks like a twister blew through here," Coren said, grimacing as I pressed my fingers harder into his side.

"I guess we could simply take off. We can't explain this without being admitted to a looney bin." I grimaced. "God, Coren, you're really bleeding. You may need stitches."

"I heal pretty quickly, but I may need to bandage the wound for a day or two."

Shaking my head, I said, "I wish I had that power."

"In my world, it's a necessity, not a superpower." He hissed as I pulled a piece of glass from his wound.

"I guess when you have pissed off souls, fast healing would be a good thing."

Coren opened his mouth to say something but grunted instead when I located a piece of metal near his open wound. His blood continued to flow and I applied more pressure. The warm fluid glistened as it ran down his jeaned leg. I was worried Coren might pass out from blood loss.

I tilted my head in confusion as I stared at the liquid seeping through my fingers. The color wasn't red like a human or any demon color I had seen before. I pulled my hand away from his wound to see the blood. I held it up my hand to be sure it wasn't a trick of the light. The liquid on my fingers shimmered.

He had golden blood.

My gaze swung up to his, my mouth gaping in utter disbelief.

He frowned at me. "What's wrong?"

His attention moved down to my hand. He went stock still when he saw his shiny blood reflecting on my fingertips

"You're a fallen angel," I whispered.

Still not wanting to believe it myself, I pulled my hand closer to my face for inspection. Yep, it was the same tint as pure 24-karat gold. I blinked a few times and shook my head in disbelief.

"Mara…"

This couldn't be happening. I had a hard time with him as a demon, but I had accepted it. This was so much worse. In many ways, a fallen angel who resided in the underworld was as evil as Satan. They chose to fall and join the ranks of hell on their own accord. Demons often didn't have a choice because of birth or whatever, but angels sure as fuck did.

As the implications set in, I scrambled away from him.

Coren reached for me but flinched when it pulled against the gash on his side. "I know what it looks like, but I promise it isn't what you think."

"Tell me why you lied to me. Why you thought holding this information from all of us would work out. And why you fuckers explode when you're killed."

"I'm here to protect you. That's my mission. What I didn't expect was to fall in love with you."

I scoffed. "I'm your mission? I knew you worked for Lucifer, but this is a low blow. How can you expect me to trust you now?"

"I had to fall—."

"No. Nobody forced you to choose. You did that all by yourself." I held up a hand to keep him quiet. "Lor!" I called out, hoping he'd appear if I said his name.

"Mara, I'm still the same. Nothing has changed."

"Fuck you."

As though he'd waited for my summons, Lor appeared next to me in the alley. He took in the extent of the damage from me killing a fallen angel, but I grabbed his hand and begged, "Take me anywhere but here."

"Please don't do this," Coren whispered. "Let me explain."

Without hesitation, Lor gripped my arm. My eyes never left Coren, and I held my breath to keep from screaming as my body splintered apart when he disappeared with me.

Chapter 26

There's only one way to stop evil.
You have to embrace yours.

I stood on the edge of the Garden of Gods in Colorado again. The gorgeous morning sun filtering through the park hadn't lifted my melancholy mood.

My hand and forearm still had Coren's golden dried blood. The color shimmered in the indigo hue of the sunrise. I stared at it. How can such a beautiful color be breathtaking and disturbing at the same time?

"What do you mean he's a fallen angel?" Raven asked, her face a mask of confusion.

After Lor dropped me off in Colorado, he went to retrieve Raven and Death. Death was none too kind about it. His jaw flexed as he looked around, his arms folded across his chest.

I wasn't sure if he was upset at Lor for bringing him here, or if he was pissed at Coren. I was going with both. After I explained the situation with Coren and the fallen in the alley, they all gaped at me like I'd grown a penis out of my chin.

"You sure his blood was gold?" Lor rubbed a hand over the stubble along his chin. "There was a lot of chaos after you killed the fallen."

I held up my stained hand and shook it at them. "The fallen angel had golden blood, I know because

247

it splattered me in the face and puddled on the ground before shit went to hell in a handbasket. And, yes, Coren's blood on my hand was the same as the fallen."

"Are you really that surprised?" Death responded. "He was too good to be a demon. Too kind. Too in love with Mara. Demons don't have an ounce of love inside their evil bodies. We all failed to see his real identity, but I knew something was off. Something didn't say demon to me, but I couldn't figure him out. Guess we know now."

"What are we going to do about it?" I kicked the dirt at my feet. A reddish pebble skidded across the soil.

"Nothing," Lor said.

"Why not? He lied to us. He was a fallen angel this whole time!" I was frustrated. While I didn't want them to kill him, I wanted some sort of payback. Maybe I could give him a black eye.

"The fallen you killed," Death said, "what color were his eyes?"

"Pink. And not like pale, either. They were like bubble gum pink." I shrugged. "Weirdest colored eyes I've ever seen."

Death nodded. "If Coren was a true fallen, his eyes would turn that color within a few months. Since his eyes don't even have a hint of pink, he must be a recent one."

"Really?" Raven asked, her eyebrows raised in surprise. "Don't you find that odd?"

"Regardless, he was in hell with Lucifer." Lor shrugged. "That isn't a good sign."

Death nodded. "Hell is a far cry from Heaven. It wasn't like he fell and landed in a church."

Raven's narrowed eyes swung to me. "Speaking of churches. Mara, why did you go to the church that day?"

All eyes turned to me in curiosity. I closed my eyes in frustration. Dammit. Raven and her big mouth.

"You went to a church? Which one?" Death probed, his dark eyes watching me with such intensity the hair rose on the back of my neck.

I itched my neck. "The one across from the donut shop on Main. Why?"

"When I brought him a soul recently, Lucifer mentioned he couldn't track you for a while. He wanted to know why. I brushed him off, but now it makes sense."

My lips parted. When the priest blessed me, Lucifer couldn't find me. That explained why he searched me out and wanted to meet me at the coffee shop. And why he had sent the possessed woman. Was it the blessing, the holy water, entering a church, or all the above?

I went in search of angels when I entered the cathedral. I guess I had found two. Coren and Aralim.

"Oh my God." I pulled my phone out and searched Our Lady of Angels. I scrolled through picture after picture until I found the one I wanted. I turned my phone around. "Does this angel look familiar to anyone?"

"Holy shitballs," Raven breathed. "You weren't kidding when you suspected it was him in the stained glass."

Death took my phone from me and inspected the picture on the screen. "I thought this image was of an archangel, but Coren isn't one. Of course, most humans don't know what an archangel really looks like, so this could be an interpretation of what they saw when this was made."

Lor cleared his throat. "So Coren has been on Earth before. I have to wonder when and why."

"Does it say when the windows were made?" Raven questioned, taking the phone from her father. "No, it doesn't. But I know how to find out." She pressed a few buttons and lifted my phone to her ear. "Hello, my name is…Samantha. I'm a student and wanted to ask a few questions about your architecture." Her voice was sugary sweet and as fake as the Louis Vuitton purse I bought from a man named "Peanut."

After she said a few uh-huhs and okays, she asked, "And the cause?" After a few more minutes, she thanked the person and hung up. She handed my phone back to me and smiled. Her black eyes twinkled.

"Well?"

"The building was built in the twenties." She smirked. "However, after a fire, they had to completely overhaul the building, including the stained glass. Anyone want to guess when the newer stained glass was installed?"

"I have a feeling I don't want to know." I sighed.

"Wait, I want to try to guess," Lor said.

He scanned the landscape in front of him and tapped his chin with his finger. His eyes reflected the sun like fire. The different shades created a kaleidoscope of reds. There were times his eyes mesmerized me because they were so unique, and this was one of those times. Lor really was handsome, and if things were different, I might have hit on him if I hadn't met Coren first.

Lor's attention turned to me. "I'm estimating about twenty-five or twenty-six years ago."

Raven nodded enthusiastically. "Yep. The building burned on January 13th twenty-six years ago and the remodel was finished exactly a year later."

I took a step back. "Why is everyone looking at me like that? What does my birthday have to do with anything?"

"Mara," Death said, "the church burnt on the day of your birth. Then it was refurbished one year after you were born."

Shaking my head, I eyed my friends. What does my birth have anything to do with a church burning? Then suspicion hit me like a speeding train. My skin prickled as memories flooded my mind. "What was the cause of the fire, Raven?"

"Arson."

I closed my eyes in both understanding and anger.

My mother had worked as a secretary for a Catholic church while she was pregnant with me. She had lost her job and benefits right after I was born, and her life evolved from a single mother with a job to a jobless single mother. She eventually became hooked on drugs sometime after that. She had blamed me for it all. In her sick mind, I had caused her unemployment and her addiction to drugs.

I bet we were supposed to die in that fire. However, because she was delivering me instead of inside the fire, everything from the moment of my birth was a setup. Everything. My addict mother, her abuse, her lust for a better life that wouldn't include me. That she'd sign over my life to get her riches, and obviously Lucifer getting my soul in the process.

I knew with absolute certainty Coren hadn't set the fire. Lucifer had.

The biggest question was why. I spoke to shadows, yes, but he hadn't known that until recently. Someone had hinted he wanted me as a concubine. That didn't fit either. I was missing something. Something huge.

Even more puzzling was how Coren ended up on a stained glass inside the same church my mother had worked. Had he come to protect me as a baby? There were so many confusing details and mysteries surrounding my life. I wanted to start mapping them out on a chart, but it would probably take up every ounce of wall space in my apartment.

"Earth to Mara," Death said, tearing my attention away from my mental conflict. "Did you hear me?"

I winced. "Sorry, I was thinking."

"We need to head back. Raven and I can't be gone for long. You know death waits for no one."

Dread settled in my belly at the possibility of seeing Coren again. Anxiety was so thick it practically coated my skin, but I took a deep breath and fucking dealt with it. I had to. There was no choice when it came to him or my soul. I nodded in agreement.

Lor came forward and wrapped me in a hug. He leaned down to whisper in my ear. "My darling girl, tattered wings can still fly."

When he pulled away, I stared at him. Hadn't Aralim said the same thing? Death held my hand to fade me away from Colorado. I kept my eyes on Lor as the world faded.

Lor smiled sadly and said, "He loves you, even with your darkness."

The last thing I saw were those damn red eyes before I popped into my apartment and stumbled against the couch. *My* darkness? Sure, Lucifer had altered my life, but I wasn't evil.

"Are you okay?" Raven asked, her brows wrinkled as she watched me.

"Am I a bad person?" I whispered

"No, you're not perfect, but you're not bad. Why?" Death put his hand on my back.

I frowned and looked around my empty apartment. "Lor had mentioned Coren accepted my darkness."

Death smirked and patted my back gently. "We've all got darkness living in our hearts. We have the same amount of good in us, too. We merely have to choose whether to embrace both or let one consume us."

Raven crossed her arms. "Mara, that's not all Lor said before we faded. I think you need to talk to Coren."

My eyes searched for anything Coren had owned when he stayed here. No leather jacket hung on the back of the couch, no boots by the front door. Only a hint of his cologne hung in the air.

"We'll help you tonight when it's time to hunt." Raven gave me a hug. "Get some rest. He'll be back, I promise."

"What do I do when I finally see him?" I questioned because I had no idea how this worked. My lack of relationships and breakups only caused uncertainty.

"Talk to him, *Mi cielito*," Death said. "It's that simple, and that hard."

I sighed. "Why did he have to show up and try to break through this barrier around my heart? I'm supposed to be badass and unemotional."

Raven grinned. "While you *are* a badass, you've never been completely coldhearted. A little awkward with the emotional stuff, yes, but you wouldn't have friends if you hated everyone."

"And you wouldn't have family, either. Because whether you want to admit it, we are family. Blood be damned," Death said.

"Thanks," I said, feeling uncomfortable but humbled.

After saying our goodbyes, I sat on the couch and used a cloth to clean my sword until it shined.

Then I cleaned my bathroom and kitchen, followed by my bedroom. Honestly, I felt weird without Coren there. It had only been twelve days since I met him. How could that short amount of time change everything?

My world remained the same. Lucifer owned my soul, and Raven and her father fought to keep me above the surface of humanity. I still battled demons each night, sending them back to hell. Yet, my life had changed. I had new friends with Lor and his shadow comrades, and I allowed Coren to break through my thick walls I had built long ago.

I plopped on the bed and stared at the ceiling until I finally fell asleep. I dreamt of fighting a demon. Only the demon looked like me with lilac eyes. We clashed swords, an equal match for each other.

The demon version of me pushed me back until my back hit the invisible wall behind me.

I shivered my distorted voice came from the being. "There's only one way to stop evil. You have to embrace yours."

I woke covered in sweat, my heart beating hard in my chest.

The dream was so vivid and realistic. My arms still shook from the battle between… myself? I had no idea what to call what I had experienced. Was it a nightmare? A lucid dream?

After using the restroom to empty my bladder, I stumbled into the kitchen to my coffee maker before I started my evening. I put the filter in and filled it with water and coffee grounds. I started the machine, but I felt a presence in the room. They remained quiet and unmoving. I waited until the carafe filled, took out a mug, doctored it, and took a long sip. I sat the mug back down on the counter. I spun my mug around and turned to face whoever decided greeting me after waking up was a good idea.

A man stood next to my kitchen counter. My sword met his neck in a flash of movement. "Who the fuck are you?"

He wore a black suit with a blue tie that hugged his fit body. Salt and pepper hair rimmed his ears and deep wrinkles edged his eyes. His jawline sagged a little from age, but he still the confidence of a much younger man. Moss green eyes examined me curiously.

"Would you like to put on pants?" he said, his ears reddening.

I didn't care if I wore my panties and a t-shirt. This man was an intruder and if he didn't start talking, he wouldn't have a throat left to talk.

"Are you deaf? Who in the holy fuck are you and what are you doing in my apartment?"

"I'm sorry to meet you this way, Mara. I tried to introduce myself in public over the years, but you were never alone. When I saw you were by yourself for the first time, I knew breaking into your apartment was my only chance."

"Tell me why I shouldn't kill you and then call my friends for the cleanup?" I pushed my blade harder against his neck.

He leaned forward, allowing my sword to prick his skin. A drop of crimson blood dribbled down his neck and stained his white dress shirt. "You can kill me if you'd like, but then you'd have to explain to everyone why you killed your father."

"Liar," I said. "My father wouldn't have left me alone with an evil mother."

He held his hands up. "I didn't know your mother was pregnant when I left her. It wasn't until later that I heard she had a child. By the time I tracked her down, she was dead and you were gone."

I snorted. "So it took you this long to find me? I call bullshit."

"Your mother hid her tracks well. Argueta isn't even her real last name, or yours."

"Prove it to me," I growled.

He reached into his jacket and then paused when I bristled. "I'm getting the proof you're asking for out of my pocket."

He held out an envelope. I refused to take my sword off his throat. "Open it for me."

His eyes never left mine as me as he opened the said envelope and took out three pieces of paper. He held the first up for me to see.

I inspected the picture. My mother was young and smiling, her happiness so at odds from what I remembered. Next to her was a younger version of the man in front of me, his arm around my mother.

Shrugging, I said, "That doesn't mean you were a couple. You could've been friends for all I knew."

With a sigh, he held up a white sheet of paper. When I only stared at it, he smirked. "My name is

Marlin Foster, and this is a DNA test showing I'm your father."

Narrowing my eyes, I snarled, "How in the hell did you get my DNA?"

"I finally caught up with Jennifer, which is your real mother's name by the way. However, she had already died and you were already gone. So I grabbed some hair from your brush and had it tested."

"Your creep factor just shot up to a million, old man." While he was moving to show me each paper, he'd yet to fight the blade at his throat. Point for him.

"I'm sorry. I know this must be insane to you, but it's my job to hunt people down." He held up the last piece of paper.

Three names greeted me on an old birth certificate. Mara Foster as the child, the mother as Jennifer Carter and the father listed as Marlin Foster.

My gaze swung back up to his. "They could all be fake. People can forge documents."

He nodded. "I thought you might say that. I would think the same thing, especially in our line of work."

My brows lowered in confusion. "Our line of work?"

"You hunt demons, my dear. I hunt angels."

The blood drained from my face. Rage propelled through my body like fire. Could the man who said he was my father, be hunting Coren and that's how he found me?

I sunk the blade a little more into his skin and another drop of blood pooled against his shirt color. "Get out before I kill you. I won't warn you again."

CHAPTER 27

*Some of the most poisonous people
come disguised as family.*

Once the man sat the papers on my coffee table, he left as requested. Of course, he left with more blood staining his white shirt, too

After I locked my three deadbolts, I searched for my cell phone. I needed to do some research on my supposed father and figure out how to warn Coren. He hadn't returned, and I bet I'd have to hunt him down to find him.

Marlin Foster was a ghost. No pictures, no newspaper clippings, no record of arrests, or hospital admissions. Next, I searched myself to see what would come up. The only thing that did was an old picture from high school cheerleading, so I searched my supposed name Mara Foster out of curiosity. I sat back on the chair with my heart in my throat. Mara Foster vanished from the hospital, along with her mother. There was a grainy, out of focus picture of my mother on the front page of the Townsy paper. The articles stopped. No search, no police involvement. Nothing.

If I was indeed Mara Foster, then why hadn't there been a search or any other article about a newborn vanishing? Somebody went to great lengths to hide me, which I assumed was my mother. Then why the drug addiction if she wanted me hidden? I scoured over the paperwork again. There had to be some sort of clue I had missed.

I picked up the picture. They looked happy enough in the photo, but I spotted the man in the background. He was underexposed, but I knew him without a doubt. Nobody had the same body shape, the same wicked smile. Had my father known Lucifer?

"Hey, girl."

I grabbed my sword but relaxed when I spotted Raven seated across from me.

She frowned. "Are you okay?"

I slid the papers over to her. "This man said he's my father after he had broken into my apartment earlier."

Raven's burrows crinkled as she read everything. She read them a second time. "You don't believe him?"

Shrugging, I slowly placed the picture in front of her. "This is my mom." I pointed to her and pointed to the man next. "This is Marlin Foster. The man who says he's my father."

"They were both good looking and they look happy in the photo. This doesn't prove anything."

She started to slide it back, but I stopped the photograph with my finger. "Look closer."

Raven did as I asked. Her face morphed from confusion to disbelief. Her eyes snapped up to mine. "What in the hell is Lucifer doing there?"

"I'd like to know that, too. Did this Marlin Foster know him? Did my mother?" I let out a frustrated breath. "There's more."

Her eyebrow rose as she awaited what I had to say. I hesitated for a few minutes because I knew what I was about to tell her would change everything.

"Spit it out," she said, her toes tapping in impatience.

"So, we all know I hunt demons. That's nothing new. Well, this guy, my apparent father, does the complete opposite."

Staring at me, she blinked a few times. "The complete opposite? What does that even..." Her eyes widened as the meaning sunk in. "You can't be serious."

"Completely serious. Have you never heard of an angel hunter?"

"We never met anyone brave enough to confront an angel, let alone kill one. Well, until you." She winced. "But if he's really hunting angels, then he can't kill them. There's no way. He'd have to trick them somehow."

"But I killed one. Why can't he do the same?"

"Trust me, he can't." She smiled, but a moment later Raven inhaled sharply. "Coren."

I nodded sadly. "We have to find him before that Marlin dude does."

Her blonde hair bobbed as she nodded. "Agreed, but how?

"I have no freaking clue."

*****

Finding an angel is tricky business, especially if they don't want to be found.

As Raven and I searched for Coren, I felt eyes on us. Always watching, always barely beyond sight. Time would tell if it was Coren, my father, or one of Satan's spies.

"Do you feel somebody...?" Raven hesitated, unsure how to explain.

I nodded and whispered, "Yes."

She gave me a grim look as we turned the corner near the donut shop by the church. I glanced up at Our Lady of Angels Cathedral thinking about the pastor and the blessing I'd received. A loud chiming sound from the steeple echoed down the street.

I stopped so suddenly Raven bumped into me. The ringing sound was sporadic and too soon for the hourly ding.

"What?"

I shook my head, unable to explain. Instead, I turned on the balls of my feet and started across the street. My boots clunked against the concrete steps leading up to the door of the place, Raven hot on my heels.

Once I reached for the door, she grasped my arm. "What do you think you're doing?"

"I have to go in. I have a hunch."

"You're going to risk Lucifer's wrath based on a hunch? Remember what happened the last time he couldn't track you? He threatened all of us."

"Look," I yanked my hand out of her grip, "you can come with me or you can stay here. Either way, I'm going inside."

She let out a breathy sigh. "Fine. I'll be right behind you."

My eyebrows hit my hairline at her response. "You can come in?"

"Mara, I'm an angel of death. I can go anywhere I damn well please."

"True," I said and pulled open the doors to a quiet empty church.

We rose up the small set of stairs and came to an abrupt halt. A lone figure kneeled on one knee at the front of the space.

Neither Raven nor I wanted to interrupt him. We watched him in silence, but my eyes swung to the stained glass of the angel that looked an awful lot like the man near the altar. Coren, who I first assumed was a demon, was praying inside a holy space. Apparently, fallen angels were able to enter houses of worship and divine places. That was unsettling. This fallen angel wouldn't hurt me or Raven, or any of my friends. He wouldn't kill unless he had to, that much I knew.

Last time I saw Coren he was bleeding in an alley and I had left him there. Despite what I had originally thought about him, this man protected me at every opportunity. He hid my volunteering at

SafetyNet. He let me fight my own battles without interfering. Okay, not interfering too much.

His strong back was curved to allow his head and hands to rest on the one bent knee. There were no words said, no hushed whispers. Only silence. The scene was beautiful and serene.

"Mara." Coren hadn't moved, but he spoke my name similar to a prayer.

"Thanks for the hint on your location." I looked around the church again. "But why here of all places?"

"Honestly?" He rose and looked at me. "I knew you'd be safe."

"Well, yeah, but you know as well as I do that Lucifer will be pissed when he can't track me again. Safe is a biased word right now."

Raven snorted. "And if this holy place does the same for me, then I'm in a heap of shit."

"You'll be fine." Coren waved a dismissive hand in her direction. "My concern is you, Mara. Hell is in chaos, heaven is in an uproar, and the only one who will suffer is you."

"But what about you? Lucifer knows you're a fallen angel," I said as I took a step in his direction.

Coren lifted a shoulder. "There are plenty of fallen angels in hell, and I quickly rose through the ranks with nobody the wiser on my true mission."

"Wait," Raven looked at me, and then at Coren. "What true mission?"

"Like I tried to explain to Mara before she left with Lor, I fell for one specific person. I was tasked with infiltrating hell and attempting to keep Mara from completely losing her soul. When Lucifer put a time limit, I figured something was off. There are things in motion that I can't stop unless I have help."

My eyebrows elevated. "You mean my father?"

Both pairs for eyes focused on me. I wanted to shift uncomfortably, but I remained as still as possible.

"You met your father?" Coren blinked in what must have been shock. "Does he know what you do for a living?"

I winced. "Yes, he does. He hunts angels."

"Impossible," Raven muttered. "He's a fool."

His eyes narrowed. "What makes you think he truly hunts angels?"

"He told me. I guess he could be lying."

Raven scoffed and shook her head. "I bet he's lying. My question is why he showed up after all these years. If I ever see him in person, I'll be sure to torture it out of him."

"He can't be the real deal." Coren smirked. "You of all people know what happens when an angel is killed, Mara."

"What happens?" Raven asked, her gaze traveling between Coren and me.

A shiver ran over me. If Coren hadn't been there to shield me, I wouldn't have survived the blast. "They go kaboom."

Chapter 27

Do no harm but take no shit.

Lor stared at me with his bright scarlet eyes. "You can't be serious."

My lips thinned in annoyance. "Look, I wouldn't ask if it wasn't serious."

"So you want me to spy on your father without any details?"

"I just met the guy. Forgive me for not having his fucking address."

Lor's lips twitched at my sarcasm. "I'll see what I can do, and I'll fill the rest my gang in as well. They ask about you all the time. They want a rematch at the Garden of the Gods when this is all over, you know."

"Of course they do." I laughed with a shake of my head. "If I make it out with my soul intact, I'll take them up on it."

"You'll keep it," he said, his fingers brushing my cheek in a friendly gesture. "I'll make sure of it."

"I know you'll do your best, Lor. Thank you."

With that, he smiled and began to fade away, and the last thing to disappear were his eyes. Once he was gone, I sagged against the wall and let out a long exhausted breath. My gaze moved to the calendar on the fridge. The cute gray kitten in a basket hadn't lifted my spirits. I'd faced stronger demons, Lucifer threatened my friends, and I had an emotional upheaval over Coren.

On the plus side, Coren located a Wiccan to help cleanse my apartment and protect it from negative energy. They were due to arrive any minute. Lor assured me it wouldn't keep him or the rest of his gang out, but he felt the woman might help with demons entering my space uninvited as the âme damnée had.

I thought the whole thing was hocus pocus, but I was willing to give this person a chance to keep my apartment clean of evil. After all, Coren would know what kept demons away. When the knock sounded at my door, I hesitated. I slung open the door to see a petite, redheaded woman in a jade dress that matched her eyes. Her sandaled feet were manicured with pink toenails and she examined me from head to toe.

"I'm Everly Miles. Are you Mara?" she asked, her voice soft yet firm.

"Yes, nice to meet you." I held out my hand in greeting.

She recoiled. I clenched my teeth at her rudeness. If Coren hadn't vouched for her, I'd slam the door in her face. Taking my hand back slowly I sneered, but I meant to smile politely. I wasn't good at being courteous. I stepped back and invited her in with a wave of my hand.

She looked around the small space as she entered, but she stopped and stared at my balcony in confusion. "Have you had any recent demon visitations?"

I snorted. Was this bitch serious? She glared at me so I guess she was.

"Yeah, you could say I've had a few," I said with a shrug.

One of Everly's eyebrows rose. "How many is a *few*?"

"Did Coren not say anything about my occupation?"

"You're surrounded by so much darkness that I wouldn't touch your hand, so I can only imagine what you do for a paycheck. However, that's none of my business. I was hired to protect your apartment, nothing more." She placed a black shiny stone on the table next to the glass sliding doors. "Negativity and darkness are not welcome here."

I opened my mouth say something rude back but the sword rattling against the coffee table caught my attention. Oh shit. That wasn't good.

Everly placed a rose-colored crystal on my bookshelf. "Negativity and darkness are not welcome here."

Another clatter of the sword had me snatching it off the table before she noticed. The handle vibrated against my hand and I prepared to attack whatever entered my apartment.

"Uh, Everly?"

She placed another dark rock on my coffee table and repeated her mantra. My fingers were going numb from the vibration of the blade. Fear fluttered through me. I had to get Everly out of my apartment because I refused to put the innocent woman in danger.

Grabbing her arm with my free hand, I pulled Everly in the direction of the front door.

She sputtered and yanked her arm free. "Don't touch me."

"Look, you have to go. You know how hard it was to shake my hand because of my supposed darkness? Well, if you don't leave now, you'll meet something *far* worse than me."

The telltale aroma of hell hit me first, but I noticed the instant she smelled it. Her body stiffened and she clutched the remaining crystals to her chest. She reached into her purse and pulled out a bundle of roots and a lighter. She lit the weeds and muttered something to herself as she waved it over her body. The horrid smell of burned pepper and lemon rinds almost covered the scent of sulfur. That packet of herbs wouldn't do anything against a demon.

The sound of sharp claws on my kitchen floor had us both turning slowly in that direction. She began chanting louder with one hand holding the black stones and the other waving the burning crap.

A four-foot-tall canine growled at us, its mouth full of pointed crystal-like teeth. The canines hung over the dog's lips and red, foamy drool fell to the floor. The glacial blue eyes focused on us with rapt attention as it took a step forward. I had the distinct impression the beast was waiting for his prey to move before it attacked.

"Everly," I said as I tightened my grip on the sword, "this thing will attack us as soon as I make a move. I want you to run as fast as you can. Understand?"

"I think I can help," she insisted.

"No, you need to get the fuck out of here. This thing will slaughter you in an instant. You'll be collateral damage to the beast, but I don't want to protect you and fight for my life at the same time."

The dog growled so low it vibrated the floors. I repressed a shudder. I hadn't known if I'd survive this or not, but I'd be damned if I wouldn't go down fighting.

"Tell me to run and I will. But when you can, I want you to grab the onyx from the coffee table and toss it in the hellhound's mouth. The stone won't kill it, but it'll slow it down enough for you to do the job," she said.

I glanced at the small black rock on my table and then at the creature in front of us. "On the count of three, okay? One."

Another drop of red drool dripped out of the hellhound's mouth and it clashed its teeth at us.

"Two."

Everly's crystals clattered behind me and she took a deep breath.

"Three."

Everything happened simultaneously. I snatched the onyx from the coffee table as I darted forward, the beast leaped up as Everly ran out the apartment door, and I swung out of the way when teeth snapped near my torso.

Now that I was alone with the monster of a canine, I twirled my sword in one hand and clenched the stone in the other. The hound dove for me again and I rolled easily over the couch, my sword swinging upward as I moved. The blade connected with its cheek and it whined. With a shake of its head, those glacial eyes fixated on my face again. The thing snarled and its muscled bundled as it bounded over the back of the couch.

Claws raked against my thigh, but I had moved at the last second to keep them from sinking into my flesh. A loud cry rattled the picture frames as I jabbed my sword into its eye and yanked the weapon back. Only one eye looked at me now, and claws swiped to protect its blind side. Twisting to avoid another blow, I vaulted back over my sofa. Only the hound was too quick and knocked my feet out from under me. I landed with an oomph, barely rolling away to avoid a bite from those wicked-looking teeth.

The sour smell of sulfur wafting off the hellhound was so strong I could taste it. All demons had that horrible scent, but this ugly fucker stunk as if it had bathed in it. The creature opened its maw to snip at any of my body parts within reaching distance. I took that moment to toss the onyx inside the large mouth and I knew the instant the mutt swallowed it. Crimson foamed inside his or her mouth and it coughed. The dog pawed at its mouth.

I took that moment to give a hard upswing of my sword. I expected blood or gore, but as soon as the head went rolling, black smoke swallowed the thing's fur. Within ten seconds, the only sign anything occurred inside my apartment was the hellhound's red drool and claw marks.

Letting out a sigh, I ran my free hand over my face. I'd never get my deposit back if I ever moved.

"Is it gone?"

I swung around and gaped at Everly standing inside the door. "What are you doing? I thought I told you to run."

She smirked. "You didn't tell me how far."

Raven popped in and Everly jumped in surprise. She gave the witch a once over and said, "Where's the body?"

"There isn't one. The ugly fucker went poof as soon as I killed it." I lifted a shoulder in a shrug.

"What do you mean it went poof? Demons don't just disappear without my help and you know that."

"That's because it wasn't a demon, it was a hellhound," Everly stated. "After it ate my blessed stone, I guarantee it won't be back anytime soon."

"Wait," Raven held up a hand, "you had a hellhound in your apartment and you lived to tell the tale?"

"I'm standing here aren't I?" Sliding my sword back in the sheath, I rolled my eyes. "You act like I can't take care of myself."

"Oh, Mara. That's not it at all," Raven said. "You're one hell of a fighter, and I get that. I know you can stand on your own in any situation handed to you, but you're only human."

"Only human." I snorted. "Everly saw the darkness, Raven. If I'm only human, then I'm a human touched by hell."

"That's why…" Everly trailed off. She tapped her chin.

Raven and I looked at her expectantly. She reached into her small purse and rummaged around while she mumbled under her breath. She pulled out a small gold sphere with shimmering pits.

She grabbed my hand, placed the heavy golden ball in my hands, and then closed my fingers over it. "That's pyrite. Some may call it fool's gold, but as far as healing goes, it's one of the best protection stones from negative energy and physical danger. Some say the sun god himself created the stones; others say the color reflects angels above. Either way, I want you to keep this with you at all times."

I opened my palm, stared at the hue of the stone, and thought about the color of Coren's blood. "Can I ever use it like the onyx stone?"

"Glad you asked." Everly grinned. "You could use it in the same way as the hellhound, but I'd rather you carry it with you. No exceptions."

"What about a dress?" I asked.

Raven chucked. "You'd rather saw off your arm than wear a dress."

"You can wear it in your bra. Or perhaps your panties," Everly suggested with a wink.

"I like her, Mara. She's witty."

"Can we get back to the hellhound, please?" My eyes narrowed. "Why were you surprised I lived? Isn't it simply another demon?"

"Actually, no," Raven said. She thinned her lips as she contemplated the next words. "Demons are either soldiers or slaves, per se. A hellhound is Lucifer's creation. He made four of them by blending corrupt souls in hellfire. They are pure evil and the deadliest beings in the underworld. Other than Lucifer, that is. Even my father avoids them."

My mouth dropped. Lucifer sent a fucking hellhound to my apartment. What he hadn't counted on were Everly and her magical rocks. I bet he was pissed I had defeated it. I snickered at the thought of Ol' Luke pacing the halls of hell in a rage. Bending over, I grabbed my stomach in a fit of laughter because the hellhound probably had to sleep outside in the doghouse tonight.

Wiping the tears of amusement from my eyes, I smiled at Everly. "I don't know how you know about this stuff, but I think you need to meet a few of my friends. They'll love your insight," I chuckled again, "at keeping Lucifer on his toes."

"I'd love to meet them, but I have another client in about an hour." She handed me a purple business card with only a number on it. "Give me a call."

Nodding once at Raven and me, she left the apartment and closed the door behind her.

"Bringing a witch in is unconventional, but it might work," Raven said. "I have to wonder how she knows so much about hell." She pointed to my hand. "If that trinket works I'll be surprised."

Glancing down at the heavy stone in my hand, I sighed. "She was right about the onyx. I guess time will tell if she's right about this one."

Chapter 28

Obsession is the root of all evil.

I had changed clothes and tucked the pyrite in the pocket of my jeans. With everything going on, we slacked off on demon hunting, but I didn't want to give Lucifer any more incentive to drag me to hell.

Coren met me outside. I took in his muscular arms in the black t-shirt, the jeans riding low on his hips, and the stubble lining his jaw. *Are all angels this gorgeous?* I wondered.

"How did it go with the witch?" he asked.

"Everly is fantastic. She helped me defeat a hellhound."

He stopped short and grabbed my arm to keep me from walking. "Uh, you're joking, right?"

"Nope, but it's all good. That fucker was sent back to daddy." I tilted my head. "Do all hellhounds vanish in a cloud of smoke?"

"I'm not sure," he said. "I don't know anyone who has met one and been around to tell anyone about it. Until you."

"That's what Raven said, too." I raked a hand through my hair. "I know how it found me. We all know Lucifer is a dick."

"Well, I have more clever words in mind for him."

I covered my mouth and mocked a gasp. "You're an angel, Coren. You're pure and chaste."

He scoffed. "Right. If you believe that about me, then you don't know me at all."

Letting out a laugh, I shook my head. Oh, I knew how vulgar and crass Coren was. He tried his best to throw me off with his crass sexual talk in the beginning, He was kinder than I expected, but I knew Coren had a mouth on him far worse than any demon. Honestly, that's what I liked about him.

"You know," I said, "we have a long night ahead of us. If you could be with anyone past or present, who would it be."

"You."

"Be serious."

He smirked. "I am."

Ignoring the emotion in his eyes, I pointed in the direction of the line of people waiting to get inside the newest club. "Do you think they'll be there all night and never get in?"

"Most likely," he replied, his smirk a full-blown smile now.

That smile caused all kinds of sexual feelings to flare to life, so I inspected the street in front of us instead. This would be a long night if he kept grinning at me like that.

My sword pulsated against my back and interrupted my dirty thoughts about Coren. "Demon," I whispered.

Coren went on alert, his eyes scanning the vicinity. We both knew we might encounter a high-level demon or an unlucky escaped one. Either way, we had to treat the confrontation with caution. Double-caution after the hellhound in my apartment.

Yanking my sword free, I used my free hand to touch the gold sphere in my pocket. A couple walking by gave us a wide berth, and I didn't blame them with my wicked-looking blade. I hadn't cared about them. My only focus was whatever was in the alley ahead of us. The weapon in my hand rattled again, the metal ringing slightly.

Coren's eyes narrowed at the sound, his jaw ticking once. When we rounded the corner of the alleyway, a lone man stood in the dim lighting from the building above. He wore dark jeans and a trench coat that fluttered in the wind. His shoulder-length, blond hair shifted slightly as he turned to watch us.

He was attractive with a sharp-angled jaw and eyes the color of celery. The scar running down his left cheek said he'd been through some shit. There was a faint scent of sulfur from the man. If I hadn't smelled that, then I'd have guessed this guy to be a mere mortal.

"Hi, Coren," the man said. "So nice to see you again."

"Zagan," Coren growled. "What do you think you're doing?"

"Hello, Mara." Zagan bowed, but the gesture was sardonic at best.

My lips curled into a scowl. Although he no longer looked like a bodybuilder, I'd met this demon once before. He'd given Coren a warning about caring about me and warning him about interfering in demon hunts.

With the sword held tightly, I took a menacing step forward. "What in the fuck do you want this time?"

Zaran grinned and it pulled on his scar. "So glad you asked. I'm here to give you a warning."

"Oh no," I covered my mouth in mock shock, "I'm so surprised."

"Fine, if you don't want me to help you, then I'll just kill this shell of a human and be on my way."

My heart lurched at seeing that once in my life, and I didn't want another human to die because of me.

Coren chuckled. "Go ahead."

I glanced at him in shock at his coldness over a human dying. "Fine. What's the warning?"

"Lucifer has quite the obsession with you. In fact, he's so foolish that he's neglecting his duties and letting his generals do his dirty work. As you can imagine, that isn't going over well."

"Interesting," Coren said. "When did this begin?"

"About two months ago."

Anger flared through me. "But he didn't put a time limit on me until recently."

"Do you know why he wants Mara so badly that he'd risk an uprising in hell?" Coren questioned, his voice cold and unflinching.

"All I've heard from rumors is it has something to do with a prophecy and a sword."

Coren's eyes glanced at my weapon. "Makes sense, I guess. But everyone knows a prophecy isn't set in stone. Remember Jeanne d'Arc?"

"Who's that?" I asked, curious how this woman had anything do with a prophecy.

With a twist of his lips, Zagan said, "Why Joan of Arc, my dear."

My eyebrows rose. "You're shitting me, right?"

"Afraid not." Coren shook his head. "They said a young maid of honor and sacrifice would become the savior of France. She would be dressed in armor, carrying a sword and riding a white stallion. She was supposed to work miracles, but some of the supposed prophecies happened and we all know how that ended."

My gaze went from Coren to Zagan and then back again. "Please tell me you both aren't old enough to have met Joan of Arc."

Zagan shrugged. "Okay, we won't."

Coren grimaced.

Fuck me. Talk about an age gap between Coren and me. Age is just a number my ass. We're talking nearly to six centuries between us, but I'm sure it was far more than that. I was afraid to ask him his true age.

"Okaaay." I blinked a few times. "I'm not defined by some prophecy that may or may not be about me. We recently discovered the passage, so how could Lucifer know?"

"I'm not sure of the details. We're going off gossip and not facts." Zagan held his hands out. "But where there is hearsays, there are believers."

My eyebrows lifted. "Do you believe it?"

"I don't know." Zagan lifted a shoulder.

At the same time, Coren said, "Not all of it."

"And what's this crap about my sword?" I lifted the blade and looked at the shiny metal and decorative hilt.

"Nothing." Coren narrowed his eyes at Zagan, daring him to speak.

Zagan's face went blank. "I'm sure it's nothing to worry about." He gave another mocking bow. "Until we meet again."

In a split second, Zagan disappeared. Only a spot of black smoke floated on the breeze where he had stood.

My mouth dropped. "Did he just fade away with a human body?"

Coren shook his head. "That was really him. No possession needed this time."

"Asshole." Zagan had called my bluff on my assumption he possessed a body to speak to us and I hated him even more for it.

"Agreed."

I put my weapon away. We both left the alleyway and strolled back in the direction of the bar scene. Since it was Saturday, the place was crawling with partygoers. Different music blasted from each bar we passed, but besides Zagan, we hadn't seen a demon in hours.

The slowness reminded me of when Raven and I had hunted. We'd usually run across a couple and then stop for the night. Of course, that was before

Lucifer got a hard-on for me and sent awful creatures in an attempt to kill me. Sure, I knew hell needed somebody in charge of the tainted souls like heaven needed somebody to take in the pure ones. Still, if I had a way to maim or hurt Satan, I would.

Speaking of Raven, I missed her company. While I liked Coren, I wanted my best friend to be here, too. I had to make sure to ask her to hunt with me next time.

"This is boring," Coren said with a sigh.

I smiled. "Believe it or not, this was how it was for years. I can't help but think this is the calm before the storm."

"I wondered that, too. We've fought some bad guys for days, and then nothing?"

Puffing a breath out of my lips, I nodded.

My thoughts must have worked because Raven poofed in, her strides catching ours as she materialized.

"Hey," she said, "sorry I'm late. There's been a wave of deaths lately. I finally told Dad I needed the rest of the night off to hunt with you two."

I grinned. "I was just thinking about you. Glad you're here."

"I'm happy I'm here, too." She slung an arm over my shoulder. "I need to kick some demon ass and relieve some stress."

"Good luck," Coren muttered.

She ignored him. "So, what's new?"

"Oh, you know. Saw the demon named Zagan, and he said Ol' Luke wanted me because of the prophecy you showed us, and something about my sword. Can you believe he'd believe that bullshit or that he'd want my sword of all things?"

There was a beat of silence before Raven chuckled. "Crazy, right?"

Rap music blasted from the club to our left, the lights flashing to the beat through the large windows. Several people smoked a few feet from the door and I eyed their choice of clothing. That's when I noticed the woman in the black racy dress. Her dark skin was accented in a gold shimmer and her makeup was perfection. Her long black hair hung down to her back, and she was at least six-foot tall with legs that went on for miles. Her sexuality drew the attention of those around her, each of the smokers' never looking my way from her.

I hated how beautiful she was, but I blinked in shock when she looked in my direction. At first, I thought her eyes were hazel, but as she watched me, I noticed they were mustard yellow. The faint smell of hell wafted off her, but she'd almost covered it with perfume. Her long, blue nails tapped against the wall behind her in a rapid succession of clicks. When she spotted Raven at my side, her fingers froze. Her gaze shifted to me and I knew the instant she realized who I was. I gave her a wicked smile and pulled my sword free. Her eyes darted all around her, and then she ran. For wearing stiletto heels, the bitch could sprint. *Fuck.*

I took off after her, my boots pounding on the pavement. She turned the corner on Main Street and I followed. This one wasn't getting away that easily.

"Mara!" Raven called after me, but I heard their footsteps following shortly behind me.

When the woman hurdled over the tall chain-linked fence, I cursed. I had to climb it, but I hadn't lost her. She had trapped herself in an old industrial complex with tall brick buildings surrounding her.

"Just give up," I said, swinging my sword in my right hand. "It'll be over before you know it."

"Oh, baby, I don't want to go so soon," she crooned, her bottom lip pouting.

Her hands moved from her hips, up her stomach, and to her breasts. My eyebrows narrowed in confusion. What the fuck was this shit?

"Coren," Raven shouted, "don't get any closer! This is a succubus."

"Shit," I heard him curse and his retreating footsteps.

"I don't mind a foursome," the succubus purred. "Actually, I quite enjoy them."

The demon's hands had now moved under her shirt to caress her nipples. I wanted to gag at the heated expression she gave Coren. Now she really had to die.

"Listen, bitch, he's mine." I charged forward, my weapon raised.

She ducked at the last minute and my sword sliced into her shoulder. The succubus screeched and her once yellow eyes were swallowed by blackness. Her mouth opened wide to show a row of shark-like teeth.

"Holy fuck," Coren muttered.

Raven snickered. "Yeah, they're pretty ugly when they're feeding or pissed off."

Ignoring their remarks, I focused on my task. My goal was to dispatch this demon so she couldn't wreak havoc on unsuspecting victims again. I hated to know how many males or females she'd already killed by her sexual prowess. I wanted to slice each one of her limbs off until she was only a bleeding stump on the ground.

Despite the obvious pain the demon was in, she swung her attention to Coren and said, "I'm sure *all* of you would enjoy my company."

"I already told you once. He's *mine*." With anger coursing through me, I twisted my body around and the blade sunk into flesh. As the demon's head slid from her body, I said, "And I don't share."

Staring at the succubus's body bleed out on the concrete, I realized the blood was cherry red, which was an odd shade for a spawn of hell. The color was too humanoid, and I let out a sigh.

"What's the matter?" Raven questioned as she strolled up beside me.

Because jealousy had roared to the surface when the sex-crazed freak tried to get Coren in bed, I had admitted that I believed he was mine. If that didn't scream emotional attachment, I didn't know what did. I struggled with that for a minute and then decided some things were better left buried so deep inside it would take some torture and a shovel to dig them out.

Coren's steps echoed against the surrounding walls, and at his approach, I wanted to kick the dead, headless bitch one more time.

Instead, I shrugged and gestured to the demon with my blood-stained sword. "Nothing. Just tired of these damn surprises. A succubus? I thought they were folklore."

"We didn't talk about them in our demonology lessons. Dad hasn't said much about them, other than they literally eat the souls out of their victims." Raven shivered. "Honestly, I wonder if they are how the rumors of vampires started. If you ask me, I think vampires are real, but they're allusive as hell."

I shuddered at the mental image of a succubus eating a soul out of a body, and because vampires might be living among us without anyone the wiser. I had to be a fool to think other supernaturals didn't exist.

Coren's hand caressed my back and I stepped away, not because I didn't want him touching me, but because I wanted him to. I hated myself for both moving away from him and for wanting to feel his fingers trace the tattoos on my skin.

Raven winked. "I'll go ahead and take this beasty back to hell. The lower demons will love her."

Gross. As soon as she disappeared with the body, I slid my sword back in its holder, turned on the balls of my feet, and made my way back to the street.

"Did you mean what you said when you said I'm yours?" Coren asked, easily catching up to me with his long strides.

Of course, he would bring that up. I inwardly groaned. I hadn't wanted to admit anything, so I gave a noncommittal shrug of the shoulders. "She had her sights on you. I was trying to keep you from being succubus fodder."

He gently grabbed my arm, stopping me right before Harvard Street. "You're such a horrible liar, Mara."

He stared at me, his brown eyes reminding me of caramel, far too sweet and tempting for my liking. I stared right back at him, lost in the way he looked at me. He took a step forward and wrapped an arm around my waist, pulling me closer. His gaze went to my mouth a second before he leaned down and met my lips.

The kiss was electrifying, toe-curling, and sexy. I didn't care that I was splattered with demon blood or the consequences of making out with an angel. All I focused on was the spellbinding kiss between us. When he pulled back, he left me breathless and wanting more.

Coren's lips curved into a knowing smile. "You can't ignore what we have together forever."

"Want to bet on that?" I said. With a smirk, I strolled away from him.

His laughter reverberated behind me, sending a delicious chill deep in my bones. What he send next caused the enchanting shiver to turn cold.

"You still owe me a favor, you know."

I spun on my heels so fast he took a step back. My sword met his throat. "That *favor* won't be used for sexual acts. I'll slice your dick off and then your head, especially if you expect me to do anything like that to keep our agreement."

He held his hands up in surrender. "God, no. That's not what I meant at all. I'd never, ever ask you for anything like that."

"Good," I put my weapon away, "because I don't want to kill you."

"You must really like me, then." Coren grinned.

Rolling my eyes, I edged around him and strode in the opposite direction on the street. I had to get away from Coren. One because he has me so edgy that I nearly stabbed him, and two because I wanted to wipe away his grin with my lips.

Pulling my leather jacket tighter in the cool air, I glanced up at the cloud-covered night sky. I wondered if the snow would be early this year. Hunting demons in ice and snow was a bitch and I dreaded it. Then I realized I may not make it a full winter if Lucifer had any say in the matter.

"Want me to take you back home before it gets too cold tonight? I think we both deserve a break after the succubus."

I longed for a break, but I shook my head once.

Coren sighed. "Fine. If you want to be stubborn about it, I'll take matters in my own hands."

"No fucking—"

My protest was cut short. His hand moved as fast as a viper, snatching my arm in one smooth motion. I didn't even have a chance to say another word. My skin tingled as he faded, bringing me along for an unnatural ride.

*****

"Your father is a ghost, Mara."

I let out a long breath. "Nothing? Really?"

Lor's mouth thinned. "We all tried to locate his whereabouts. It's like he vanished."

As I leaned against the railing, I observed the sun rise over the horizon from my balcony. The morning light made Lor's skin seem pale and his eyes cardinal red. They were absolutely stunning.

Coren had left shortly after he dropped me off, knowing damn well I'd berate his ass for fading me without permission. I'm sure Lor had waited until I was alone to deliver the news, anyway. He and Coren had a shaky truce. I think they avoided each other for my benefit.

"How could somebody disappear like that?" I questioned, more to myself than Lor.

He answered anyway. "Do you know how long it took us to find you? One year."

"But I had signed a contract and could see you. That doesn't count."

"That could be true, but what if you're father sold his soul, too? A man like that doesn't show up without a reason. I have to wonder what his angle is and why. Why did he show is face after all these years?"

"Honestly, I think he has an ulterior motive for his visit." I pulled a picture out of my pocket. "He gave me this picture the day he showed up.

Supposedly it was his way to prove that he knew my mother. But I think you may be on to something in regards to his soul."

He took the picture from me and studied it. His crimson eyes narrowed as he saw the character in the background. "And the plot thickens."

I snorted. "No shit. Welcome to the life and times of yours truly."

"Be careful. I don't want anything bad to happen to you. You're only human, after all."

"So everyone keeps reminding me," I replied and massaged my temples. "I wish you guys had faith in me."

"It's not that we don't. You're not as resilient as your friends and me. You can't deny that." When I scowled, Lor reached up and removed my hands from my head. "While you're a badass and slaughter demons, you're also my friend. From where I come from, that means you're family, and we take care of family. We care deeply about you and don't want to see you hurt. Or worse."

All the tension left my body at his confession. "Is this how you feel, or all of them?" I whispered.

"If I had to guess, I'd wager all of them. Coren most of all."

The stakes kept rising higher and higher, and before too long, those same stakes might be my undoing. Especially if Coren was involved.

I threw my arms around Lor in a hug. He hesitated before he hugged me back. Without saying anything, he slowly dissipated until I held only air. My gaze went back to the city before me. I went to put the picture back in my pocket and I had to tamper down my anger. He had dematerialized, along with the photograph of the man who said he was my father.

"Lor!" I screamed. "Give me the fucking picture back!"

There'd be no response. Lor had probably arrived in Colorado right after he disappeared.

Shit.

Chapter 29

Don't get mad, get evil.

After sleeping the day away, I stumbled into the coffee shop down the street.

As soon as I entered the space, I breathed in the earthy scent of toasted beans and vanilla. The cool hilt of my sword rested against my back and I adjusted my jacket to hide it. After my recent experiences, I refused to go anywhere without it. I'd be prepared if the pretty blonde barista came from the netherworld.

"Cooffeeee." Raven chanted like a zombie talking about brains.

I jumped at her rapid appearance next to me. I glanced around to make sure the patrons weren't paying attention. They weren't, thank goodness. The dark circles around her eyes and her wrinkled clothes were more startling than her entrance into the shop.

"Are you okay?"

She focused on me. "Dad and I are swarming with deaths and we haven't slept in days. I don't know how much longer we can keep up with this type of workload."

Concern for my friend took over. I'd never seen her like this. "Is there a war or an epidemic or something?"

"Or something," Death said, his deep timbre softer than usual.

Starling for the second time, I whirled to face Death. The same exhaustion lined his handsome face and his dazzling eyes were dull.

Glancing between them both, I frowned. "What's going on?"

"I wish I knew, but I know Lucifer has something to do with it." He ran a hand over his face. "The souls have gone to both heaven and hell, therefore we have no proof of his involvement. These last two weeks have been unusually busy."

"This has been happening for two *weeks*?" My mouth gaped before I snapped it shut. "Why haven't either of you told me this?"

"We haven't had time, *mi cielito*."

We all placed our orders with the barista and took a seat near the back so we all faced the front door. I sipped on the vanilla macchiato and observed my friends chug theirs. I doubted five coffees would cure their fatigue.

Spinning the cup around on the table, I listened to the scraping sound for a bit before I spoke. "Why now? How are these people dying?"

Raven's eyes stared at my cup as it rotated on the hardwood. "They're random things. Pandemics in hospitals, unexpected fires, accidents, you name it."

"So what makes this any different than any other time? Those types of horrible events happen every day, as awful as that is."

"Because," Death answered, "we've seen these events double, if not triple lately. Sure, we may have one awful day and things go back to normal. Yet, we're going on two weeks of this shit."

I sat back in the chair in shock. "This isn't a coincidence."

"Agreed." Death gave a short nod.

"Who's doing your job right now?" I asked after taking a sip.

"Nobody. The ghosts can pile up for a couple minutes. They'll be there when we're done with our break."

The detachment in Raven's tone sent chills up my spine. I knew they were both used to death, but lack of sleep was taking a toll. I wondered if the dead were a distraction technique to keep them busy while I fought for my life.

Guilt tore through me. This wasn't fair for them. Lucifer had to be stopped and his obsession over my soul thwarted. I knew how to get information, but I didn't fully trust the source. I had nothing to lose at this point.

Clearing my throat, I took a chance. "Can you send word to a demon for me?"

Both of their eyes widened in surprise.

"I must be dreaming because you did not ask me that." Raven's lips thinned.

"Can I ask why?" Death questioned, his penetrating stare never leaving my face.

"It's a long story, and I promise I'll fill you in as soon as I can. His name is Zagan. Tell him to come find me. I need his help."

Raven rubbed her temple as she gave me an exasperated look. "You can't be serious. He is *dangerous*."

"I know he's dangerous, but I think he'll be invaluable. Of course, no demon can know you talked to him."

Death gave a quick nod. "Well, we'll try to get word to him. I'll be the one to say I think it's a horrible idea to ask the general of hell for his company, but I trust you."

Now it was my turn to stare at them. Zagan is the general of hell? For real? I was in over my damn head.

They both gave me a tight hug and said their goodbyes. Death waits for no one it seems. Not the reaper, but the deceased.

As I finished my coffee and threw the cup away, I wondered if Lor found any more information on Marlin Foster. If he hadn't, was the bastard of a father watching me now? Or had Lucifer sent one of his spies. I resisted the urge to flip my middle finger as I exited the shop. My hands fisted at my sides to keep from doing just that.

"You look like you could punch a wall," a deep accented voice said from beside me.

I reached for the hilt of my sword and then stopped. The man, or demon, was Zagan. Death and Raven worked fast.

When I didn't answer, he continued, "So, I heard you wanted to speak to me. I'm honored, truly. But make it snappy. I don't have all day."

Seeing as how I didn't want him to know where I lived, I pointed to an abandoned business across the street.

"Ah. Privacy is of utmost importance, but we don't have to have a conversation in a dilapidated building, you know."

My eyebrows knitted together. "What do you mean? Where else are we going to go?"

He beamed at me and the scar on his left cheek twisted with the movement. I barely got out a curse before he wrapped his arms around my waist and faded with me.

*****

The salty, warm air caressed my skin as we materialized. I landed haphazardly on the white shore of a beach.

"Get off your ass and walk with me," Zagan said in a patronizing tone. "It won't be long until your boyfriend finds us."

"He's not my boyfriend." Glaring at him, I stood and wiped the sand off my clothing. "Where are we?"

"A small island off the coast of Antigua." When I only looked at him, he sighed. "We're in the Caribbean."

I scanned the area, noting a few small buildings in the distance. Despite those, it appeared we were the only inhabitants on the island at the time. Maybe that's why he chose this location over the rest of the islands.

"If you're wondering if we're alone, yes. A hurricane damaged a lot of the island making it nearly unlivable at the moment. Demons often avoid places that have little to no humans."

"But not you, though."

"Not me." He nodded once. "I enjoyed this place immensely when I need a short break away from my duties."

"You mean as the general for hell?" I rolled my eyes. "That must be so exhausting."

"Don't you wish for a hiatus from your job, too? We all deserve a few hours of peace."

With as much strength as I could muster, I kept my retorts about peace and demons to myself. I needed information from Zagan, not to piss him off. I inhaled and exhaled through my nose and then said, "I need your help."

An eyebrow rose. "Oh? What makes you think I'll help you?"

"You brought me to this deserted island. I doubt you want to talk about the weather."

"The weather is gorgeous." He smirked as he stared at the crystal blue water.

With the sun on his face and the ocean breeze lifting his shoulder-length hair, he was handsome. His eerie light green eyes glimmered in the light, and

I swore his skin appeared tanner than when we arrived.

I got right to the point, only because I knew Zagan would stall as much as possible. "You said that hell was in an uproar because of Lucifer's fascination with me. How can we stop him?"

"Now that's a loaded question. If I knew how to, I would've put a stop to the bullshit already."

"I'm not asking you to do this alone. I'm asking you to be an ally."

"You mean a spy. You realize if I do this, I'd forfeit my life for treason. What do I get out of it?"

"Hell would be back to normal again. You'd be general and continue your life as usual."

He chuckled. "Try again."

Frowning, I racked my brain for anything I had in my arsenal to bribe him with. I wasn't giving up any of my friends, nor would I offer myself in exchange for his help. I didn't trust Zagan not to kill me and deliver me to Lucifer on a silver platter.

His arms crossed as he waited on my response. My eyes lit up as I thought of the only thing I had to offer. I smiled sweetly and Zagan's eyes narrowed in suspicion.

"What if I know a human that kills fallen angels?"

"Now I'm intrigued," he said. He tapped his chin with an index finger. "Gotta name?"

"I'll supply the name once you and I come to an agreement." This time I crossed my arms and waited.

"Go on."

"No gossiping about me with other demons, angels, or any creature that resides in heaven or hell. Once I have proof of this, you'll get the name." He gave a short nod, so I kept going. "I need information on Lucifer, and how I'm going to save my soul."

His head titled back as he laughed. When he looked back at my stony expression, his laughter faded. "You're serious."

"Yes."

He looked me over once. With a resigned sigh, he nodded. "Fine. I'll do what I can. I can't promise to save you, but I'll do my best to get you the information that may be helpful. It won't be easy. When I meet up with you again, I want the name of the angel hunter."

"Deal. How will I get in touch with you?"

"You won't. I'll find you." His head tilted. "Time to go."

He seized my arm and the scene of the beach evaporated a split-second later.

Chapter 30

When you dance with the devil,
he doesn't change. You do.

Lor's eyes narrowed as he sniffed the air. "You reek like sulfur."

"I do? That's weird."

He gave me a pointed look. "Mara, what's going on? Why did you appear out of nowhere smelling like that?"

"It's a long story, but I'll fill you in soon. I promise. There's nothing to worry about."

"I can't help you if you don't tell me everything," he said.

Deciding to change the subject, I glanced around. "Where's Coren?"

His breath came out in a huff. "How should I know? I'm not his babysitter."

"He was supposed to meet me at the coffee shop," I looked at the time on my cell phone, "five minutes ago."

"You were late, too. He's probably doing something important."

More important than me? I thought but wouldn't dare say it out loud. Instead, I scrutinized our surroundings. Had Zagan lied to me and used me as a distraction? What if my estranged father captured

Coren? A million scattered theories rattled through my mind, but maybe Lor was right. Maybe he was following up on something.

"Anything new?" I asked.

"This isn't over. You'll have to tell me why you smell like hell eventually" He took a long inhale through his nose. "Fable and Zen have a promising lead in the remote parts of the desert. Char and Vex are off to Italy for research in a historic church library. Other than that, nothing to report so far. I wish we had more, but alas, we're hoping for a miracle."

I hoped for the same. I wrapped an arm around him in a friendly gesture. "Next time you talk to them, will you tell them all that I'm thankful for all their sacrifices? The same goes for you, too. I'm so happy you're in my life, Lor."

His eyes narrowed. "Where is Mara and what did you do with her?"

"Yeah, yeah. Don't get used to this caring and emotional shit. I only let it out for a short time before I lock it up behind an impenetrable lock."

Lor squeezed me back and smiled. "I'm surprised you even let that beast out to play."

"Don't get used to it." I chuckled.

When we began walking back to my apartment, my sword gave away an evil presence nearby. I let out a frustrated breath through my lips.

"What's wrong?" Lor asked, his gaze darting all around us.

"I can't get a damn break."

Black smoke hovered near the entrance of my apartment complex. Lor froze when he spotted it, too. The haze twisted and darkened into a human form. As the being made a few steps in our direction, it dissipated slowly. First black boots appeared, then black pants, and next strong arms dressed in a black button-down shirt. The last thing to materialize was Lucifer's angled face and obsidian hair.

Rage throbbed through me like it had its own heartbeat. Seeing him brought up all my pent up anger roaring to the surface. I unsheathed my sword and scowled.

"Mara, put that dismal blade away," he said, his voice so deep it reverberated against the buildings around us. "I'm only here to follow up on your progress."

"Oh, I'm still alive. No thanks to you," I growled, tightening the grip on the decorative hilt.

His gaze went to my sword and back up to my face. He rolled his glossy midnight-colored eyes. "We both know that weapon won't hurt me. But if you attempt to use it, I'll make sure to end your contract right here and now."

Lucifer knew I wanted to slice him to shreds and he dared me to try. If I did, it would give him an excuse to end my existence.

"You can't do that," Lor said, his red eyes glowing from fury.

With a nonchalant hand, he waved Lor off. "I can do whatever I damn well please, shadow."

A few things happened at once, Lor shoved me behind him, Coren appeared next to me, and Lucifer gave a frightening smile full of teeth.

"Coren," Lucifer snarled. "So fancy seeing you here. I've yet to receive a progress report on her. That's unacceptable behavior."

"My apologies, sir," Coren answered. "I've attempted to keep her under control, but as you can imagine, that's nearly impossible."

My mouth hung open at his response.

"Liar," Lor hissed so low only Coren and I could hear him.

"What do you recommend for her punishment?" Lucifer questioned, his head nodding once.

"I need more time with her, my liege. If we can't come to a conclusion, then we can move forward with our plan. I'm sure I can break her eventually."

Shock and betrayal cut me so deep I'm surprised I didn't bleed from it. My nostrils flared once as I stared at Coren. His eyes met mine for a split second before he focused on Lucifer. My breath caught in my throat as I reigned in my temper, but a seething vortex of anger swirled in my gut. My breathing increased as my heartbeat thundered behind my ribcage. I wanted to punch Coren in the face and watch his golden blood gush from his nose. He deserved much worse, actually, but I knew I couldn't kill him if Lor and I wanted to keep the humans in the nearby buildings safe.

"Fine. I expect weekly updates from here on out." Lucifer concentrated on me. "Don't make this more difficult than it needs to be, Mara. Your life depends on it."

I wanted to scream "fuck you" but I held it back. Barely. Instead, I made no move to acknowledge Coren or Lucifer. I grabbed Lor's hand in mine and he squeezed once.

"Coren, let's go back to my liar and talk about how to break this wild girl."

He nodded, and with one last look at me, Coren left with the devil.

As soon as he disappeared, the rage exploded and I screamed so loud my voice cracked. "Mother fucker!"

"My sentiments exactly," Lor whispered.

Chapter 31

The devil always cheats.

Instead of going to my apartment, I stormed off in the opposite direction. Lor followed silently beside me, for both moral support and protection.

I felt like a sucker for believing Coren for so long. Oh, but he'd made himself so damn charming for me to think otherwise, didn't he? And to think I opened up my heart to the backstabber. I still owed him a fucking favor, too.

This reminded me why I remained unemotional for so long. The only thing my heart was good for was pumping blood through my body. Other than that, I'd close off any and all feelings until I felt that delicious numbness that followed me most of my life. Damn emotional shit only resulted in betrayal and heartache. I'd focus on the rage bubbling beneath the surface to fuel me.

"I don't like that look on your face," Lor said softly.

"Get used to it," I snapped. "All my life I've been fucked over by those who said they *loved* me. I opened my heart and guess where it got me? Fucked over *again*."

"Don't let a fool make you bitter. Life is too short for that. Get mad, get pissed, cry, whatever. Don't shut yourself off from those who truly care for you."

Emotion flickered through me but I swallowed it back. "I'm doing this for my own good. It's nothing personal."

Lor gripped my arm and pulled me to a stop. "The hell it is. You expect your friends to simply let you withdraw from us because of a broken heart? Fuck that. You think we've never experienced disappointment and heartache? You think we've never been betrayed?"

"Look, as a child—"

"Yeah, yeah. You had a rough childhood. That's no excuse for being a shitty human being."

"Don't you dare judge me," I barked, irritation simmering to the surface.

"I'm not." His jaw muscle ticked once. "But I'm not going to stand here and let you wallow in self-destructive pity. Your past either breaks you or strengthens you. Make your choice wisely, Mara. One lets the devil win."

His body dissipated and I stood alone on the sidewalk with my mouth sagging open. He was right. Lor had seen right through my defense mechanisms to see the real reason behind my unemotional state. My mentality from a damaged childhood left me broken. Now I needed to work on strength and resilience instead. My life depended on it.

"Mara? Is that you?" a soft feminine voice said.

My head jerked up. Everly stood a few feet in front of me with two paper grocery bags in her arms. Her red hair curled about her shoulders, and her bright green sweater complimented her jade-colored eyes.

"Hey." I tried to smile but it was forced. "Sorry, I was deep in thought."

Her head jerked to the side as she watched me. Her ruby-red lips thinned. "Your aura is mixed with a bit of purple today. Why so melancholy?"

"My aura? You can see mine?" I blinked a few times in disbelief. "What color is it usually?"

"As black as crude oil." She gave me a sad smile. "I think that's because your soul is covered in a hellish filth, though."

I held up a hand. "Wait. I still have my soul?"

"Well, of course. You can't live without one." She shifted the bags in her arms. "The color of yours means it's marked by something evil. A demon perhaps? It would explain the bloodhound."

"No, not a demon. Let's just say the being who owns my soul goes by many names and has a few songs about him. You know, like the one where he went down to Georgia."

She gasped and about dropped one of her sacks. When she recovered, she set the bags down. She dug in her purse and pulled out a dark, shiny stone. "Here. Put this in your pocket along with the pyrite. At night soak both stones in saltwater to cleanse them. It won't save your soul, but both of those together are pretty powerful protection. You'll never know when they might come in handy."

"Thanks." Taking the stone from her, I placed it in my pocket next to the gold stone. They clinked together as they settled.

"Take care of yourself, Mara. Evil isn't anything to mess with, and the devil always cheats."

"Don't I know it," I said with a snort.

We said our goodbyes as Everly retrieved her bags. I watched the witch while she strolled down the walkway and wondered how she knew about such evil. She knew how to hurt a hellhound, after all.

Letting out a breath from between my lips, I twirled on my feet and walked back in the direction of my apartment. I pulled my leather jacket over my chest to fight off the nip in the air. The colorless sky revealed the colder weather ahead. I reminded myself to buy a thicker jacket soon.

Once my key slid into my door, I froze. What if Coren was inside? What would I say to him? I might punch him square on the jaw before I said a word. He deserved that much.

Thankfully, the apartment was silent as a tomb. The only sign Coren had been there recently was his long, leather coat slung over the couch. I guess he didn't need it in hell. At the thought, anger raked against my insides. I squelched it back and placed my sword on the coffee table.

I yawned and decided coffee was needed as soon as possible. First, a trip to the restroom was in order. After I did my business, I practically trotted to Mr. Coffee. Once the machine gurgled and sputtered, I turned to grab a mug. A note on the counter caught my attention.

My name was written in a blue script. I stared the calligraphic lettering for a long time before I had the courage to pick it up. I felt the texture of the paper and ran a thumb over my name. Dread settled in the pit of my stomach, but I unfolded the note anyway.

It read *"Mara, don't believe anything I said. I'm going to challenge Lucifer about your soul. If I don't come back, I love you forever. Coren."*

My heart stopped in my chest and then lurched as it beat again. Lucifer would punish Coren for falling in love with me and for challenging him over something he wanted so badly. He sacrificed himself to save me. All the betrayal and hurt over his callousness earlier dissipated. Instead, my fury roared to life. Rage surged through me as hot as molten lava. I'd always heard rumors about seeing red from anger, but I'd never quite experienced it before. Now I had. My entire apartment and belongings turned a hazy shade of crimson.

At that moment, Death and Raven showed in a wisp of red-tinged smoke. They took one look at me and froze.

"What's wrong?" Raven questioned, her eyebrows knitted together.

"Take me to hell. *Now.*" I shoved the note in Death's face.

"We can't storm hell without a strategy. He's an angel. Lucifer can't kill him." Raven said. "We have some time to formulate a plan."

The note shook in my hand. "If Coren hasn't confronted him yet, we need to stop it from happening. What would Lucifer do if we're too late?"

Death swallowed and avoided my gaze. "I don't know. Lucifer invented all manners of torture for his own sick sense of humor. He gets off on pain and suffering. If we're too late, Coren is in deep shit."

I slammed the note down on the counter and seethed as I attempted to come up with a plan. Lucifer may own my soul, but he had the man I loved.

The fucker had no idea what I was capable of. He was going to find out.

About the Author

Emma lives in Indiana with three adorable but crazy cats. She has a degree in Fine Arts & Design and Photography. When she's not busy writing her next novel or taking photographs, Emma enjoys spending time with family and friends, listening to music, taking naps with her cats, or curled up with a good book.

Please sign up for her newsletter on her website www.emmashadeauthor.com. You can also find Emma on Facebook and Twitter.

Books by Emma Shade:

Acknowledgments

First I want to thank my friends who've been there throughout the rough couple of years. The stress of college, the loss of Gizmo, and the not so normal home life jaded me for a while. You constantly remind me that my circumstances don't define me.

C.J. Pinard, thanks for telling me to always get the words on the page! I'm so glad you're a great friend! Maybe the next time you take me to the Garden of the Gods we'll see some shadows.

Beta readers are always amazing. Pam, Hannah, Jen, Cami, and Kim, you're feedback always means the world to me.

Lastly, to the ones who are going through a rough time right now. Don't let anyone tell you how you should feel or that you should feel guilty for saving your own damn soul.